RALPH SHERMAN'S
BAG OF WIND

• •

"Did you feel that?" I said.

Instantly Roxanne and I both dove offf of our seats taking cover under the table. Marvin was a microsecond behind us.

"It was just as the air conditioner," he insisted, his head beneath the table, and his butt sticking up into the air like an ostrich, "It was just the air conditioner, right? Right?!"

Are you certain of that, marvin?" we both asked.

By the tone of his voice, we could tell he wasn't certina of anything anymore. "It's . . . it's impossible, "he blathered.

Wind can't stay in a bag!"

"It can if it's charmed, " I said.

"Charmed?"

Roxy picked up where I left off. "Yeah. You know like a snake?" She pulled up where I left off. "Yeah. You know, like a snale?" She pulled on his collar until the rest of his body fell under the table to join his big old moon face. "You can controlit, if you know the secret incarnation. As long as the incarntation is said right, it will never harm the person who opens the bag."

"We took the bag on vacation with us, " I told him. "We used it for skydiving."

"No way!"

"Way! Have you ever skydived down the mouth if a tornado funnel?"

It's a real trip!" said Roxy.

Also by Neal Shusterman

Novels

Scorpion Shards*
The Eyes of Kid Midas*
Dissidents*
The Shadow Club
Speeding Bullet
What Daddy Did

Story Collections

MINDSTORMS: Stories to Blow Your Mind*

*Published by Tor Books

MindQuakes

Stories to
Shatter
Your Brain

NEAL SHUSTERMAN

TOR®

A TOM DOHERTY ASSOCIATES BOOK
NEW YORK

This is a work of fiction. All the characters and events portrayed in this book are either products of the author's imagination or are used fictitiously.

MINDQUAKES: STORIES TO SHATTER YOUR BRAIN

Visit Neal Shushterman's Website:
www.storyman.com

A Tor Book
Published by Tom Doherty Associates, LLC
175 Fifth Avenue
New York, NY 10010

www.tor.com

Tor® is a registered trademark of Tom Doherty Associates, LLC.

ISBN: 0-765-34188-3

First edition: May 1996
First mass market edition: February 2002

Printed in the United States of America

0 9 8 7 6 5 4 3 2 1

Dedication

*This
book is
dedicated to
my teachers: Hertha
Paustian, who challenged
me to write a story a week in
ninth grade; Randy Perrezini, who
gave me the* Collected Stories of John
Cheever; *Gilbert Weatherby, who left too
soon; Lori Aguera-Arcas, who taught me how
to paint a canvas of possibilities; and Oakley Hall,
who gave me the confidence to write that first novel, and
reminded me that even the pyramids began with a single stone.*

Acknowledgments

Many thanks to all the movers and shakers who helped create *MindQuakes*. Thanks to Peggy Black, and the students at Longfellow, Irving, and Whittier Middle Schools in Norman, Oklahoma, for their contribution to *Yardwork*. Thanks to my sons Brendan and Jarrod, for their undying fascination with a certain Scottish Monster. Thanks to Terry Black, for whom I wrote *Dead Letter*, and whose formidable writing talents rest in fertile soil (but usually not for long). Thanks to Sean Ponce, whose labors inspired *Retaining Walls*.

And my deepest gratitude to Kathleen Doherty, Jonathan Schmidt, and everyone at Tor Books for their remarkable persistence of vision!

N. S.

CONTENTS

YARDWORK

● ●

As I step outside, a strange feeling tugs at my spine. Perhaps that's what it feels like when you first step into a nightmare.

Don't be silly, Jeremy, I tell myself, *there's nothing to be afraid of.*

Today the wind has brought an unpleasant smell sweeping across the neighborhood. It's tinged with a slight scent of fertilizer.

The smell's coming from Mr. Jackson's house. My mom told me all about Mr. Jackson—how he used to live here before I was born. How he spent most of his life in that house; how his beautiful garden had been the envy of the neighborhood.

He had a family, but no one knows what happened to them. They left, he left soon after, and the garden just died.

By the time I was born, the house was an ugly blotch on our neighborhood. People would live there for only a few months before leaving, and then it became completely abandoned. Now it was covered with graffiti and filled with broken, boarded-up windows. It bothered me to have a place like that next door, but like anything, I got used to it.

Then last week, Mr. Jackson just came back, like he'd never left. Since then, I've been watching the house . . . and watching him. The house hasn't changed—he hasn't had anyone come to fix the windows or paint over the graffiti. All he does is work in his garden. He sure loves that garden.

Now, as I step outside, I can hear him back there. I can hear the *skitch . . . brummp, skitch . . . brummp* of his little trowel digging up the dirt and throwing it over his shoulder. I know he's planting more flowers. Until Mr. Jackson came back, there weren't any flowers in *that* garden. Nothing grew there but ugly weeds that got filled with torn rags, Kleenex, and candy wrappers. Whatever the wind brought to our neighborhood got snagged in the thick weeds of that abandoned backyard and stayed there.

Until last week, that is. That's when Mr. Jackson showed up and began hacking those weeds, putting them into trash bags, and hauling them out to the curb. The weeds are all gone now, and bit by bit that wasteland of a yard is filling with flowers.

"Jeremy, don't go bothering the man," my mom had told me. But what she really means is "Stay away from him, Jeremy, because he's not quite right. Leave him to his business, and maybe when his business is done he'll leave forever and they'll tear that ugly house down."

But Mom's asleep on the couch now, so she doesn't have to know, and I can't resist the curiosity itching at my brain. It's a few minutes after dark. A night chill has set in, and the sun is long gone, leaving a ribbon of blue on the horizon that's fading fast. I stand at the edge of our property, peering at the upstairs windows of the old house, nervously running my fingers through my hair. Boards have covered most of those windows for years now, and thick spiderwebs fill the space between the boards.

Taking a deep breath, I cross over, through the gaping hole in the old wooden fence, into the world of Mr. Jackson. Here that dark and earthy fertilizer smell is stronger. There are no lights on in the house. I don't think Mr. Jackson has had the electricity turned back on.

He's back there all right, doing his yardwork—I can see his shadow now as I make my way down the side of the house toward the backyard. I can see that shadow on hands and knees in the dirt.

Skitch . . . brummp, skitch . . . brummp.

Holding on to a rusty old drainpipe snaking down the edge of the house, I round the corner to see him in the light of the half moon. He's setting a fresh row of flowers in the growing garden. I can't tell what they are, because all I can see is black and white.

"Are those zinnias you're planting?" I ask, remembering that my mom liked to grow zinnias.

He doesn't look up at me. I figure he's too deaf to hear me—and good thing too. I've got no business here. I can just go back home, turn on the TV, and forget Mr. Jackson; no one would be the wiser. But then he speaks in a soft whisper of a voice that sounds filled with gravel and wrapped in cotton.

"Marigolds," he says. "Man-in-the-moon marigolds, they are."

Skitch . . . brummp. He plants one more, then finally turns to look at me. I don't see his eyes, just dark shadows where they should be.

"You the Harrison boy?" he asks.

I nod, then say "Yes," figuring he can't see my nod in the dark.

"I see you lookin' out your window at me," he says. "Am I putting on a good show for you here?"

"It's not like that," I try to explain. "I've just been wondering why you're . . . I mean, look at the house. What's so important about the yard when the house looks like hell?"

"How would *you* know what hell looks like?" he asks me. *Skitch . . . brummp.* Dirt flies over his shoulder, and in goes another marigold.

By now I'm feeling all tongue-twisted and bone cold, and fear is clawing at my gut. I grip that cold drainpipe as if it can give me some comfort, and it comes loose in my hands.

Yelping, I fall to the ground, right into the bed of flowers.

"I'm sorry," I stammer, scrambling to my feet, wishing I was anywhere else in the world. When I look down, I shudder at the sight of the imprint I made in the flowers. The way the moon's casting shadows tonight, I can see the shape of my whole body, as if I'm still lying down.

I figure the old man is going to have a fit and start scooping out my brains with his planting trowel, or bury his little hand rake in the side of my neck, but he doesn't. Instead he just looks down at the crushed flowers.

"Those're no good anymore," he says calmly. "I gotta put in all new ones now."

He looks at me, and now I can see his eyes. They are ancient, the lids almost closing over them in tired sags of skin.

"I don't need you here," he tells me in that gravel-cotton voice. "I can do this myself. I don't need you."

Well, I don't need a second invitation to leave. I step back, stumbling over the broken drainpipe, and tear out of the yard, through the hole in the wooden fence and back onto my own property where the moon doesn't seem to shine quite as coldly.

I can't sleep that night, because I hear him through my closed window. Only now do I realize that he doesn't sleep—he works all through the night in that garden. *What is it about that garden?* I wonder as I lay awake. *Why is it so important to him?*

When the sun comes up in the morning, I drag myself out of bed and peer out the window. In the light of day, the garden doesn't look quite so creepy. In fact, it looks kind of pretty and peaceful. Rows of flowers of all different colors surround a single open patch of dirt. I wonder what he's going to put there.

Downstairs, I force myself to drink Mom's coffee so that I can stay awake. "I think Mr. Jackson's going to put a fountain in the middle of his garden," I tell my mom as she tosses a couple of waffles on my plate. "What do you think?"

"His business is his business," Mom says. But what she really means is *"I don't want you to go sticking your nose in that garden."* Mom's always been a mind-your-own kind of person.

"Lock the door when you leave," she tells me, like she always does when she heads off for work. Like if she didn't I'd leave the door wide open.

As I eat, I can hear the rattle of a wheelbarrow next door. Mr. Jackson's busy with his endless yardwork. I'm about to leave for school, but before I do, I get an idea. You see, I'm not quite as mind-your-own as Mom is.

In a couple of minutes, I leave the house, but instead

of turning right and heading toward school, I turn left and slip through the hole in the wooden fence.

Mr. Jackson is where I knew I'd find him, in the corner of the yard, turning up the earth for a new batch of flowers and tossing the bigger stones into the wheelbarrow. He wears a long-sleeved shirt, buttoned all the way to the top, even though the day is hot. His hands are covered with dirt and they're just as leathery and wrinkled as the skin on his face.

"I . . . I thought you might like some breakfast," I tell him. I hold the plate toward him. "Waffles. I didn't know if you liked syrup, so I put it in a little cup on the side, see?"

Still across the yard, he stands there looking at me like he's looking through a wall. Then he slowly makes his way toward me, careful not to trample his flowers with his heavy work boots. His feet drag as he moves, as if he's got no muscles in them—as if he's pulling his legs up from the seat of his pants like one of those marionettes. He reaches out and takes the plate and cup from me.

"Thank you," he says simply, then puts the waffles down on a cinder block and reaches into his pocket, handing me a wad of crumpled dollar bills.

I shake my head, not wanting to take the money, and, for that matter, not wanting to touch that dirty, puffy hand. "No," I tell him, "no, you don't have to pay me—the waffles are my treat—to make up for messing up your flowers last night." When I look down, I see that he's already replanted the area.

He shakes his head slowly. "I'm not paying you," he tells me. "I'm asking you to do something for me." He clears his throat. It crackles like eggshells breaking. "I was wrong," he says. "Last night I was wrong. I *do* need someone to help me. You understand?"

I shrug. "Sure. What do you want me to do?"

"Flowers from the nursery. Lots of flowers."

"What kind?"

He thinks about that for a moment, then smiles, revealing just a sparse scattering of rotten teeth. I have to cast my eyes down because I can't look at that terrible mouth.

"Any kind you like," he tells me. "Pick your favorites . . . and buy a shovel," he says before I go, "a bigger shovel."

After school, I head right out to the nursery with the old wagon I used when I was a little kid. I don't know much about flowers, but I pick out a few trays of really nice ones for Mr. Jackson's garden. Then I pull it all home in the rusty old wagon and present it to Mr. Jackson.

"Help me plant them," he says.

I look at my watch. Mom won't be home for another hour. I've got no homework, so I figure, Sure, why not. No good deed goes unrewarded, right? Anyway, I head for the patch of dirt in the middle of the yard that definitely needs some color when Mr. Jackson shouts: "No!"

It nearly makes me jump out of my skin. Then he quickly changes his tone. "No, not there."

"Oh, right," I say. "I forgot about the fountain. It *is* going to be a fountain, right?"

But he doesn't answer me. He just directs me to a far corner with my trays of plants.

For a few minutes we work quietly, but my mind gets to working overtime. I start wondering about that patch of dirt. Not what's going on top of it, but what's underneath. I start wondering how deep this garden is planted.

"Mr. Jackson, whatever happened to your family?"

He plants three geraniums before answering in his gravelly toothless voice. "People break apart sometimes" is all he says.

I think of my own parents. Once my parents got divorced I saw less and less of my father until I didn't see him at all. Maybe I'll never see him again, I don't know. *People break apart.* I imagine my own dad fifty years from now, an old man in a garden. No way to find him; no way to talk to him even if I do find him. Just the thought of it makes me plant the flowers faster and faster, trying to drive the thought out of my mind.

"Your family didn't go with you when you left here?" I ask, unable to keep my fool mouth shut.

"Nope. There were just old folks where I went," says Mr. Jackson. "Old folks, nurses, and more old folks."

"Did they treat you okay," I ask, realizing that he must have been in a retirement home.

Mr. Jackson thinks about it. "They cared for me, which is about the best I can say for them." Then he stops planting for a moment. "They cared for me," he says again, "but that wasn't home. *This* is. You understand?"

I glance over at the bald spot in the center of the yard again. "What's over there, Mr. Jackson? Is there something . . . under the dirt?"

"Nothing," he tells me. "Nothing but worms."

The light is growing dim now. I listen for the sound of my mother's car. Above us I can see large birds circling. Vultures. I can't remember seeing them in our neighborhood before.

Then I hear Mr. Jackson grunt, and when I look up, something awful has happened. He was digging with his little trowel and somehow slit his right arm, leaving a gash as wide as all outdoors—at least four or five inches.

"That's not good," says Mr. Jackson, in the same calm voice he used when I fell in his flowers last night.

"I'll go call a doctor!" I shout, but as I start to take off, he yells: "No! No doctors."

"But your arm."

"It's *my* arm and *I'll* deal with it."

He grabs a dirty rag from his back pocket, and I catch sight of the words stenciled on it. It reads DADE COUNTY CONVALESCENT HOSPITAL. He slaps the rag over the wound. I can't imagine a rag keeping back the flow of blood, but it does. Still, a dirty rag isn't something you use on an open wound.

"Mr. Jackson, maybe I should—"

"Get on home," he tells me. "Go on, your mother's home, I can hear her."

And he's right. My mother has just driven up.

"But. . . ." I don't know what to tell him. He holds the rag over his wound, the expression on his face unchanging, as if a tear in his arm is no more dangerous to him than a tear in his shirt. It looks as though the flow of blood has stopped, but to be honest, I never really saw a flow of blood begin.

I leave, thinking all kinds of troubled thoughts. As I head out of the yard I see, sitting on a cinder block, the waffles I brought him that morning, uneaten.

It's later that night. Mom's asleep on the sofa again, her book open in her lap. I dial the number it took me half an hour to track down and hear it ring once . . . twice . . . three times.

"Dade County Convalescent Hospital," answers a tired-sounding woman on the other end.

"I'm calling about a Mr. Isaac Jackson," I say.

A long pause on the other end, and then, "Are you a family member?"

"No. Listen, I think he's not quite right. I mean, he's here, and I think he's still supposed to be with you. I think he kind of . . . ran away."

"What do you mean he's there?" the woman says, sounding alarmed. "Who is this? Are you from the medical school?"

"I'm just a neighbor, that's all."

"It says right here that Isaac Jackson was transferred to the medical school last week."

I take the number of the medical school, and after we hang up, I try that number. One ring . . . two rings. The guy who picks up the phone talks to me in between bites of his sandwich.

"Says here we were supposed to get him," he tells me. "But he never showed up. Probably just a clerical error."

By now I'm beginning to get upset. "Well, somebody should come and get him," I say. "I mean, what if he's in trouble?"

And on the other end I hear the creep laugh. "Ha! That's a good one!" he snorts. "No, he's not getting into any trouble anymore. Not unless those med students are playing practical jokes with their cadavers again."

My heart misses a hefty beat.

"Cadavers?"

"Yeah," says the guy as I hear him take another bite from his sandwich. "You know, as in *corpse*. As in *stiff*." He laughs again. "Yeah, those med students sure are clowns. Those things end up in the darndest places sometimes!"

I slam the phone down as if hanging up can somehow change what I've just heard. I don't believe it. And yet somehow I do. And somehow I understand.

Outside the clouds hide the moon, and it's as dark as if the moon weren't even there. As I step outside, it takes a few moments for my night vision to kick in. When it does, I find the hole in the wooden fence and cross over into the cold loneliness of Mr. Jackson's world.

I can hear him back there—hear him moaning. I can hear him working with his trowel. *Skitch . . . brummp, skitch . . . brummp.* Slowly I round the corner where the drainpipe once stood, and there, in the center of the yard, is total darkness.

There isn't going to be a fountain there. That bald patch of dirt was not for a fountain at all. It was for a grave.

I peer into the hole, and see, at the bottom of a shallow hole, Mr. Jackson covering himself with dirt. With one hand he weakly slices into the dirt wall and pulls it down around him.

"No time," he whispers to himself. "No time left. No time."

My eyes are full of tears, but I wipe them away.

"When did it happen, Mr. Jackson?" I ask him. And then I force out what I really mean to say. "When did you . . . die?"

He takes a deep breath, and it comes out like a raspy wheeze. "It'll be two weeks tomorrow," he says.

I swallow hard, choking down my own terror. "And you don't know where your family is, and no one would bury you?"

The only answer is that raspy wheeze.

I reach into the shallow hole and take the trowel away from Mr. Jackson. He begins to panic as I drag him out.

"No!" he says. "No time. No time. Getting too weak."

"Shhh!" I tell him gently. "Shhh. Someone will hear."

And then I look into those empty eyes that can barely stay open at all. I force myself to *keep* looking, this time refusing to look away from that awful face, trying to see the man he must have once been.

"What do you want me to do?" I ask.

In those ruined eyes I see tears beginning to form.

"Care for me," he says.

But I won't do that. Nurses and hospital workers care *for* him. But they can't care *about* him. Not the way I can.

I look at the grave. "It's not deep enough," I tell him. Then I grab the large shovel leaning up against the house, step into the hole, and begin digging, throwing dirt over my shoulder.

The old man tilts his head. I hear it creak and fracture on his slim neck. "You're a good boy, Jeremy," he says with a voice that keeps moving farther and farther back in his throat. "A good boy."

"Rest easy, Mr. Jackson. I'll give you a decent burial; you don't have to worry. I'll take care of everything, I promise . . ."

Mr. Jackson smiles his awful smile, but somehow that smile doesn't seem awful at all. It seems wonderful and warm and filled with the kind of peace that comes from knowing things are all right. That things are in order.

I watch as Mr. Jackson lets his shoulders relax, his eyes close, and his head sink to the ground, finally giving his spirit over to the death that had been trying to claim his body. In a moment I know that he is gone—*truly* gone, the way he should have been two weeks ago.

Now I'm alone, as I stand here in the darkness of his backyard garden, digging his grave.

I will bury you, Mr. Jackson. I will bury you in the place where you lived your good years. I will cover your grave with flowers, so it will be our secret, and you can rest, knowing that there was someone in this world willing to see you off into the next.

And I will not be afraid.

Skitch . . . brummp.

Skitch . . . Brummp.

CALEB'S COLORS

A dark hat. A dark coat. A tall figure standing in the doorway, silhouetted by the stark streetlight.

"My name is Quentin Prax. I'm here about your son."

I didn't like him. Not at first. The way he spoke, it was so slow, so practiced and smooth. The way he said his name—hissing it like a snake. *Praxsssssss.*

"We've been expecting you," said my father.

The man stepped into the light of the living room, where I could see that his dark coat was not black but brown. Not just brown though—it was woven of many different colors, all intertwined until they blended perfectly into a rich mahogany. His eyes locked on mine, and he smiled. I had to look away. His smile was unnerving. It could not be read. Like his coat, it seemed to be woven of so many different thoughts and meanings that I didn't know what that smile was for.

"You must be the sister," he said to me through that smile.

I didn't like being called "the sister." "My name's Rhia," I told him. He smiled again.

"Rhia. What a colorful name."

He strolled across our living room as if he were welcome, and my parents didn't do anything about it. His presence was so powerful, my parents had no response.

Prax turned to Caleb, my little brother. Caleb sat at the kitchen table, the place he could most often be found, with a box of Crayolas. His left hand moved across a piece of paper, leaving periwinkle streaks.

When you first watch Caleb and his Crayolas, you might think his marks are random—just wild firings from a ruined brain—but watch long enough, and you'll see shapes forming out of those wild lines, until you suddenly realize that you're looking at a sailing ship, or a mountain range, or a lion that seems so real you'd swear it might leap off the page at you.

And Caleb does all this without even looking at the page. He'll just sit there, staring forward, rocking back and forth, in a way that could make you seasick just watching him.

"This must be Caleb," said Mr. Prax. "How are you, Caleb?"

"He won't answer you," I told the man. "He doesn't talk."

But Mr. Prax only smiled that many-colored smile once more and said, "Oh, he does. He just doesn't care to use words." I tried to stare this Mr. Prax down, but I couldn't. People who came to help Caleb promised us the moon, then they took our money and left Caleb no better than they found him. Caleb's condition gave my parents enough to fight about without having to argue over quack doctors—which is exactly what I figured

Prax was. He smiled at me again, then he turned to my
parents. "May we talk in private?"

"Rhia," said my mother, "why don't you take Caleb
upstairs and get him ready for bed."

I was irritated that I couldn't be a part of whatever
was going on, but also relieved that I could be out of
Mr. Prax's sight. I didn't trust him. He seemed far too
calculating and mysterious. I didn't like mysteries—
especially when they were strutting around my house.

I took Caleb's hand and lifted him to his feet. He followed me upstairs quietly tonight. Sometimes it's not
so easy. Sometimes he would whine and pull his hair.
Sometimes he would scream like the end of the world
had come. I had grown used to all of that—I had had
to, because putting him to bed was a responsibility I
had chosen to take on. But tonight he didn't kick and
scream; he merely followed.

I took him to his room and dressed him for bed. All
the time he stared forward with that blank, nonseeing
look of his. He could stare for hours at the TV like that,
and I always wondered what he saw there. Light and
colors? Shapes moving back and forth? There were
times when he would take a crayon to paper and recre-
ate, line for line, the image of something he had seen
on TV, as if his mind was a VCR, recording everything
it saw. Then there would be the times he would draw
things too strange and exotic to have come from anywhere in this world. In one moment he would draw a
place of terror so dark I could not bear to look at it, and
then in the next instant turn the page over and draw a
world of such intense beauty it would make me truly
know that there was a God somewhere, because who
else could put such a beautiful image into the head of a
small, autistic boy?

That was life with Caleb. A never-ending gallery of

Crayola wonders that papered the wall of his room, floor to ceiling. Me, I could barely draw a stick figure . . . but it didn't make me jealous. How could I be jealous of a brother whose whole world had no room for anything but himself and his Crayolas?

I finished dressing Caleb for bed and left him. Sneaking out onto the stairs, I peeked down into the kitchen, where Mr. Prax sat with my parents.

"I've done much work with idiot savants," said Mr. Prax. I bristled at the expression "idiot savant." That's the label the world gives people like Caleb. People whose brain somehow got wired to do one thing and one thing only. There were people who could do instant math like a super-computer but had to be taught to feed themselves. There were some who could memorize hundreds of books just by skimming through them but couldn't hold a conversation. I'd even heard of a little girl labeled as severely retarded who designed an aircraft for the military.

Dad sat with his arms crossed. Mom had called Prax on the advice of a friend, but it had been a long time since Dad trusted therapists.

"Caleb's had every therapy in the book," said Dad. "I doubt yours will help any more than the others did."

"You don't understand," said Mr. Quentin Prax sharply. "I'm not here as a therapist, I'm here as an employer. I'm the owner of a small but prestigious art gallery specializing in unique works of art. Perhaps you've heard of it: the Galleria du Mondes."

My parents seemed as surprised as I was. If he wasn't a doctor, then what did he want with Caleb?

"We don't know of it," admitted my mother. "We're not really art patrons . . ."

"My gallery seeks out . . . special artists with unique talents," Prax told them. "A colleague of mine came across one of Caleb's sketches and sent it to me. I was quite impressed."

Mom stiffened in her chair. Until now she had watched Prax with wide and hopeful eyes. But now it seemed her hope was draining fast.

"Just what is it you want, Mr. Prax?" she said coldly.

Prax grinned at her. "Simple," he said. "I would like to commission a large work from him."

Mom laughed, and Dad, well, he just got angry.

"Listen," said my father. "We've got a little boy with a lot of problems. I don't like the idea of hiring him out as some sort of creative freak for the amusement of a bunch of snobs."

Mr. Prax looked down at his perfectly manicured fingernails, unconcerned with my father's anger. "You misunderstand," he said. "The sole purpose of my gallery is to give expression to creativity that would otherwise be lost. Your son has a gift, and I'd like to help him share it with the world." Mr. Prax paused for a moment, then took a deep breath and said, "I have a special interest, you see, because my own daughter was very much like your boy."

"Was?" questioned Mom.

"She's no longer with me."

"I'm sorry," said Mom.

My father sighed, on the verge of giving in. "How much will this cost?" he asked.

Mr. Prax laughed heartily at that—loud enough that it made me jump. "It won't cost you, my friend, it will only cost me," he said. Then he pulled an envelope out of his pocket and handed it to my father, who opened it and began laughing. There was a check in the envelope.

"All right, who put you up to this?" he chuckled.

"Was it Joe at work? He's always pulling practical jokes."

"No joke," said Prax, completely serious. "And that's only half. The other half is payable on completion of the work."

My mother was gasping as if she were hyperventilating.

"A million dollars? For a drawing by Caleb?"

"My gallery has some very wealthy patrons."

I could hardly believe it myself. I thought of the way Mom and Dad always bought those stupid lottery tickets, even though a person's more likely to get struck by lightning five times than to win once—and now the jackpot comes walking right into our living room.

"I'm sure Caleb's condition has left you with a great many medical expenses," reminded Prax. "This will pay those expenses with more than enough left over for you."

Well, Caleb might not talk, but money does, and Mr. Prax had himself a deal. As they came walking out of the kitchen, I tried to scoot up the stairs, into the shadows, where I couldn't be seen—but Prax saw me nonetheless. He stared at me with that strange smile again.

"Rhia," said Mr. Prax. "I would very much like you to come to my gallery and assist your brother in his creation."

I shrunk back even further.

"I don't do what he does," I told him.

"Of course not," said Prax. "But every artist needs an assistant."

"No," I told him. I wouldn't be bought, like my parents were.

My parents turned to me in shock, as if I had just

thrown a stone through a plate glass window, then my mother turned back to Mr. Prax.

"Rhia will be happy to go," declared my mother. Then she turned to me. "After all, it's summer vacation, so she has plenty of time, don't you, Rhia?"

I didn't trust this Mr. Prax, no matter how much money he had. He wasn't just a rich guy who liked to help autistic kids—there was much more to him than that. Still, this was a battle I knew I couldn't win. Three adults and a million dollars against little ol' me. No matter how far I wanted to be away from Prax, I knew I was destined to spend days, maybe weeks, with the eerie man, watching Caleb paint.

"Fine," I said. "I'll go, but only because I want to make sure Caleb's treated right."

"Splendid," said Prax. "I'd like Caleb and Rhia at my gallery at nine o'clock sharp tomorrow morning."

After Mr. Prax had gone, I went back up to Caleb's room, where he sat on the edge of his bed, exactly where I'd left him.

I stretched him out and pulled the covers over him. He lay there looking up at the ceiling—a ceiling that was covered with his Crayola creations.

"Do you know you're worth a million dollars, Caleb," I said to him. He blinked, but showed no signs of hearing me. "Do you even know what a million dollars is?" Still no response. I don't know why I always expected him to say something.

"Good night, Caleb. I love you." I turned off the light, went to my room, and slipped into a sleep filled with nightmares I couldn't remember.

Caleb and I took a bus to Mr. Prax's gallery, but instead of bringing us inside, he took us for a ride in his white Mercedes limousine. The limousine, he told us, was a gift from one of the clients of his gallery. I wondered how anyone—even a rich person—could give away a limousine.

We drove for an hour, into the heart of the city, until we stopped at an immense museum of art. All afternoon we wandered through the maze of exhibits.

"See how Manet uses light to capture the moment of sunset here," Prax said at one point. "See how Van Gogh's thick textures bring the night sky to life," he said at another. "See how the tiny points of color in Seurat's work blend together the farther away you stand." Gallery after gallery, he had something to say about every artist, every painting, until my mind was so full of color and texture that all I could see was gray.

"Why are you doing this?" I finally asked him. "Caleb doesn't care. He's not listening to you. He doesn't know a Monet from a Manet from a Schmanet. He's retarded," I hated the word, but I was angry. "He's worse than retarded. Don't you understand that?"

Then he looked at me with that same cold stare he gave my father the night before. "I'm not talking to him. I'm talking to *you*."

"Me?"

I looked at Caleb, whose eyes wandered around, giving as much time to the thermostat on the wall as they did to the paintings.

"Caleb needs no words to tell him about these paintings," said Mr. Prax.

"So why are you telling me about it?" I asked.

"So that maybe you'll be able to understand some of the things he already knows," was Prax's answer. Then he asked me something I'll never forget.

"Do you think that these artists were masters?"

"Sure," I said. "I guess."

Prax shook his head. "No. These artists could only

bring a hint of greatness to their canvases. Shadows of possibilities, nothing more. They are failures." And then he leaned in close to me. "Would you like to see the work of real masters?"

And although I didn't want to go anywhere else with Mr. Prax today, curiosity had already begun to drill deep into my brain. I nodded my head and said, "Yes. Yes I do."

He took us back to his gallery, where the walls were cov-ered with canvases filled with dripping splotches of brown paint.

"You call these masterpieces?" I asked. "Looks like a lot of mud to me."

He shook his head. "This isn't the gallery. The real gallery is upstairs."

He opened a door and took us up a narrow staircase into a huge loft. It must have once been a factory or something, because it had brick walls, and lots of win-dows—but those windows were all painted over.

Surrounding us were dozens upon dozens of sheet-covered canvases, all five- or six-feet tall, and all rest-ing upon heavy wooden easels. In the dim light of the huge loft, they looked like ghosts all facing in different directions.

He locked the door behind us.

"These are the works of the masters," he said and began to pull away the sheets that covered them one by one.

Any doubts I had were gone the moment I laid eyes on that first canvas.

It was a landscape like nothing I had ever seen, and trying to explain it now is like trying to explain sight to a blind person. These were colors the human eye had never before seen. Colors that had no names, depicting a place too strange and surreal to be of this world.

The second masterpiece was in a different set of hues, but just as incredible: A scene of clouds billowing upward toward a sun that actually shone, lighting up the room. Deep within the painting, golden winged beings seemed caught in a glorious journey toward that sun.

The third was the most magnificent of all. A forest of impossibly exotic trees, swirling in a greenish mist. Hills rolled into the distance, and in the foreground the single limb of a tree curved downward, with a smattering of red leaves. It seemed so real I could almost smell the rich fragrances of the forest and feel the slow breeze that made the mist swim and shimmer. It was unearthly, and otherworldly, like the other paintings.

"You wish to touch the painting," said Prax. It wasn't so much a question as a statement of fact. "You may do so. These paintings are meant to be touched."

I reached out toward one of those redder-than-red leaves to feel its velvet texture . . .

. . . and when I drew my hand away, I was holding the leaf between my fingers!

I gasped, and let the leaf flutter to the ground.

Prax smiled. "The task of the artist," he said, "is the creation of worlds. Very few succeed. Many die trying."

In a small room behind the great gallery was a paint-splattered studio, and in that studio were a palette, brushes, and about a thousand brand-new tubes of paint. All set up in front of a canvas the same size as the others in the gallery. Only this canvas was empty.

Caleb stood just a few inches away from the canvas, staring that blank stare of his, and Mr. Prax put a paintbrush in Ca-leb's hand.

"Do you believe in miracles, Rhia?"

To be honest, I didn't know. But then my brother began to paint. Thick, heavy brush strokes. In moments Caleb had begun creating a bright, wonderful work of art.

Then I saw something out of the corner of my eye. There was something shiny in Prax's hand. Shiny and sharp. I gasped and pulled Caleb away from the canvas as Prax brought the carving knife down . . . slashing through the center of the canvas. The fabric shredded from top to bottom.

"No!" he screamed furiously at Caleb. "Look at those brush strokes! This is Van Gogh!" I was so shocked, all I could do was push myself back against the wall in disbelief.

Caleb screamed as if he himself had been stabbed and didn't stop screaming until Prax brought another canvas. He quieted immediately and silently resumed painting. He dabbed his brush against the canvas lightly, creating tiny little points of light. Again Prax's knife came down, shredding the emerging work.

"No!" Prax yelled. "This is Seurat."

Caleb wailed again and began to rock feverishly back and forth. Once more Prax brought a fresh canvas.

I wanted to grab Caleb and run, taking him away from this ranting, insane man—and yet part of me must have understood what he was doing, and why he was doing it. Because I stayed. I stayed to witness Caleb's terrifying ordeal.

"We're not leaving here," shouted Prax, "until we're done. Even if it takes days. Weeks. Months."

On and on it went. I began crying, begging Prax to

stop, but he wouldn't. He shredded canvas after canvas—one that looked like a Manet, and another like a Picasso. Caleb barely had a chance to get down a single brush stroke before that awful knife would come down again, sending him into a screaming fit, each one worse than the one before.

And then Caleb just shut down.

Prax put a new canvas in front of him, and Caleb didn't move. He stood there, red in the face, staring at the white fabric with an expression of emptiness worse than ever before—as if he were staring through the canvas with no emotion. No mind. He didn't even try to paint.

"Now you've done it!" I shouted at Prax through my tears. "Now he'll never paint or pick up a crayon ever again! You've ruined the one thing he can do, you monster."

Prax didn't answer me; he just looked at Caleb, waiting. Then I heard the faraway jingling of bells, and Prax left to greet a customer who had just arrived downstairs. He closed the door behind him, and Caleb and I were alone with the horribly empty canvas.

"Caleb," I whispered. "Caleb, you don't have to paint. You don't have to do anything. We'll get you home. I'll tuck you in bed. It'll be just like it always was. You'd like that, wouldn't you?"

Nothing. Caleb didn't even rock back and forth. Something was very, very wrong, and I cursed Prax for doing this to him.

That's when I heard voices outside the door. I peeked through the keyhole to see Prax—his slick, smooth self leading a couple through the great secret gallery. The man and woman hardly looked rich enough to invest in great works of art. In fact, they looked poor, worn, and tired, as if they'd seen more trouble and pain than most.

The man knelt down on the gallery floor, opened up a suitcase, and showed its contents to Prax.

"It's all there," said the man wearily. "Every penny we could find. Everything we own."

"I'm afraid it's not very much," the woman apologized.

Prax waved the remark away. I guess he didn't care how much it was. "Have you chosen a work that suits you?" he asked.

The man and woman stepped toward the surreal landscape with the red leaves.

"Ah," said Prax, smiling his multicolored smile for them. "My daughter's. I hope you enjoy it."

And with that I could see the look of world-weariness leave the couple's faces. How would they carry it out, I wondered—it was such a huge canvas.

I leaned back to brush some hair from my face, and when I peeked through the hole again, the couple was gone . . .

. . . and a single leaf, redder than red, fluttered to the floor at Prax's feet. My heart missed a very long beat.

Prax immediately covered the painting with a sheet, and turned.

"Come out, Rhia," he said, knowing I was there all along. "The door isn't locked."

I stepped into the gallery and helped Mr. Prax adjust the sheet on the painting so it hung just right.

Prax seemed to sigh in satisfaction, then closed the suitcase. I noticed it only seemed to have a few crumpled bills.

"This world we live in," said Prax, "is kind to some, but cruel to others. For those who would rather not be here, I provide . . . alternatives." Then he smiled at me, and although his smile still seemed filled with many strange colors, I felt I could understand some of them now. "Perhaps there will come a time," he said, "when everyone will have to choose a masterpiece."

The smell of oil paint seemed to grow stronger around me, and I turned to see that Caleb had begun painting. He was working feverishly—and this time it was different from before. As I stepped back into the studio, I could see the speed at which his fingers were moving. They were a blur. Even the colors he was putting on that canvas seemed far brighter, far more special than the colors that came from the tubes of paint.

All the time he stared through that white canvas as if the work was already there behind it and he wasn't so much brushing on paint as he was brushing away the emptiness. Soon he threw the paintbrush away and began to use his fingers, spreading and blending the colors from corner to corner. For half an hour we watched in awed silence, and half an hour was all it took.

"My God!" I said when it was done, but my words seemed far away, lost in the depth of the painting.

It was something entirely new, nothing like what any artist anywhere had ever created. The world Caleb had made was both wilderness and city, both earth and sky. Wild winds swept through magnificent trees toward gleaming crystalline spires. Brilliant shafts of light spilled upon peaceful hills, and yet the light was balanced by deep shafts of darkness that swam with unknowable mysteries. Still, as new as all this was, it was somehow familiar. It was then that I realized that everything in this great work I'd seen before. A fragment on the refrigerator door. A sketch on Caleb's wall. Everything Caleb had ever drawn was just a shadow of this, his great work. His one work.

I reached toward it, wanting more than anything to

reach into it—and instead I got my fingers covered with paint.

Caleb smoothed over the smudge I had made with my fingers.

"It's not finished," said Mr. Prax. "It needs a signature."

"But Caleb can't write his name."

Mr. Prax shook his head. "That's not the kind of signature I mean." Then Prax leaned over and whispered into Caleb's ear. "Go on, Caleb. Finish it."

And with that, Caleb reached forward and pressed his spread fingers against the center of his creation. He grit his teeth. He squinted his eyes and pushed that hand against the canvas with all his soul, until finally his hand punched through . . . into a world rich with colors. I could see the canvas changing, the flatness of it stretching out and back like a wave was rolling through it, until its depth reached the infinite horizon.

Caleb looked at his fingers there inside of his painting, watching the light playing off of them . . . then he lurched forward and leapt into it. Once inside, he threw his hands out. He spun around. He was dancing— Caleb was actually dancing! And then for the first time in his life he turned his head to look at me. And he smiled. It was a smile filled with more colors than Mr. Prax's. That's when I knew Caleb was finally where he belonged. Caleb didn't waste time saying good-bye. He turned and ran, hopped and skipped deep into his world, until he disappeared in a place the canvas did not show.

My joy to have seen him so happy overwhelmed my grief at knowing he was gone. With my eyes full of tears, I reached my hand into that world too. I felt the warmth of that strange light. How I wanted to launch myself in there as well, but Mr. Prax had something else in mind.

"I need a gatekeeper," he told me. "Someone to decide whom Caleb would want in his world. Will you do that for me?"

I didn't answer him. Instead I went to a shelf, opened a sheet, and together we gently covered the canvas.

That night we brought Mom and Dad to the gallery, to show them the masterpiece—and although my parents can be thick as a brick sometimes, one look at the painting and they understood. My mother cried tears of both joy and loss, as I had. My father hid his feelings by comforting her.

Since then, I've been taking my own art lessons. I still don't know much about art, but I do know that there are places inside of us—palaces of glorious light and caverns of unknowable darkness. Magical places filled with brilliant, unimaginable colors that we suffer to bring forth.

I know I could never suffer the way Caleb did—to imagine a place so perfectly that it becomes real—but if someday I can paint just a shadow of the possibilities . . . perhaps that will be enough.

RALPHY SHERMAN'S JACUZZI OF WONDERS

. . . .

We were sitting in our hot tub, minding our own business, when *she* came out to join us. Vermelda.

Roxanne, my younger sister, let out a groan. "Ugh! Here it comes," said Roxanne. "Do you think it will want to sit in here with us?"

"Pretend we don't see her, maybe she'll go away," I said, but unfortunately Vermelda did have a mind of her own—amazingly small though it was—and she was determined to warm up to us and force us to like her. She was my father's girlfriend, you see, but we knew she was after his money, just like all the others. Needless to say, we didn't like her very much.

"Hi Ralphy, hi Roxanne," she said with a pretty capped-toothed smile. "Can I join you?" Her skimpy polka-dot bikini made her look like she'd walked right out of a Coppertone ad.

"I guess," I told her. "It's a free country."

She dipped a pink-painted toe into the water. "Ooh, it's hot," she said.

"The better to boil you with," responded Roxanne.

Vermelda chuckled uncomfortably, slipped her foot in inch by inch, and descended into the bubbling tub of chlorinated water. She sat next to us and tried to make conversation.

"We were talking about foreign languages," I told her, "and how funny some words are."

"Really," she said.

"Yes," I told her. "For instance, in Mexico, the most popular brand of bread is called *Bimbo*."

Roxanne nodded. "Bimbo bread," she said. "Only in Mexico, they pronounce it like this: *Beeembo!*"

I looked at Vermelda and smiled widely. *"Beeeeeeembo,"* I said, very slowly.

"Well, that's certainly interesting," said Vermelda, lowering her shoulders into the water. "So," she said, "your father's told me a lot about both of you."

I kicked my feet just enough to get her hair wet. "Really," I said. "He hasn't told us anything about you."

"But," added Roxanne, "I think we know everything we need to know."

Vermelda smiled uncertainly.

"Be careful where you sit," I told her. "People have been known to disappear in this Jacuzzi before."

"Disappear," repeated Vermelda. "What do you mean 'disappear'?"

I raised my eyebrows. "Exactly what you think, Miss Hyde: They come, they have a soak, and they're never heard from again."

"Yes," chimed in Roxanne, "it's a mystery never fully explained."

Vermelda wagged a press-on nail at us. "You two!"

she said. "Your father told me about you and your stories." But the way we just smiled when she said that made her even more uncomfortable. So she changed the subject.

She looked up at the trees, then down the long expanse of our sizable backyard. "It must be nice," she said, "to live in such a big house. Your father must get lonely with no one to share it with. No one grown-up, I mean." And then she added, "I'm so sorry about your mother. It must have been terrible for you to have her taken from you so young."

"Oh," sighed Roxanne, "she'll be back."

Vermelda looked at us with the clueless eyes of a lab rat. "But . . . but I thought . . ."

"Yes, that's what everyone thinks," said Roxanne.

"But the truth is," I told her, "she was abducted by aliens."

"Oh really," said Vermelda, clearly not believing a word of our testimony.

"Mm-hmm," I said. "Right here in this very backyard. The ship came out of the trees and sucked her up through a straw."

"Pretty amazing," added Roxanne. "I saw it through my window. It's one of my earliest childhood memories."

"We get postcards from her occasionally," I said.

"But we can't read them," finished Roxanne. "On account of they're written in Alien."

A pulse of water surged in the Jacuzzi. A big bubble surfaced. It was getting dark, and the lights in the hot tub made it look like a bubbling vat of radioactive acid.

Suddenly, Roxanne sat up straight.

"I think it's down there," she whispered. "I felt it brush past my toes."

"Felt what?" asked Vermelda, pulling in her knees.

"You know," I said with a friendly grin. "The Loch Ness Monster."

Vermelda sighed, relaxed, and crossed her arms. "Now come on, Ralphy," she scolded. "I mean, some of the stories I've heard you tell are good—really good—but the Loch Ness Monster? In a Jacuzzi? How could that be possible?"

Roxanne looked at her with scientific seriousness. "We think there might be a space-time worm-hole."

"This Jacuzzi's much deeper than it looks," I explained. "It's so murky—Dad never cleans it out. You can't even see the bottom, can you?"

"No," said Vermelda. "But . . ."

I lowered myself into the water until my lips were just above the surface. "I sent my toy submarine down there once, with a camera attached," I said. "It went down, but it never came back."

The water continued to churn. The pump sounded like the engine of a great ship, a submerged groan, deep and hollow. I grinned.

"You know," announced Vermelda, her face getting more twisted and furious-looking by the minute, "a good boarding school would help the two of you learn the difference between fact and fiction. Someone ought to persuade your father to send you to one."

Roxanne folded her arms and stuck her nose in the air. "If you don't believe us, ask Dad."

"Of course, Dad probably won't tell you," I added. "He's trained to conceal the truth, no matter how much he's tortured."

Vermelda looked at us sideways. "Excuse me?"

"You know. They teach you that stuff when you're a spy," Roxanne whispered.

I rapped my sister on the arm. "Roxanne, we're not supposed to tell!"

"Oh yeah, I forgot."

"Your father's an accountant," insisted Vermelda. "I met him when he was doing my taxes."

"A *cover*," I explained. "I mean, do you really think an accountant could afford a house like this?"

Vermelda looked at us like a snooty poodle. "Maybe he got the money from the aliens," she said, painting on the sarcasm as thickly as she applied her mascara. "And they pay to keep him quiet about your mother's abduction."

My sister's lips quivered and I could see her pushing the tears out of her eyes. "You think that's funny?" shouted Roxanne, through the tears. "You think it's fun to tease small children who have no mother?"

Vermelda took on that laboratory rat look again. "But . . . but I was just playing the game—you know? Playing along with you two."

I took Roxanne under my arm and shot Vermelda an accusing glance. "You really don't have to be so cruel. Making fun of us. Calling our lives just a game."

"And I thought you were nice," pouted Roxanne.

I stared across the surface of the pool. The currents of the churning water seemed to change slightly.

"Ooh!" said Roxanne suddenly. "There it goes again. Did you feel it?"

"That," proclaimed Vermelda, "was not the Loch Ness Monster. It was your foot."

I shrugged. "Maybe it was, and maybe it wasn't."

Vermelda shivered.

"Cold?" Roxanne asked.

Actually, the water around our toes *was* beginning to feel a bit chilly.

"Hmmm," I said. "It's as if water is being pumped in from a different source."

"There!" shouted Roxanne. "Don't you see it?" She was pointing to the center of the huge tub.

Vermelda jumped in spite of herself. Her knees were locked up tight against her ample chest, and she was staring wide eyed at the bubbles. It's amazing the things you can see in the shifting shapes of hot tub bubbles. I don't know what she saw, but she did start to look just a little bit anxious.

"Oh!" growled Vermelda, furious. "Now you listen here, you little mucus-nosed brats! There's nothing in here but you and me. The bottom is only four feet deep, and I'll prove it by standing up!"

"I wouldn't do that if I were you," I warned.

"Shut up, you!" she barked.

She stood up. She went down.

I shrugged. "I tried to tell her," I said to Roxanne as we both gazed into the bubbling water. Then with a *blub-sputter-cough!* up came Vermelda, her perfectly coiffed hair now a wet mess hanging over her face.

"Help me!" she gurgled, reaching out her hand.

Roxanne and I just looked on with pity. "Can't you swim?" asked Roxanne.

And that's when *it* appeared.

Suddenly, from the center of the Jacuzzi, the creature's immense head rose up from the water and grabbed Vermelda in its wide, tooth-filled mouth.

Vermelda tried to scream, but the thing swallowed her in a single gulp. We watched a bulge slip down the creature's long neck, like a snake swallowing a mouse.

The monster roared, then pulled its head back down through the Jacuzzi, squeezing way, way down to the bottomless depths, where, in some way that we don't quite understand, our Jacuzzi connected to that famous Scottish lake.

Of course the monster never came after us. After all, we fed it.

The tub returned to normal, except for the fact that it wasn't hot anymore. Now the only sound was the endless churning of the murky water. A single press-on nail came floating on the current of lukewarm bubbles and bumped against the side.

Roxanne shook her head. "Some people just don't listen," she said and reached over to turn up the heat.

Dad came out into the backyard a few minutes later, wondering where Vermelda had gone.

"Nessie ate her," we told him.

He shook his head sadly. "Not again. Didn't you warn her?"

"Of course we did," I told him. "But she had a mind of her own."

"How awful," said Dad. "Who's going to eat that extra steak tonight?"

"You can take it with you," I suggested, "and eat it on your way to the Pentagon tomorrow."

Dad sighed in resignation and turned off the Jacuzzi. The light went out and the bubbles settled. "All right, come on inside, you two. There's a postcard from Mom in the kitchen."

"Really?" Roxanne raced off into the house, still dripping wet, and I followed.

Of course we couldn't read the card, but man, the picture on the front was great!

NUMBER TWO

● ●

A *purpose,* he thinks, *a purpose in life. Everyone has a purpose in life.* Yes, this is true—it has to be true—but what is his purpose? Will he have to search it out in a long quest, or will it come to him on wings, in a vision or a dream? Someone with great wisdom has brought him into this world—would that someone ever tell him why?

And how long would he have to wait for an answer?

Not long.

Not long at all.

Pulled out of darkness, and into a bright light he has never known before. Shapes swirl all around him, moving colors and lights, all out of focus. An eye, a face, a soft, warm hand lifting him up, making him feel wanted, needed. He wants to cry out with joy, if he only knew how to cry. Sounds of voices, talking, laughing.

And a grinding noise.

Moving now. Moving across the room, through the light, and toward the noise.

"Wait your turn," a voice says sternly.

In the center of the light is a round shape, and in the center of that round shape is a dark hole.

Moving out of the light and into darkness again, into the dark hole, filled with a strong, musty odor. His head is firmly caught in the darkness.

Tight.

Uncomfortable.

He begins to panic.

And the grinding noise starts once again. Loud, all around him—around his head, grinding and slicing.

Spinning blades.

Sharp gnashing gears, grinding against each other— they slice deep into him, cutting away. He screams, but no one can hear over the grinding. *Help me! Help me, please! Something's gone wrong!*

If someone listens, someone has to hear.

I'm alive.

If someone knows, someone has to care.

But the slicing, gnashing knives carve deep, taking pieces of him away forever. Cruel. Unfeeling.

Until all that is left of his head is a dark pinpoint. His soft sensitive core, once protected, is now exposed to the world.

Out of the darkness, into the light again, moving through the air that painfully blows across the pale open wound.

The soft hand that had given him so much warmth before now holds him too tightly and flips him upside down. His aching face is pressed against a rough, flat surface and scraped against it, like a nose to the grindstone, until bits of him are left behind, silver-gray traces of his life draining away onto the clean coarse surface.

This can't be it! This can't be my purpose! he

screams. *I am meant for more! Much, much more! Doesn't anyone hear me?*

But all that can be heard of his screaming is a gentle *hissssssss* as the little girl presses his face to the rough page and writes:

How I spent my summer vacation

THE SOUL EXCHANGE

. . . .

Down the long, empty corridor, in the chrome and tile bathroom of Bloomingdale's, Nina closely examines a zit in the mirror.

Her face, in every other way, is perfect, but that's not what Nina sees. She sees the ugly whitehead on her cheek and thinks it's Vesuvius about to erupt and wipe out Pompeii. She imagines half of Manhattan must know about the zit by now. Her stunning green eyes, her shimmering red hair, mean nothing to her as long as that *thing* sits on her face.

"I hate myself," she mumbles. "I'm sooo ugly!"

The lonely restroom is not so lonely. An old woman has entered. She comes to the mirror beside Nina and tries, with bony, shaking hands, to put lipstick on her thin lips. Nina notices how the crone's rouge sits on her wrinkled cheekbones, round and far too red. She looks like a clown. Nina has no love, nor patience, for the elderly. To her, a woman like this has no business wearing makeup. What good is it going to do? You'd need a cement mixer to hold the makeup it would take to spackle in those wrinkles. You'd need a machete to cut through the hairy mole on her chin.

The old woman steals a sideways glance at Nina in the mirror. Her eyes are narrow, and cloudy.

"What are *you* looking at?" says Nina. Her voice booms far too loud around the gray-tiled room.

"You have a pimple," says the woman, her voice as rough as sandpaper. Probably from smoking, thinks Nina. Stupid woman. It's a miracle she's even lived this long.

"I know about the pimple," says Nina, striking an irritated pose. "So why don't you mind your own business."

Nina dots the solitary spot with Clearasil. Still the old woman looks at her sideways. The woman, Nina notes, wears an ill-fitting coat that must have been very expensive once. Some sort of fur. But now it's moth-eaten, and mangy. She wears jewelry also—not the cheap imitation stuff, but the real thing. A diamond as big as an almond. What a waste for something so precious to be on someone so wretched, thinks Nina.

"I couldn't help but hear you, dear," says the old woman. "You sound very, very unhappy with yourself. You poor thing."

Nina looks at herself in the mirror again and grimaces at her own reflection. It's not right. It's not perfect enough. She wants to rip her awful face off and flush it down the drain. Her best friend, Heather McKnee, is prettier. She hates, hates, hates Heather McKnee, but most of all she hates her own face, and the zit it gave birth to.

The old woman smiles, and her thin lips disappear, revealing two rows of yellow teeth. "I understand what you're going through," the old woman says.

"How can *you* understand anything?" snaps Nina.

"My bones may be old," says the woman, "but my mind is still keen. I remember my youth." Then she reaches into her pocket and pulls out a business card, holding it out to Nina with a quivering hand.

"Give him a call," she says. "He's sure to help. He knows what you need."

Then the old woman turns and limps toward the door. Nina follows her out and watches as, cane in hand, the woman makes the long trek down the empty hallway to the department store.

Nina looks at the card. Burgundy lettering on a shiny gray background.

Dr. Morgan Taylor Voyd
Discorporeal Physician
Extractions and implants while-u-wait

Nina, not being blessed with vocabulary skills, has no clue what any of it means, but the chicken salad in her stomach doesn't feel too happy about it. Suddenly, Nina doesn't feel like shopping today.

Tonight is pizza night for the "in" group at East End Private Academy. On pizza night, they go out to Little Guido's and eat pepperoni pies with extra cheese, then talk about all the people they hate, such as teachers, parents, and anyone who's not at the table with them.

Heather McKnee is there, and as she arrives Nina says a silent die-slowly-and-painfully prayer to herself, about Heather; then they sit to eat. Nina sits next to Brent, her boyfriend of the month. But she'd much rather be sitting next to Heather's boyfriend. He's a ninth-grader, and goalie of the junior varsity soccer team. Brent, on the other hand, is in eighth grade like the rest of them. He's captain of the eighth-grade wrestling team. Big deal.

Brent sits there, with his arm clamped around her shoulder, like they were Siamese twins, connected at the wrist and neck.

"I'll just have a salad," says Heather. "I don't need all that grease." And then she looks at Nina and adds, "It could give me zits."

Nina smiles, pretending that it doesn't bother her. She can feel the zit on her face, like a big, fat pepperoni. She turns her face away so that the others can't see it, but they do. Her friends have radar when it comes to how a person looks. They can spot an out-of-place hair from a hundred yards. They can smell a dying fashion trend like body odor.

Brent looks at Nina's face, as if she had pulled off a mask to reveal she was the Phantom of the Opera. He takes his hand from her shoulder, releasing her from his boyfriendly headlock. "You know," he says, "there's soaps you could use for that."

"Ha, ha," says Nina, covering it with her hand and intensifying her silent death-prayer toward Heather. When the pizza comes, Nina refuses to eat. Instead she pulls out the card the old woman gave her. Dr. Morgan Taylor Voyd.

"Who's he?" asks Brent, looking over her shoulder.

"Some doctor," says Nina. She tries to hide the card, but Brent pulls it away. He looks at it, but it might as well be written in Chinese.

"What is he, a zit doctor?" asks Brent.

"No, he's a discorporeal physician," she says, trying to sound wise, as if she knows what it means.

Brent passes the card around the table to Nina's humiliation.

"Must be a shrink," says Heather. "A good therapist can really help with emotional problems."

"He's not that kind of doctor!" insists Nina. "And anyway, I'm not going to see him." She grabs the card back, crumples it up, and hurls it across the room. It lands right in the trash.

"Two points!" announces Brent and slips her into his boyfriendly headlock again, in spite of the zit.

Brent talks about himself as he walks Nina home. How annoying. Nina much prefers the boyfriends that will talk about her. Brent is in the middle of professing his undying belief that there's nothing fake about professional wrestling when Nina interrupts him.

"Brent, do you think I'm pretty?" she asks.

Brent shrugs. "Yeah, sure, why not?" he says—which doesn't mean much, because Brent would say anything as long as he got to show her off to his friends in public places.

"Am I prettier than Heather?" Nina dares to ask.

Brent hesitates. "Well . . ." he says, "you're both pretty. You're just pretty in different ways."

The answer infuriates Nina. She takes his hand and pulls it behind his back in a move that rivals the best of wrestlers.

"Ow!" yells Brent. "Lemme go! What's the deal?"

"You were supposed to say 'yes,' " she tells him. She pushes him away and heads off in the other direction. Brent, still dumbfounded, doesn't follow.

She retraces her steps down First Avenue and ducks

back into Little Guido's. Then she digs through the trash, past greasy half-eaten slices of pizza and sticky soft-drink residue, until she finds the crumpled business card.

Deep in the unknowable parts of Brooklyn, overgrown sycamores line the streets of the old neighborhood where the doctor lives. Their roots buckle the sidewalk into concrete accordion folds. The homes are brown brick, and although it's a bright day, the trees block out every trace of the sun.

Halfway down the street, a shingle hangs outside the doctor's home office. M. T. VOYD, reads the shingle. *Appointments required.* Nina has already made her appointment.

She rings the bell, and a moment later the doctor answers the door.

"Come in, Nina, I've been waitin' for you," he says with a heavy Jamaican accent. He is a tall man, as gaunt as a skeleton, with skin the color of dark chocolate. His head is clean-shaven, and buffed to a perfect shine. There is no way to tell how old he is.

"Did you have a time findin' tha place?" he asks. His voice is soothing, yet at the same time cold and slippery, like wet ice on a glass table.

"No," answers Nina. The truth is, she barely had to look for the place at all. It's as if she was drawn right to it.

The doctor has a huge cherrywood desk, spotlessly clean. His walls are covered with diplomas and certificates from the best universities and finest medical associations. He folds his long fingers together and sits at his giant desk across from Nina, smiling.

"Just what kind of doctor are you?" asks Nina.

"I began as a surgeon," Dr. Voyd tells her. "A brilliant one, oh, yes. Surgical techniques have been named after me. I am in textbooks."

"But you're not a surgeon anymore?"

"I got bored with that kind of medicine," he tells her. "Too easy. No challenge. And where I come from, I have seen many things that science cannot explain." He smiles, revealing spotlessly white teeth. "That is the kind of medicine I practice now. The kind of medicine *you* need."

Nina can feel her knees shaking. "How do you know what kind of medicine I need?"

Dr. Voyd laughs deep and heartily. "These things are obvious to a trained professional like me," he tells her. Then he gets deadly serious. "You are unhappy with yourself. You are thinkin' there must be a way to change those features of yours. Those green eyes aren't green enough, maybe. Or your nose comes to too sharp a point. And then there's that unsightly blemish on your cheek. Am I right?"

Nina nods, entranced by the way this man has examined her soul the way another doctor might examine her throat.

"Well," he tells her, "I am in the business of makeovers."

Nina's heart pounds with anticipation. "You can fix my face?"

"Not just your face, but everythin'. I can give you a new look—a new feel. I can give you a new body." And with that he stands and ushers Nina to a door that opens up into his spacious house. Only it is not a house. It looks more like a hospital from the dark ages. Or a morgue.

The walls are painted black and covered with strange symbols Nina cannot read. Hanging from the ceiling are voodoo dolls, with a single pin piercing them through the heart . . . and beneath each doll is a body, lying on a narrow steel gurney. At least a dozen of them, their slow breathing the only sign that they are alive.

"Welcome," says Dr. Voyd, "to the Soul Exchange."

Nina steps into the room to get a good look at the people in there. They are not the most beautiful specimens of humanity. Very unattractive by Nina's standards.

"It's a simple procedure," explains Dr. Voyd. "I extract their souls and implant them into new, more desirable bodies."

"How come they're all so ugly?"

Dr. Voyd sighs. "Once my clients trade up, I sometimes get left with bodies no one wants."

Nina can understand that. It's just like at last month's cheerleader bake sale. The lousy cookies never sold— and here was a whole roomful of lousy cookies.

"But . . . I don't want any of these bodies."

Dr. Voyd smiles his toothy grin. "I have one coming in tomorrow that is perfect for you." Then he reaches into a folder, pulls out a wallet-sized photo, and presents it to Nina.

And the moment Nina sees the face in the picture, she knows it's right! The girl in the picture is about thirteen, like Nina—and perfect. Thick locks of wavy blonde hair. Smooth skin, a wonderful smile, in a photograph rich with bright colors. She is far more beautiful than Nina—or even Heather. Yes, this will be the perfect exchange.

"It is my policy," explains Dr. Voyd, "that if you agree to the exchange, you may take nothing with you. Your personal belongings, your money—all must go to whoever inherits your old body. You understand?"

Nina nods. It will be worth it. Now only one question remains.

"How much?"asks Nina.

"For you," says Dr. Voyd, "two hundred dollars."

Nina thinks about it and nods. "It's a deal."

During school the next day, the anticipation hangs heavy over Nina. That morning she had "borrowed" her mother's ATM card and taken out two hundred dollars, which she brought directly over to Dr. Voyd. The exchange is to take place at four o'clock in the afternoon, *sharp*.

Throughout the day, she keeps glancing at Heather and can barely contain her mocking laughter. *Ha!* she thinks. *Tomorrow I'll walk into school—everyone's eyes will turn away from Heather and turn to me!*

By the end of the day, she can't keep it to herself anymore. She has to tell someone. On the way out of school, she pulls Brent aside.

"I want to show you something," she tells him. Then she ever so carefully pulls the picture of her new self out of her purse. "What do you think of her?" she asks him. "Don't you think she's beautiful?"

Brent's eyes go wide as he stares at the picture, then he looks at her worriedly. "Is this a trick question?" he asks.

"Just answer me; Do you think she's beautiful?"

"Well . . . yeah," he says. "But . . ."

"But what?"

Brent holds the picture closer. "Her hair's kind of goofy looking . . ."

Nina lets out an irritated puff of air. "Well, she can change her hair. That's easy."

Brent hands her back the tiny picture. "So, what's the point?" he asks.

Nina smiles slyly. "You'll see."

* * *

Four o'clock sharp. The wind blows through the thick sycamores, and the rustling leaves are so loud Nina can't hear herself think as she races down the street.

"Everything is prepared," says Dr. Voyd as Nina steps in. "Follow me."

They pass through the room full of unwanted bodies to a smaller back room, lined with a dark and gritty metal Nina guesses must be lead. A body lies on a stone slab, covered with a sheet from head to toe, and above it dangles a voodoo doll, pinned like the others through the heart. A second stone slab waits for Nina. Dr. Voyd closes the heavy leaden door, and it seals the room like a bank vault.

"Lie down, Nina," says the good doctor. "This will take only a little while."

Nina lies down and watches as the doctor takes another doll from a shelf, then comes toward her with scissors. She tenses, terrified of what he might do. He brings the scissors to her face, then moves them off to the side, snipping a lock of her ginger hair. Then he takes that hair and carefully sews it into the seam of the doll's cloth head, calmly humming to himself.

"Just about ready."

Nina tries to fill her mind with thoughts of the perfect face she will have. At last, Dr. Voyd takes a long hat pin with a round pearl-colored head and holds it in one hand, the doll in the other.

"Take a deep breath and hold it," he instructs. She does, then watches as he jams the pin through the doll's heart.

Sudden blackness colder than the dark side of the moon, and emptier than death.

Nina feels herself moving through the darkness. It

*could be a million miles, it could be a million years;
time and space have no meaning now. The cold is
unbearable, but she has no mouth to scream, until—*

She gasps, a deep breath of air that rattles in her
lungs, then opens her eyes to see the cloudy cloth that
covers her face. She pulls it back, revealing a bright
light above. Out of focus. Then the light is eclipsed by
Dr. Voyd's dark round head.

"You can get up now. The exchange is complete."

Nina sits up, feeling achy and weary. She looks to
the other stone slab, but her old body is not there.

"You were in transition for an hour," explains the
doctor. "During that time, the other client took posses-
sion of your body, and left."

Nina reaches up to her face. It doesn't feel right.
Something is wrong. Her face feels cracked and rough
like elephant skin. There is something round and fuzzy
on her chin. A hairy mole!

She looks at her hands and screams. But no one can
hear her but the doctor in the leaden room.

Her hands are old. More than old—they are ancient:
wrinkled and weak, covered with the age spots of
thirty thousand sunrises.

Dr. Voyd smiles coldly. Mockingly. "Another satisfied customer," he says and hands her a mirror.

Nina is now the old woman—the same old woman
who gave her the card. *This* was the body she has
exchanged for her own!

"No!" shouts Nina, but her voice sounds frail and
thin. "This can't be me."

"What's the matter?" says Dr. Voyd. "Mrs. Ditmeyer
is a beautiful woman! Of course, not as young as she
was in that picture. But beauty is ageless."

Now Nina understands why the hairstyle in the picture didn't seem right. Why the photograph's color seemed to be almost painted on.

"You can't do this to me!" she screams. "I'm only thirteen!"

"Correction," says the doctor calmly. "You *were* only thirteen."

She cries through her blurry aged eyes.

"Of course," says the doctor, "if you're not happy with Mrs. Ditmeyer, I could give you one of the people in the other room."

"I don't want any of them!" wails Nina. "I want someone young! Someone beautiful."

Dr. Voyd crosses his arms. "Well," he says. "I can make such an exchange for you, if you bring in a young subject to exchange with."

At last some hope! "Yes!" she cries. "I'll bring you someone as soon as I can!"

"And then of course there's my fee," explains Dr. Voyd. "To put you in a young body . . . that will cost you an even million dollars."

She gasps for air, her breath taken away by the mere thought.

"But I don't have a million dollars!"

Dr. Voyd puts a large firm hand on her shoulder. "Come now, Mrs. Ditmeyer. Of course you do! Have you checked your bank account lately?"

An early fall day, several weeks later. The old woman feeds pigeons in the park, all the while looking sideways at a group of loud young kids. Faces she recognizes. She wears jewelry so heavy she can barely lift her hands. But she does. She lifts one to her cane and painfully forces herself to her feet, making her way down the cobblestones to the group of kids.

Her former body is there, with someone new inside it. Brent, and Heather are there as well. They laugh and make fun of anyone who walks by. The kids see her coming and start to laugh hysterically.

"Here comes your last girlfriend," says the Nina-body to Brent. Brent thinks it's just a joke.

The old woman hobbles forward, her weary eyes fixed on Heather. She takes a card out of her pocket and holds it out to the gorgeous young girl with her trembling old hand.

"I've been watching you," says the old woman desperately to Heather. "I know a doctor who can help you. He can make you look even better than you do now. He knows what you need."

The Nina-body laughs cruelly as if it is one big joke. She can afford to laugh; she is no longer trapped in Mrs. Ditmeyer's body.

Heather looks at the card with disgust and hands it back to the old woman. "Thanks, but no thanks," says Heather. And then she smiles. "I've already been to Dr. Voyd. In fact, I was there before you were."

The Nina-body laughs again. In fact, both girls laugh; evil and cold, like two members of a dark and secret club.

The old woman feels dizzy. She begins to fall backward, and Brent catches her. "Hey, are you okay?"

He helps her up, and she shrugs him off. "I'll be fine," she says and limps away, not daring to look back.

So Heather had been a client. Of course! She should have known! The fact was, Nina had come to realize that there had been many, many others who had been through Mrs. Ditmeyer's body. She was certainly a rich old woman. When the whole thing began, a year ago, she had fifteen million dollars according to her bankbook. Then about once a month, she wrote a check for a million dollars—always to Dr. Voyd, as different people were tricked into her body and bought their way out. It's like a game of musical chairs, and every turn costs a cool million—until someday soon the money will run out, and someone will get trapped in poor Mrs. Ditmeyer's chair for good.

Voyd is a genius. And now he is very, very rich. She admires him almost as much as she hates him.

As she makes her way toward her decaying mansion across Central Park, someone comes running up behind her.

"Yo, old lady, wait up!"

It's Brent.

"What can I do for you, young man?"

"That doctor you're talking about," he says. "Is he a doctor for guys too? I mean, can he make a guy better looking too?"

The old woman looks him over slowly. This is something she has not considered. "Perhaps," she says, then reaches into her pocket and pulls out the card, handing it to him.

"I think he'll know what you need, too," she says. "Call him for an appointment right away."

"Thanks," says Brent with a big smile. Then he turns and runs off.

The old woman grins at the new prospect. It's not what she expected—and of course there will be many, many adjustments . . . like getting used to the wrestling team for one—and then there's the problem of dating her old self.

But she'll learn to adapt, because, in spite of everything, his youth is certainly worth a million dollars. And beggars can't be choosers.

DAMIEN'S
SHADOW

•••••••••••••••••••••••••••••••••

With power beating through my muscles, I drove around Max, controlling the basketball with such incredible skill it seemed to be a part of me. On the sidelines, music pounded out a rhythm with the same intensity that my ball pounded the rhythm on the pavement. It was starting to get late, but the heat of the day had not yet given way to the comfortable cool of a late summer evening. I knew the hour by the length of my shadow, stretched across the asphalt, making my legs look even longer, like a real basketball player's, and making my arms seem monstrous, like the arms of a spider.

I drove around Max, around Jason; I even got past their center who was so tall and broad everyone just called him Tree. I broke for the basket! With my powerful feet, I flew into the air, and once airborne left my shadow orphaned on the pavement. With the ball cupped in my hand, held there as if by a magnet, I swung it toward the basket. I was not tall enough to dunk, but I could bounce it off the backboard like a pro and get it right into the net.

Then as I released it from my fingers, out of nowhere a hand eclipsed the light in my face, smashing the ball back into my nose. I saw a bright flash before I felt the pain, which came sharp and jagged. I tumbled and was down once again, meeting my shadow in a bone-bruising hug on the concrete. Cupping my hands to my nose, I cursed. My nose was not broken—at least I didn't think it was—but it was bleeding. I stood up trying to fight the pain, trying to pretend it didn't hurt. Then I screamed at that sycamore of a center, "Goaltending, you moron!"

My best friend Max—who also happened to be my greatest adversary when it came to basketball—just shrugged.

"It wasn't goaltending. You weren't close enough to the basket for it to be goaltending."

"What are you talking about, I was right up there!" I yelled.

I brought up my shirt and dabbed the drops of blood com-ing from my nose. I looked to my own teammates. They backed me up—they pointed fingers at Max and their choose-up teammates.

"You guys cheat like there's no tomorrow!" I said.

Max crossed his arms. "Are we gonna play, or are we gonna stand here picking each other's noses?" And he whacked the wagging fingers out of his face. My teammates backed down and just shook their heads.

"C'mon, we're still winning," I said, which was true.

It was then that I saw something strange. At first I didn't think much of it. My shadow was long and dark, cast by the setting sun. Although I made no move, I saw my shadow reach out and slap Max's shadow hard on the back. I saw Max's shadow stumble, then recover.

When I blinked, both shadows were exactly where they should have been, and I wondered if it was just a trick of the light, or if perhaps I was getting sunstroke from playing basketball for too long in the heat of the day. I thought nothing of it until the following day.

Summer school.

Day after day of math and science, math and science. Not the summer school you might think. I was there by choice. I wasn't there to make up for work I didn't do, but to get ahead on work I didn't want to do next year. I had always been a good student and a good athlete, too. I was competitive in everything I did, and I *always* won. When they said that I might be able to skip eighth grade by doing extra work during the summer, I knew it was a challenge I wanted to take. I knew it was a game I could win.

"You're just not smart enough," said Melanie, who was taking the summer classes with me. She was always first in class, getting A's and A-pluses in everything that she did. I liked Melanie almost as much as I hated her. It was good having her around because it kept me on my toes.

"You're just dumb," she said as we worked through math equations. "It's a fact: boys are dumb—girls are smarter. No matter what, I'll always get higher grades than you."

I gritted my teeth and sneered at her. "Don't count on it, Melonhead." I turned back to my work, concentrated on the numbers, and tried to solve the equations faster. I processed those numbers in my brain at the highest speed that I could and was about to announce the answer when Melanie shouted it out.

"Forty-two," she said. "X equals forty-two."

"Very good, Melanie," said the teacher. I pounded my fist on the table, and the teacher turned to me laughing. "Gotta be a little bit faster, Damien."

Melanie smiled her superior smile at me. I was so angry that my eyes were about to tear. I looked away, catching sight of the shadow of my head against the cabinet. I could see my profile, my nose elongated, my lips, my hand.

My hand . . .

I held my hand up and moved my fingers, remembering what I had seen on the basketball court yesterday. The shadow-fingers moved along with me. I put my hand down . . . but my shadow-fingers did not go down. I saw them grab Melanie's shadow by the hair. I watched as another hand came up and around the neck of Melanie's shadow. I saw Melanie's shadow begin to struggle—and all I could do was stare, slack jawed.

"What are you looking at, dweeb?" I snapped my eyes to Melanie, who was staring at me as if I was from outer space.

"Just the wall," I said. "Is it against the law to look at the wall?"

When I turned to the shadows again I still saw it just as clearly as before. My shadow held Melanie's shadow tightly by the neck until Melanie's fell into a heap, just a clump of gray light where the wall met the floor. It stayed there like a discoloration in the green linoleum tile, and I imagined that the dead, dark spot would never wash away. I shivered.

"Damien," Melanie said to me, this time a little bit more worried than before. "Are you all right?"

I guess my eyes must have peeled way too wide. "Yeah, yeah, I'm fine," I said. Then I asked her what she saw when she looked at the wall.

"Just your shadow," she said with a shrug.

"Me too." I raised my hand and wiggled my fingers. My shadow did exactly what it was supposed to do. When we were done with our assignment we left the room. I never mentioned to Melanie what she should have noticed about herself: She saw my shadow, but she did not see hers.

The news was out by the next morning. Gossip traveled through our neighborhood like a scent on the wind, and the day's gossip was about Melanie Defalco.

"Did you hear?" shouted a neighbor to my mother as she came out to pick up the newspaper. "Melanie Defalco ran away."

"Ran away?" my mother said.

I shook my head. "No way, Melanie's not the kind of girl that runs away. The only thing she'd run away from would be a bad grade."

But as I walked around the neighborhood that morning and listened to what people had to say, it seemed clear that Melanie was gone. For most of the morning I had completely blocked out what I had seen in the classroom the day before. See, there are things you deal with every day, and there are some things you keep to yourself not because you want to but because you have to—because nobody, not the people who love you the most, not even your closest friends, would ever believe you.

What I saw or what I *thought* I saw, I kept to myself for a long time. Each day I went to school and prayed that Melanie would show up, but she didn't. And every time that I caught sight of my shadow, in stark sunlight or in the faint incandescent glow of a single lightbulb, I shuddered. It seemed so innocent. Always doing what it was expected to do while I was looking. But then every once in a while it would make a move that looked slightly wrong—that was slightly different from what I had done. But I'd tell myself that it was my imagination.

A week after Melanie disappeared, I spent an afternoon over at Max's house reading comic books, talking about sports—and girls. We spent a whole half hour trying to figure out the best way one might ask out Sondra Marsh, whom all the guys liked, but no one dared date.

I guess it was our talk about girls that got Max thinking about Melanie.

"You think she'll ever come back?" asked Max.

I didn't answer him. I knew it would be a disaster to say anything. But even disaster would be better than what was going on inside my head just then.

"Max," I said quietly. "Have you ever taken a look at your shadow? I mean, really taken a look at it?"

"My shadow?" He thought about it and shrugged. "Sure, I guess. I mean, it's just my shadow."

"Yeah," I said to him. "But what if it wasn't *just* your shadow? What if it had ideas of its own? What if it had the power to do some of the things that you thought about doing in your darkest dreams, but wouldn't dare in real life."

Max returned his attention to his comic book. "Get real!" he said.

I pulled the comic away from him, and it tore. I thought that he'd get mad at me but instead he just looked at me strangely, like I was from the moon.

"Damien? What's up with you, huh?"

I tried to pick my words very carefully, arranging them in my head before I spoke them out loud.

"Max," I said. "I think something's happening to me. But it's not just me. It's happening to people around me, too. People . . . like Melanie." I could almost see a wall fall between us as I spoke. Max backed up.

"What about Melanie?"

"My shadow strangled hers," I told him.

Max looked around, picked up his torn comic book, and headed toward the door.

"Listen, I gotta go," he said.

"This is your house," I reminded him.

Max took it in stride and nodded. "Right. Well, I gotta go anyway." And he left me alone in his living room. So much for my best friend.

The next morning I smoothed the whole thing over, doing my best to convince Max that it was just a joke that he took too seriously. Then, at summer school, I didn't talk to anyone all morning. I even ate lunch alone, in the corner of the cafeteria. The fluorescent lights above gave off an even, diffused light—the kind of light that is flat and smooth and casts no shadows. It was the kind of light I tried to hide myself in these days. I sat there moving my semi-liquefied beans back and forth on my Styrofoam plate, trying to make my over-achieving brain figure out some way to control my shadow. Is there a way to grab it? Is there a way to hold it? And if I could, what might it feel like in my hand? Would it feel light and airy like a black silk stocking or would it feel cold and empty like a swirling winter wind? I would probably never know because whenever I tried to reach for it, it would reach away, copying my moves precisely until the moment I stopped looking.

The thing about isolating yourself in a huge cafeteria is that suddenly you become a target—suddenly you get noticed, even if disappearing is what you are really trying to do.

Someone sat down across from me. When I looked up my heart stopped painfully suspended between beats. It was Sondra Marsh. Of all the times for Sondra Marsh to come up and talk to me, why did it have to be today?

"Hi," she said. "You looked lonely. I thought you might want some company."

I shrugged, barely even daring to look at her. "I'm not lonely," I told her. "Just alone."

She went on talking about how she hated having to take summer school science and how she wished she could have brains like me. "Maybe, if we have some of the same classes in the fall, we could study together," she suggested.

"Yeah, sure," I told her, trying not to sound overly enthusiastic. "Yeah, that'd be great." It's amazing how girls have the power to wipe a guy's mind clean. Suddenly I couldn't remember what I had been thinking about before she'd gotten there.

She smiled at me again. "It was nice talking with you, Damien." Then she got up and left.

The cafeteria was clearing out now, everybody getting ready to go home since summer school was only half days. I watched Sondra leave, and before I knew what I was doing I was up on my feet and hurrying after her. I just couldn't leave it alone. I had to push forward, just like I did in the classroom, just like I did on the court. I never waited for success at anything; I always pushed it. I had never been pushy with girls, but this time I had been handed the ball. I couldn't keep myself from driving down the line.

I caught up with her just outside the school gate.

"Sondra," I called.

She turned and smiled just as the sun came out from behind a cloud, making it seem as if her smile had lit up the sun.

"Sondra, you doing anything tonight?" I asked.

She shrugged. "Nothing special."

"I was thinking of going to the movies," I told her. "Maybe you'd like to come?"

She had no hesitation. "Yeah, that'd be nice," she said.

Suddenly I realized that I had done too good a job catching up with her and that I was standing a little too close. Embarrassed I looked down to see our shadows short and squat in the midday sun against the pebble-marked concrete.

My shadow was kissing hers.

The sight stupefied me, and all I could do was look up at Sondra, gaping.

"What's wrong?" she asked.

"Nothing, nothing," I covered. "I'm just glad about going to the movie together, you know?"

She took me for my word and left saying "See you tonight." I looked down as her shadow pulled away from mine and left with her.

I knew that I could never let her shadow meet mine again, so instead of going to the movies that night, I found a broken-down basketball court that no one wanted to use and played by myself, trying to lock my mind on my layups. I went home when it got too dark to see on the court—too dark to have a shadow—and I stayed out of streetlights all the way home.

But at night, when I was alone in my room, sitting at the head of my bed, I couldn't get the shadow out of my mind. The moonlight painted a sharp-edged shadow against my closet door of the tree outside my window. The long and twisted bough seemed like an octopus tentacle, and I kept on expecting it to move.

I reached out my hand into the moonlight, daring to catch a shadow on the wall. Five fingers, so much darker than my own and just as powerful. Then I dared do something I had been afraid to from the very beginning. Quickly, impulsively, I threw my hand to the wall, grasping at my shadow . . .

. . . And I actually caught it! I held it, but only for a second. I felt it slip out of my fingers like a snakeskin.

So, I said to it, *you can be caught.*

It was a glimmer of hope, and I held on to that glimmer as I fell asleep.

Nothing could have prepared me for what happened next. It was one of those strange twists of fate that damns everyone it touches. It turned out that Sondra went to the movies looking for me, but instead found Max. From what I was able to find out, they never went into the movie. Instead they went to get a burger and talk. They talked a lot. They got to know each other a lot better—and the next day I saw them walking down the street, much too close to one another.

I said "Hi" as I passed them, and didn't dare look at them. Only Max said "hi" back, his nose up in the air, like a proud victor. After all, he had wanted to go out with Sondra as much as I had. I kept walking, determined not to look back, but I felt my feet start to drag as if my shoes had suddenly become lead weights. It wasn't my shoes. Tall and thin in the morning sun, my shadow stretched behind me, trying to crawl away from me like a spider, trying to crawl to them. I picked up my pace and dragged it away.

At home, I closed the door to my room, pulled the curtains, and shoved blankets in the cracks. Then, when my eyes had adjusted to the dim light, I took a roll of masking tape and sealed out the light coming from around the door frame. I unplugged the digital clock and sat alone in absolute darkness. I knew a shadow couldn't exist without the light to create it, and I wondered if it was possible to live the rest of my life in total darkness.

Max showed up later that afternoon. I heard him ring the bell. I heard his muffled call up to the window.

Maybe he'll go away, I said to myself. But best friends don't go away. He must have found an open window, because he found his way in and creaked open my door, flipping on the light. I must have looked like a vampire as I sat there on the bed, squinty eyed.

"What are you sleeping for? It's the middle of the day!" he said.

"You don't want to be here, Max. Just go."

"You're mad at me because of Sondra, aren't you?" he said. "Well, you had your chance. You're the one who stood her up."

I felt my hands ball up into fists. How could he be so stupid to think that all of this could be just because of that?

"I don't want to hurt you," I told him.

He looked at me, jutting his jaw out. "What's that supposed to mean? You want to fight me, is that what you're saying?"

"No, no, no!" I screamed at him. I reached out and pushed him hard, trying to get him out the door.

"You've got problems," he yelled, and then he yelled a whole lot of other things. But I didn't hear his words—I was too busy watching my shadow, which had already crossed paths with his. See, there's this plastic sword leaned up against the corner of my room. It's just a stupid prop from a school play I was in, but I've always kept it because it looked kind of cool. Max kept talking on and on while I watched my shadow grab the shadow of the sword . . . and mercilessly run Max's shadow through!

I screeched as my shadow pulled out the sword. Max's shadow crumbled to the ground and lay there, leaving the same gray stain that Melanie's had left.

"And one more thing," continued Max. "You stink at basketball, too!"

He turned and stormed out.

I knew I couldn't just leave it like that—I didn't know exactly what would happen to him, but I still had to warn him!

I caught up with him on the street and forced him to stop and listen.

"Max, remember when I was talking to you about the shadows?" I said to him.

"Yeah, what about it?"

"I want you to look at yours." Max was the kind of guy who didn't believe a thing unless he saw it. He looked down. The afternoon sun was bright, casting my shadow on the concrete. Where his shadow should have been there was nothing; only unbroken sunlight. He looked at it for a long time. He didn't get scared. Not yet.

"So what's the trick?" he asked.

"No trick," I told him. "Your shadow is dead. I watched it die."

But I suppose even seeing wasn't believing this time. He hardened his gaze.

"I don't have time for this noise," he told me and walked off, looking at the ground, at his feet, at his arms, and everywhere around him for the slightest trace of his shadow.

I skipped dinner. I told my mom that I had a stomachache and sat alone in my room and watched TV, trying to lose my mind to the blaring box.

Max came by around eight o'clock that night. I don't know what had gone through his mind between when he left me on the street and the moment he showed up at my door, but whatever it was, it had left him tired and terrified. He asked if he could spend the night at my house—a sleep-over—like we had when we were younger.

We sat together watching TV. The early evening shows and the late evening shows, the news and the late late movies. Then we played board games, long after my mother had gone to bed, long after the moon had set in the sky. We sat there keeping each other awake, terrified of what might happen to Max if he fell asleep.

"Maybe it's not going to happen to me," said Max at around three in the morning. "Maybe if I stay awake, the sun will come and will give me a new shadow."

"Maybe," I said. For after all, he had gone this long and he was still here. Maybe knowing it was about to happen would keep it from happening. I tried to stay awake, but my eyelids dropped and my consciousness fell away from me, as if it had fallen through a trapdoor.

I remembered no dreams. I remembered no time passing—until I was woken by a desperate whisper at dawn.

"Damien! Damien, help me!"

I snapped my eyes awake. The first rays of dawn were pouring through the room, creating shafts of light filled with floating dust. I watched as the light passed through the air and shone on Max's unbelieving face. If you have ever seen a person vanish from existence, and I doubt that you have, it's not something that happens all at once. It takes a while—seven minutes to be exact. The amount of time it takes the sun to break over the horizon.

Max lost his dimension first, not all of them, just one. As I looked at him, he seemed to go flat against the wall. I reached up to touch him, but instead banged my hand against the plaster. He was a flat projection against the white wall of my room.

"Do something, Damien. I'm afraid!" he cried.

But how can you help a projection? As the sun peaked higher above the horizon, his color went next. His bright blue shirt faded, and all his colors became different shades of gray like an old black-and-white TV. The sound of his sobs became more and more muffled as all the grays of his form began to swirl and merge together, the hard lines dissolving into one another, like a stain washing out of a wet rag.

"I'm sorry, Max," I whispered woefully. "I'm so sorry . . ."

In a moment, there was only a dull shape where he had been, and in a moment more, it faded completely, leaving nothing but a daylight-painted wall.

That was yesterday.

In the neighborhood, people are still trying to figure

out what happened to Max. The police questioned my mom and me. I told them that he must have disappeared sometime during the night.

There'll be more questions, I'm sure—but that doesn't matter anymore.

It's night again. Outside the moon shines bright. Mom stayed up late after the trouble-filled day, but finally dozed off around midnight. As for me, I'm staying up all night.

I don't need to worry about my shadow anymore. It's not going to hurt anyone. Because now it hangs from the shadow of the tree limb, against my closet door. It was hard to catch, and harder still to loop the shadow of the rope around its neck, but in the end I won. I always win.

Amazing to think that the limp blotch dangling against my closet door could have caused so much trouble. But I can rest easy, knowing that it will never bother anyone ever again.

So I'll wait out the night, playing board games alone and listening to the ticking of the clock. It was a fine thing to beat my shadow at its own game. Now all I have to do is beat the dawn.

TERRIBLE
TANNENBAUM

••••••••••••••••••••••••••••••

Endless rows of pine trees stretched as far as the eye could see, all pruned to a perfect point. It was Christmas again, and Tammy McDaniels trekked with her parents and brothers to select this year's tree.

"See all these trees," said Brett, Tammy's older brother. "Well, in six weeks, they'll all be dead."

Eight-year-old Michael, Tammy's younger brother, stared at Brett with wide-eyed shock. Apparently he had never thought of such a thing—that trees could live and die like people.

"That's right," continued Brett. "They'll all be axed so that we can have presents under a tree." Brett gave his little brother a nasty smile. "Merry Christmas."

"Brett, kindly keep your thoughts on the subject to yourself," said Dad.

Tammy, who was almost twelve, wasn't bothered anymore by the things Brett said. But it did bother her to see Michael tormented so.

"Will you look at this one," said Mom as she

pushed through the pine branches of the lot. "This is a healthy one."

"Too small," said Dad.

"How about this one?" said Michael.

"Too thin."

"How about that one?" said Tammy.

"Too fat."

"Gimme a break," said Brett. "What is this, 'Goldilocks and the Three Trees'?"

"Brett," said Mom, "why don't you just go sit in the car."

"Are you kidding," mocked Brett. "I'm having too much fun."

It was easy for Tammy to ignore Brett. She had grown used to him and his sick sense of humor. And anyway, she had her *own* philosophy when it came to Christmas trees. To Tammy, the trees on the lot were grown for one purpose only: to celebrate Christmas. Naturally, it was what the trees lived for. If a Christmas tree did have a spirit, Tammy knew it wanted to be taken from the lot and brought into a warm home where it could be adorned and surrounded by love. Each Christmas, Tammy could feel the goodwill breathing from those happy trees. She wondered if there were ever any Christmas trees that didn't feel that way.

Brett, however, never got into the Christmas spirit. When the family had purchased an aluminum tree one Christmas, he had complained that it was tacky. "How silly," he had said, "to have a tree made of metal." To Brett, it had been as ridiculous as the pink plastic flamingo Mom maintained on the front lawn. Then, when the family decided to buy a live tree, Brett complained that they were brutally killing a tree just to celebrate Christmas. As if that weren't enough, each year on Christmas morning Brett would pout that he never got what he wanted, even when he got exactly what he wanted.

It had become a family tradition that all of them go to the U-Cut Christmas tree lot and pick out a tree, even though everyone would rather Brett stay home, including Brett.

"By the way," said Brett, "don't count on Santa coming this year. There's no such thing as Santa."

Michael's lower lip started to quiver. True, Michael was getting a little old to believe in Santa, thought Tammy, but just because he did believe didn't mean that Brett had to tease him about it.

"You take that back!" screamed Michael.

"Brett," said Dad, "it's bad enough you pull the wings off of flies. Do you have to torture your poor brother, too?"

"Make him take it back," bawled Michael.

"Take it back, Brett," warned Mom, "if you know what's good for you."

"Fine, fine," said Brett. "I take it back. There is a Santa Claus, okay? He comes down our chimney every single year with nice gifts for all the good little boys and girls, and he does lunch with the Easter Bunny in the off-seasons. Are you happy now?"

Michael stopped crying, and Mom sighed with relief.

"Santa knows you're a good boy, Michael," she said—but said no such thing to Brett.

They pushed their way through hundreds of trees until they lost all sense of direction. Tammy played hide-and-seek with Michael, hidden in the dense forest of evenly spaced trees. Michael would occasionally get lost and cry until someone found him—but that was all part of the fun. Dad forged on, holding the heavy ax by its neck until they came to a little bald spot in the tree farm. In the center of that bald spot stood what looked like a single perfect tree. It wasn't until the family got closer that they realized several unusual things. First, the tree was surrounded by a thin layer of snow, even though the first snow of the season had not yet fallen. Second, all the other trees on the edge of the bald spot were leaning away from this tree in the center. It looked like they were actually growing away from it.

If trees had legs, thought Tammy, they might be running away.

"Well, isn't that odd," said Mom.

"Not at all," said Dad, "trees don't always grow straight."

It was cold inside that clearing, colder than anywhere else on the tree farm. Mom zipped up her jacket and made sure Tammy and Michael's were zipped as well.

"Cold front coming in," said Dad.

Brett stepped up to the tree and reached into it to see if there was any rot.

"Ouch," he said and quickly withdrew his hand. He had pricked his finger on a pine needle.

"I don't like this tree," said Brett. "It has an attitude."

But if any of them had reservations about the tall, lonely pine, those reservations were wiped away when they saw the price tagged onto one of its lower limbs: eight dollars. The tree was eight feet tall, and any of the other eight-foot trees went for at least fifty bucks.

Dad was overjoyed. But Tammy was feeling more and more unsettled by the tree. A tree shouldn't make a person feel that way, she thought.

"Maybe," said Tammy, "the people who run the tree farm know something we don't. Maybe that's why it's priced so low."

"Nonsense," said Dad, hefting the heavy ax he used only once a year. "They must have mispriced it by mistake and I'm not going to pass up a bargain like that." He swung the ax low.

THWACK. The heavy head of the ax buried itself deep in the tree's soft, wet wood. He pried it out and swung again.

THWACK. The tree groaned and creaked; the cold wind blew stronger. The surrounding trees seemed to take on a greater tilt away.

THWACK. At last the tree could hold on no longer.

TIMBER! Severed from its roots, the tree collapsed down, its branches flopping to the side.

"We're going to have a fine Christmas," said Mom.

"The best ever," said Dad.

"Another one bites the dust," said Brett.

And the tree said absolutely nothing.

At home they sawed the base smooth and wrestled the tree onto the large stand, where an iron spike dug itself deep up into the tree's trunk.

Ten minutes later the tree had already started to tilt. No one seemed to notice since they were busy hanging ornaments. First, they hung the lights. Then came the glass ornaments. Next, the special ornaments: baby's first Christmas, first Christmas together, and the like. They adorned the tree till its outer branches were shining and beautiful . . . while deep within, the twisted branches remained dark.

It was by far the tallest tree they'd ever had. Eight feet did not look that big on the lot, but here in the house, even with its vaulted ceilings, the tree seemed huge and imposing. When the family finished trimming the tree, Mom sat at the piano, and they gathered 'round. As was family tradition, they sang "O Tannenbaum"—which none of the kids could sing with a straight face, as this was what they always sang to tease Joey Tannenbaum, who lived across the street.

It wasn't until after they were done that they noticed

how cold it was getting in the house, although the heater was turned on full blast. Even Moby, their goldfish, seemed to shiver in his bowl on the piano. They decided to have a fire, which warmed the fireplace, but little else.

"It's the humidity," said Dad.

"Bad insulation," said Mom.

But it was Michael who was first to suspect the truth.

"It's the tree," he said.

Tammy and the others looked over to him, as he stood next to the tree.

"That's odd," said Mom. The tree seemed to be leaning toward Michael.

"It doesn't like us," said Michael.

The way Tammy saw it, the tree wasn't just leaning—it was looming. Looming over Michael like a tidal wave waiting to crash.

"Get real," said Brett.

Tammy went over to the tree and put her hand near it. It did seem colder near the tree than anywhere else. Tammy thought to reach her hand into that tree, but then changed her mind. There should be some light in there from all of those lights strung around the outside of the tree, she thought. Why was the inside of the tree so dark? She turned to her parents.

"Weird," she said, but they both shrugged. Then she felt something soft and spiny like a caterpillar rub up against her arm. She gasped and slapped it away.

But it was only a bough of pine needles.

She was about to laugh, until she realized that she was not the one who had moved closer to the tree. *It was the tree that had brushed against her!*

A red ornament jangled ominously on the branch.

"Smile, sweetie!"

A bright light flashed in her face as Mom snapped a

picture of her beside the tree. Did the tree flinch at the flash, or was it just Tammy's imagination? She couldn't be sure—but there was one thing she *was* sure of: this tree, unlike any other tree she had known, had no feeling of Christmas love and goodwill.

That night, after the fire had burned out, the only glow came from the multicolored lights of the Christmas tree. They cast spiny shadows of red, blue, and green on the white walls.

Brett was in his room being antisocial, and before Tammy went to sleep she went in to give him a piece of her mind.

"What are you doing in here?" challenged Brett. "I thought you were downstairs sucking in some Christmas spirit."

"Brett," she said, "sometimes you're such a creep. Just because you don't like Christmas doesn't mean you have to ruin it for the rest of us . . . telling Michael there is no Santa, and all."

"Why should you care?" said Brett. "Maybe I'm trying to protect him—maybe I don't want him to be disappointed later."

"Maybe you just like to make people feel lousy." Tammy turned to leave but just as she reached the door, Brett said something that made her stop.

"There is a Santa Claus."

Tammy turned back. "What?"

"I said, there really is a Santa Claus."

"Shut up, Brett. I don't like it when you tease me."

"Who said I was teasing?" Brett was looking down at the video game he was playing. He paused the game for a moment and looked at Tammy.

"He can fit down the chimney 'cause he doesn't have any collarbones. His reindeer fly because nobody told them that they can't. He gets to every kid's house 'cause he knows how to stop time and travel in between the seconds. And every once in a while when he finds a bad kid, a *really* bad kid, he wakes him up in the middle of the night and tells him, 'Hey son, I'm sorry, but you don't get a gift from me this year 'cause you've been way too naughty.' Just like he said to me when I was nine." Brett shrugged "And I guess I've just been naughty ever since."

Tammy stood there for a minute, almost taking it seriously. Then she shook it off.

"Ha ha," said Tammy. "Very funny."

"Laugh all you want," said Brett, "but that's why I don't like Christmas, and I hope someday Santa gets his."

Downstairs, their father unplugged the Christmas tree lights and the whole house was plunged into pine-scented darkness.

At three in the morning, everyone was awoken by a heavy THUD and the tinkling of breaking glass. It was the kind of dead-of-night sound that brought terror to any household.

"Daddy," Tammy wailed, "someone's breaking in!"

Tammy came out of her room to see Dad racing downstairs with a baseball bat—all set to do battle with a burglar. He flipped on the light . . . but there were no burglars. In an instant it became clear what had intruded into their night: The tree had fallen onto the piano, leaving shattered glass ornaments all over the keys.

The fear that had woken Tammy up still raged inside. She kept telling herself that it was just a fallen tree, but it didn't quiet the uneasy feeling that pounded through her. There was something about the sight that was terrible—like a car wreck.

Michael, who was peering down through the banister, began to cry.

"I don't like that tree, Daddy," he whimpered.

"It's okay, Michael," said Mom, "we'll fix it in the morning."

She and Dad lifted the tree off the piano. Pieces of broken Christmas ornaments rained to the ground. Baby's first Christmas, first Christmas together. All smashed to bits.

"We'll have to get a new base," said Dad. The steel legs were horribly twisted out of shape. "Funny," said Dad, "they said it could hold a tree up to fifteen feet. Metal fatigue, I guess."

Then Tammy noticed that among the fine fragments of shattered ornaments were shards of glass much thicker than the rest.

"Moby!" she gasped. From behind the banister, Michael began to whimper harder.

"It's okay," said Dad, trying to exercise a little damage control. "We'll get a new fish tomorrow. Maybe we'll get two. Maybe a whole family—how's that?"

Michael settled down and Tammy helped her parents clean up the mess, and when they were done, Tammy stared at the tree until Dad turned out the light. Lying on its side, the branches of the tree all swayed down toward the ground—but somehow those branches seemed to be moving, squirming, and it occurred to her that they never did find Moby.

Tammy went to bed that night dreaming of a tree whose branches were octopus tentacles and whose trunk was the scaly body of a python.

By the time Christmas Eve arrived, the tree had fallen a total of five times. Dad had tethered it to the light hanging from the ceiling above it, and still it pulled loose from the cord. Now it was tied to three different spots in the room—the light above, the banister, and the upstairs railing. There was no way it was moving—it looked like King Kong in shackles. As for its trimming, they had given up on glass ornaments, since there were only two or three left. All that remained on the tree now were the unbreakable things—silver tinsel and popcorn chains. The walls in the corner of the living room were filled with gouges, and green marks from where the tree had fallen, as if some battle had taken place there.

Michael wouldn't even go into the living room anymore, and Dad joked that they would probably have to put their presents under the tree—literally *under* the tree—to prop it up.

"When's the Christmas tree burn this year, Dad?" Michael asked. Everyone knew Michael hated to see the trees burn, but this was one year he was actually looking forward to it.

Although he wouldn't admit it, even Brett steered clear of the psychotic pine as best he could.

It was Tammy who kept a close watch on the tree, puzzling over it. She imagined that if trees truly did have personalities, then a tree could be bad, the way some people might be bad.

She sat alone across from the tree as Christmas Eve faded into twilight. While everyone else watched *It's a Wonderful Life* in the family room, Tammy peered into its darkness—watching it the way a guard might watch a prisoner. Its limbs blew with the breeze, even though there was no breeze, and when she looked into it long enough, she could swear she saw faces in there, staring out at her, but she was certain it was just her imagination. Why did they have to take this tree? Why couldn't they have chosen a tree that *wanted* to be a part of the celebration, as did all the trees they had in the past? Trees that weren't selfish. Or evil.

"I'll bet Santa will come and take it away," said Michael, peering in from the hallway. "Santa would never let a tree like that ruin Christmas."

It took a long time for Tammy to fall asleep that Christmas Eve. She kept thinking about what gifts the morning would bring, but mostly she thought about the tree.

In her dreams, the tree, with its snake trunk and octopus arms, spoke to her in a slippery whisper of a voice.

"Have yourself a Merry Little Christmas," the dream-tree told her, then wrapped its tentacles around her and pulled her into its darkness.

Christmas dawn was frigid. Cold drafts had blown down the open flue of the chimney, filling the house with icy winter air and fireplace ash.

Tammy awoke to the sound of bells jingling somewhere outside and met her brothers just coming out of their rooms farther down the hall. Not even the icy cold could blunt the joy of Christmas morning, thought Tammy. Not even the tree. Tammy smiled as she and her brothers reached the edge of the stairs.

"I know Santa brought me a new bike!" said Michael.

"I'll bet I got a whole mess of video games," said Tammy.

"I'll probably get stupid clothes that don't fit," said Brett.

And with that, they clambered down the stairs.

Brett saw it before Tammy did. He gasped, and his face became as green as the Christmas cookies they had eaten the night before.

Santa, it turned out, had indeed come.

Michael instantly began to cry and buried his face in Brett's chest. Brett, who normally would just push him away, held Michael tight. Tammy could only gape. Holding onto the banister, she felt as if her legs would buckle beneath her.

The tree had fallen sometime in the dead of night. This time it didn't engulf the piano. Instead it pinned one brightly dressed, bearded old man to the hardwood floor.

Outside the sleigh bells impatiently jangled, and deer hooves restlessly scraped the roof.

Where were Mom and Dad? thought Tammy. Had they drank so much eggnog last night that they were sleeping through this?

The man trapped beneath the tree turned his head weakly and spoke in a raspy, wheezy voice.

"Muh-muh-merry Chr-Chr-Chr—"

Tammy looked to Brett. The corners of Brett's mouth had turned up in a sinister, Grinch-like grin. He raced off into the garage and returned moments later with their father's ax. Then he looked at the man beneath the tree.

"I've had about enough of you," he said, as he raised the ax high above his head.

"No!" screamed Tammy. She grabbed Michael, turning his head so he wouldn't see.

The blade came down and sank deep into the dark trunk of the tree. From the tree came a hideous wailing cry.

"Watch out!" warned Brett. He swung again. Pine sap splattered in all directions, leaving thick, sticky clumps in Tammy's hair. A third swing. *Thwok!* Then a fourth. *Thwok!* The tree shattered, its limbs tangled around the ax, but Brett pulled it free and raised the ax high above his head one last time.

"You're sawdust!" he said, and with that brought

down the blade for a final blow that split the terrible tree in two, freeing the not-so-jolly man trapped beneath.

Michael and Tammy helped him up. Brett, dropping the ax to the ground with a thud, stared the silver-haired visitor in the face.

"Well," said Brett. "What am I now? Naughty or nice?"

"Please, I'm in no mood," said Santa. He turned to look up at the closed door of their parents' room. "Tell your parents to stay away from cheap trees. You get what you pay for." And with that he turned to go.

"Thankless old man," grumbled Brett beneath his breath—but apparently nothing escaped the man's large, pink ears.

Santa turned back to Brett. "Very well," he said reluctantly, tossing Brett a small box. "I suppose you've earned it. It's in the driveway."

Inside the box Brett found a key.

"And Brett," said Santa Claus. "Do stop being such a royal pain, or I'll have to send the tooth fairy to punch out some of those pearly whites."

Once their guest had made his exit, they bundled up the remains of the tree and Tammy set it on fire in the backyard. She watched as it burned with a furious flame, its darkness completely consumed and reduced to ashes in a matter of minutes. Then, she set up the old aluminum tree.

In the end, Tammy had to admit that Christmas morning turned out the same as always—for by the time Mom and Dad finally dragged themselves out of bed, the house was clean and there was nothing out of the ordinary to explain.

Nothing, that is, but the Porsche in the driveway.

DEAD LETTER

∎ omb it may concern, I have, for much too long,
suffered from the insults, cruel attacks, and bla-
tant discrimination in your newspaper. As the only
newspaper in the town of Rancid Falls, one might think
you would learn to be fair and objective with the items
you report. But in fact, in your paper, my kind have
been treated with more disrespect than we can stand.

Haven't you ever heard the expression "show
respect for the dead"? I suppose not! Let me tell you, it
makes quite a few of us roll over in our graves—as you
can probably tell from that rumbling sound you occasionally hear from the graveyard on the hill.

Oh sure, you write all these nice, flowery notes the
day we go on to our final rest—but the second we try to
return from the grave, we are no longer welcome. Suddenly those sweet flowery things you've written
become big banner headlines, turning our simple home-
comings into horrible events, as if we were criminals.

For instance: Your headline last week read CORPSE

TERRORIZES FAMILY. I would hardly call climbing in through a window in the middle of the night and playing Beethoven on the family piano an act of terror. If the woman fainted and the children ran screaming down the street, that's their problem, don't you think?

A week before that, you ran a headline that read HEADLESS WOMAN CARJACKS CADILLAC. As if it had been her intent to steal that car. *She was headless*—the last thing she wanted was to be behind the wheel—but when that inconsiderate driver ran away in terror, what was a poor headless woman to do? She had to drive the car if she was ever going to make it home.

What's so awful about it? Why would you deny a cold lonely soul the right to slip into their home in the middle of the night and have a nice long talk with their family? Surely you would be thrilled to wake up one night to find your own dear sweet grandmother, whom you haven't seen for so many years, suddenly there beside your bed, smiling that wise grin of the dead. No doubt she's often thought of paying you a surprise visit (or at least that's what she told me).

The fact that more and more of the dead have been returning home should be a clear indication to you that your newspaper ought to be publishing more articles of interest to the dead.

Perhaps a story on facial creams. Maybe a whole section devoted to death-styles of the rich and famous.

But all you seem to dwell on is how, after we've risen, we attack the living, turning them into one of us. Surely you can't see any harm in that—after all, we're just doing what creatures do naturally: increasing our numbers. Who are you to deny us that simple right?

And by the way, we resent the way your newspaper, and others, has referred to us in such insensitive and cold ways. We are not "zombies," we are not "moldering bones." The correct term for describing us is quite simply the "Living Dead"—and should you continue to refer to us in such unkind and bigoted ways, you will most certainly be hearing from the International Association of Living Dead Persons (IALDP).

And now I would like to set the record straight on this business about us eating the brains of the living. Don't you see how ridiculous that sounds? Why on earth would a person who has risen from the grave want to eat a human brain (no matter how tasty and delectable it might be)? After spending all that time wasting away in the graveyard, don't you think we might have developed a craving for something better— like maybe a steak, or some Häagen-Dazs? And anyway, I'm sure you'll agree there are quite a few people out there who could do with having their brains eaten. Oh, there are quite a few brains I personally can think of that would not be missed. And yours is high on my list. In fact, it's on all our lists. (That is . . . it *would* be if we actually *did* eat brains, and I'm not admitting that we do.)

But what gets me most, sir, are your laughable articles that announce the doom of mankind, and how you cheer the military's pathetic attempts to stop us from populating the finer neighborhoods of Rancid Falls. Why is it that you never mention that *we* are becoming the majority population of this lovely town? In fact, the only empty neighborhood in town is the graveyard. The dead have no use for it anymore, as we've decided if we must return to ashes and dust, then we might as well live out our deaths in a comfortable home, spending eternity watching old reruns of "I Love Lucy" (which are certain to be on for all eternity).

In the end, sir, I'd like to remind you that in this world of five billion living, breathing people, *we* are the majority. We've been here longer than you have, we will be here after you're gone—and believe me when I tell you that we have all decided it's time to come back.

So when you hear that knock at your door this evening, and when you open it to reveal a hungry, grinning crowd, their heads tilted to one side in the dim streetlight, don't be afraid. It's only us.

BOY ON A STOOP

A row of abandoned tenements rotted on a neglected city block where few people had reason to tread. There were a million ways to get where you were going without passing down that ruined street; nevertheless, Martina took that path to school every day. The buildings had been that way for years, and Martina felt a strange sort of affinity toward them. In many ways, they were like her: ignored . . . forgotten . . . friendless. Nothing, not even a row of buildings, deserved to be that unloved—so she limped her way down the broken weed-choked pavement of the condemned street every day.

That's where she saw him.

He sat on the stoop of one of those empty buildings, halfway down the block. It was the only one without a board nailed over the entrance. There was no door, just a dark rectangular hole, rimmed in chiseled plaster. Like her, the boy on the stoop seemed thirteen. He had jet black hair and features so handsome she couldn't help but stare at him out of the corner of her eye. She could feel his eyes following her as well, and it embarrassed her—because no boys looked at her. More often than not, they just looked away. Martina's glasses were thick, and one eye was slightly clouded from a childhood accident involving a neighbor boy and a stick. Then of course there was that horrible leg brace she was forced to wear on her weak right leg. She had been self-conscious about both her eye and her leg for as long as she could remember, keeping to herself and shying away from other kids. She preferred sticking to her books, and her many collections.

So naturally when she noticed this handsome boy looking at her, her face went red, and she hobbled out of his sight as quickly as she could.

He was there again as she walked home that day, still sitting on that porch as if he had nothing better to do than calmly watch life pass on the city pavement before him—and he was there the next day too, and the next. Each time he followed her with his eyes as she passed, like a portrait that always seemed to stare at you, no matter where you stood. It was easy to deal with being invisible, but being *noticed*—that was something entirely different.

Did he look at everyone like that or was it only me? wondered Martina. She concluded that there must be something wrong with him in the head, otherwise why would he be looking at her?

Her parents were not problem solvers when it came to talking through Martina's troubles. Her father, who worked two jobs, was rarely home, and when he was home, he was too exhausted to take much time for her. Martina's mom, who worked at a day-care center, was always frazzled, and the last thing she wanted to hear at the end of the day was a child's voice—even her own child's. Still, Martina knew she tried her best to be a functional parent.

One night she approached her mom, who sat up in bed, reading a sappy romance novel. "Mom, am I a good person?" she asked.

Her mother answered without hesitation, "Of course you are, honey."

"Then why don't more people like me?"

This time her mother did hesitate and began to rub her forehead as if the question had given her a headache. "It's not that they don't like you," she answered, "it's that they don't *know* you. If you let people know you a little better, then they'll like you a whole lot."

It was easy for her mother to say, but it just didn't work that way at school. There was a cruel pecking order in junior high, and once you found yourself at the bottom, the other kids wouldn't let you rise above it.

But the boy on the stoop wasn't a classmate. He didn't know her place in the pecking order.

Martina knew these were dangerous thoughts, because they filled her with the kind of hope that could be her ruin. So she returned to her room and tried to drive thoughts of the boy out of her mind. She read a book, recatalogued her various collections—rare coins, stamps, even exotic insects, pinned and labeled in a glass case. But not even her insect collection could keep thoughts of the boy away. In the end, she gave up, and closed the case on her tiny impaled bugs, locking it with a shiny silver key. She wished she could lock away her thoughts of the boy as easily.

The following Monday, a wind blew through the city, marking the arrival of fall. The leaves had already turned and were dropping to the pavement, where they would soon dry into brittle brown shells crunching underfoot. Martina wore a coat that was too heavy and out of style as she left for school.

When she peered down the boy's street, she could see him sitting on the porch again, leaning back on his elbows, relaxed and calm—such a stark contrast to the tension of the city. She approached him at a slow, steady pace, trying to hide her limp as best she could. Then, when she was in range, she turned to him—looking at him directly, rather than sneaking a glance. He smiled at her and she felt trapped in his deep green eyes. Her heart pounded a mysterious rhythm in her chest—a rhythm of fear and wonderful anticipation—because she knew that today she would say something to him.

But instead she gagged on the gum she was chewing and launched into a coughing fit.

"Are you all right?" he asked, getting up and taking a step closer to her.

Feeling like an imbecile, Martina cleared her lungs with a strong solid cough. The gum flew out and became one with the rest of the muck on the broken sidewalk. "I'm fine," she said.

"Good," said the boy. "I wouldn't want you to die. Not here on the sidewalk, anyway."

There was an uncomfortable moment, so Martina tried to fill it. "Don't you ever go to school?" she blurted out and immediately realized how nasty she must have sounded.

She thought he might make a nasty comment back to her, and that would end it forever. But instead he just kept smiling. "I get tutoring at home," he answered.

Now that she had the chance to study his face, she could see how irresistibly perfect it was. It should be illegal, she thought, for a face to be that perfect. He seemed smart too. Not just smart, but sharp. Sharp as a blade.

"What's your name?" he asked her.

"Martina."

"I'm Forest." He held out his hand, and as Martina reached forward to shake it, she dropped her books. They clattered on the cracked stoop and lay splayed and limp, like accident victims, on the sidewalk.

Martina quickly knelt to pick them up, but her brace didn't afford her such quick movements. Forest helped her, and when the books had all been collected she found herself sitting beside him on the stoop, like it was the most natural thing in the world.

"Why do you sit here?" she asked him.

Forest shrugged. "It's where I live."

Martina looked up at the ugly tenement. Five floors of windows, either broken or boarded over, graffiti scrawled on the soot-stained bricks—and if she listened, Martina imagined she could hear the scuttle of rats. "How very sad for you," said Martina.

He gave her his strange enigmatic smile again, and it penetrated her like a sudden blast of radiation. "It's not what you think," he said. "Would you like to see?" He gestured toward the entrance.

Martina turned to look into it. It was a dark cavity, and the wind echoed inside it, making it sound as if it were breathing. A heavy vine grew out of the darkness disappearing off the edge of the stoop, and she wondered what could possibly grow in a place like that.

"Uh . . . I'll be late for school," she answered and stood up, suddenly afraid of his friendship, and the place in which he lived.

He grabbed one of her books before she hurried off. "Maybe I can read this," he suggested. "And the next time you come we can talk about it together."

She nodded, feeling her familiar shyness closing up her throat so she couldn't speak. Then she turned and hurried down the street and around the corner to school.

As luck was no friend of Martina's, it turned out the book he borrowed, *Oddities of Nature*, was the subject of an oral report she was supposed to give that day. Still, she was glad that he took it . . . because it was one of her favorites, and when she worked up the nerve to walk down his street again, they'd have a lot to talk about.

"It doesn't make sense," she told her mother over dinner that night. "He's living in an abandoned building, but he says he has tutors."

Tonight her mom rubbed the back of her neck, instead of her forehead, which meant that her usual sinus headache had been replaced by her biweekly migraine. "Maybe we should talk to the police about him," she said, trying to hide the suspicion in her voice. "He could be a runaway."

Martina fiddled with the spaghetti on her plate. "If he's a runaway, he wouldn't be sitting out there like that, for the whole world to see."

"Well, whatever he is, I'd leave him alone if I were you."

Her mother's words lingered for the rest of the night, like the heavy taste of her over-spiced pasta. Her mom had always pushed Martina to make more friends, but at the same time injected her with a heavy dose of paranoia. Here was someone who seemed to welcome her friendship. Was she going to throw that away? As Martina prepared for bed, she studied her plain face in the bathroom mirror and wondered what the boy on the stoop saw when he looked at her that could possibly make him smile.

* * *

"It's a really interesting book," said Forest as they sat together after school the next day. Always on the stoop—never moving from the stoop. Together they flipped through the pages of *Oddities of Nature*. "It's full of weird things," said Forest.

"I know, isn't it great?" Martina flashed him a rare smile.

They turned to a page that featured a bird with both of its eyes on the same side of its head, then Forest pointed out his favorite—a frog that could freeze solid as a rock, but would come back to life when you defrosted it. Martina turned to a dog-eared page toward the back of the book.

"This is my favorite," she said. "The anglerfish."

The picture showed a strange-looking thing with small eyes, sharp teeth, and a wormlike stalk growing out of its forehead. "It hides behind rocks, or in the dirt," Martina explained, "so passing fish only see its stalk. The fish think it's a worm and try to munch on it, then the anglerfish jumps out and munches on *them*."

Forest took a long look at her. "You really like strange things, huh?"

"Yeah," she said excitedly. "I collect them—strange coins, strange stamps—I even have a whole case full of strange bugs."

"You're not like the other girls," said Forest, never taking his eyes off her.

Martina looked away. "Are there lots of other girls that you talk to?"

"A few," said Forest, "but you're the most fun."

Martina couldn't look at him. She blushed. It was as if he knew exactly what to say, exactly what she wanted to hear. When she dared to glance up at him again, he was grinning mischievously.

"I'll bet I can show you something weird you've never seen before!"

Martina closed the book. "What?"

He stood up, taking her hand, and moved her toward the dark peeling hole of the dead tenement building. Martina grabbed the rusting iron railing of the stoop, not letting herself be dragged in.

She thought of all the things her mother had told her about strangers—and all the warnings she had heard in school, ever since an eighth-grade girl had vanished the week before.

"It's okay," said Forest in the softest of voices, "you can trust me."

Somehow she felt certain that she could—that this boy would never do anything to harm her. And besides, everyone was sure that missing girl had just run away.

Martina loosened her grip on the rusted iron railing and let herself be led into the dank, decaying building.

Forest led her through the dismal building, following the trail of that long, thick vine that grew out the front door. Around her, the mildewed paper peeled in thick layers, and the termite-eaten wooden floors felt soft beneath her feet. Then he led her through a back door, into paradise.

In the city, most low-rise buildings faced back to back, and between them one could usually find a courtyard. Those narrow brick courtyards rarely saw the sun and were usually filled with weeds and trash. This hidden courtyard, however, surrounded on all sides by condemned buildings, held a garden.

Martina had read a book called *Lost Horizon* about a beautiful, magical place in the midst of snow-covered mountains. If there could be such a place in a concrete and steel city, then this was it. She had never seen trees and plants so beautiful—wide leaves dense and green, flowers blooming with every color of the rainbow. They all seemed to sway in the breeze. They seemed to gently reach toward her. Everywhere else in the city, leaves were turning, and trees were dying for the winter, but not here. This was a lush urban jungle. Barely able to catch her breath, she touched a large purple petal that felt like silk.

"But . . . how?"

"Must be an underground spring," suggested Forest, "or maybe just a broken hot-water pipe. Anyway, it's here."

She explored the dense garden with Forest, and he explained the many plants: one that only opened up in twilight and let off a rich blue light; another that had large round seeds embedded in its branches that looked like eyes, the same shade of green as his. Martina could swear she had seen one of them opening and closing.

It was then that Martina finally began to feel just a bit apprehensive. It was getting late; the courtyard had fallen deep into shadow, and the sun had left the sky. The afternoon had quickly become dusk.

"I'm glad," said Forest, "that you're not afraid. The others were all afraid."

There were too many things wrong with this picture. Martina knew just about all of the oddities creation had spat out—but none of the plants here were familiar at all.

And then there was the vine.

Down every path, that singular vine grew, ropy and dense. She followed it with her eyes to find where it ended, for it no longer grew through the door and into the tenement. Now it looped back into the garden, as if someone had moved it. At last she traced a path to its end. It only took a moment for her to realize the truth—and exactly what it meant.

With the sun gone from the sky, a huge leafy pod, two stories tall, had opened up in the southern corner of the garden—and inside was a flower a perfect shade of ocean blue, with a dozen soft petals each as large as her hand.

"Would you like to pick it?" asked Forest.

Martina looked at him sadly. "Are you my friend?" she asked him.

"Yes, Martina," he answered. "We're friends to the end."

Martina looked at the beautiful flower, and at the beautiful boy, then she reached down and lifted up the heavy green vine. As she held it, she could clearly see how it grew right into the base of his spine, like a tail— or more like an umbilical cord. "I knew you were special," she said to him, her voice barely a whisper. "But I didn't know how special."

The truth was, there was only one plant in here; it just had many different faces. Whether it evolved from the slime of the city, or whether it came here from someplace else, it thrived, like an anglerfish.

This handsome, charming boy was merely the worm to lure its prey.

She was terrified now, but told herself that she didn't care—that her fear didn't matter. Something as beautiful as this garden, as beautiful as *him*, deserved to live . . . even if it meant that she had to die. There was almost something soothing and comforting to being devoured by this strange, exotic creature. Becoming a part of it.

Forest took her cold hands in his. "I need you to pick the flower, Martina . . . Please."

Gently he guided her toward the large lovely leafed pod in the corner of the garden that loomed like a giant cavern. As they drew closer, she could see thick, black thorns, like jagged teeth, hidden beneath the leaves. "We'll be together forever," whispered Forest, "and you'll never feel lonely ever again."

She would have let him throw her inside—she wasn't afraid to die. But she was afraid of pain. In the end it was that fear that drove her to action.

Those thorns would hurt more than the teeth of a shark.

Just as Forest gave her one final push toward the open mouth of the cavern, Martina dug in her heels, reached up, and tore off one of the cavern's tooth-thorns. With a rush of air, the giant mouth snapped shut on the hem of her dress.

"No!" she screamed. The green cavern opened its mouth once more, baring its black teeth, and the entire thing lurched closer. It clamped down on her leg—she could feel the pain shoot up her whole body. Forest backed away, his vine trailing into the thick underbrush.

"I'm sorry," he said. "I'm sorry, Martina." The giant jaws opened once more and chomped down again, getting more of her.

But it wasn't over yet. The thorn in her hand was sharp as a carving knife. She knew she couldn't fight the thing trying to eat her, so she reached out and grabbed the vine—Forest's vine—and she sliced into it.

"Don't!" screamed Forest, in a sudden terror more powerful than her own.

She felt the jaw behind her loosen its grip on her leg. She sliced into the vine again. Around her all the leaves, all the flowers, began to rustle and shake. She pulled on the vine, and Forest fell over. Then at last she found the thinnest part of his umbilical cord, jammed the knife into it, and sliced through it again and again, until she had cut it in two, separating Forest now and forever from the plant.

The boy-thing screamed, and his chilling wail echoed off the brick walls of the condemned buildings around them. Then she felt the pressure on her leg release. The leaves around her wilted and dropped, the flowers disappeared into their buds, and in a moment all was silence.

She pried open the jaws of the cavernous plant. She was bleeding, but not as badly as she had thought. It was her horrible curse of a leg brace that had saved her. The thing couldn't bite through the steel! She pulled herself free, and the dead green jaws closed with a sickening *thwump*.

She went over to Forest, who lay on the ground, as still as the rest of the garden, not breathing. But then, he had never breathed in the first place, had he?

She cradled his head in her arms, brushed his dark hair out of his face, and with tears in her eyes, she kissed him. Then she grabbed him by the arms and dragged him across the dark ground of the dead garden.

A few weeks later they tore the whole block down and found just what they expected to find in the court-yard—the dry, crumbled remains of dead city weeds, although the weeds here seemed to have grown much thicker than most other places.

Since that day, Martina always left for school early—but she didn't go straight to school. Instead, she went to the basement of her apartment building. There was a storage room down there, a room that few people knew about, and no one—not even the building manager—ever went into. It was one of the many forgotten places of the city.

Inside the claustrophobic room sat a beautiful boy with sparkling green eyes. His eyes stared up fearfully at Martina as she entered.

"So you're finally awake," said Martina. "You've been unconscious for over a month."

Beside the boy was a clay pot filled with rich potting soil, and above him hung a fluorescent growlight that made his soft skin look blue. He was very thin, but Martina knew that would be only temporary. The boy shifted to reveal the knotty vine growing from the small of his back and into the clay pot, where it had taken root. Martina poured in a pitcher of water spiked with a healthy dose of Miracle-Gro. Then she took a hamster from her pocket and released it on the ground.

"You're going to be fine," Martina told him calmly. "I have a green thumb, you know. I'll nurse you back to health."

A small tuber had already grown from the pot, and at its end was a fist-sized pod. The hamster sniffed at the pod; the pod opened and snapped closed around the hamster without a sound. The boy barely seemed to notice. Eating was an automatic response.

"Eventually you'll need larger things," Martina whispered, "but I'll take care of that too. I'll take care of everything."

The boy opened his mouth to speak, but his voice was raspy from his many weeks of sleep. "Why?" he asked. "Why have you done this?"

"Because you're my friend," she answered, happy and in control. "You're *my* friend . . . and you'll talk with me, and you'll play games with me, and we'll have good times together for the rest of our lives, won't we, Forest?"

And as she said it, she brought out a huge pair of gardening shears and set them gingerly on a shelf.

Forest shuddered at the sight of the shears. "Yeah," he said in weak but terrible dread. "Yeah, uh . . . it'll be . . . great."

Martina smiled again as she gazed lovingly at him, then she turned and limped out the door. With a shiny silver key, she locked all three deadbolts behind her.

Outside, the day was cold, but that didn't matter, because now something warm and wonderful filled Martina's heart. How good it was to be blessed with a friend like Forest.

RETAINING
WALLS

••••••••••••••••••••••••••••••••••

On a morning full of cold clouds, my father sweeps me out of bed and into his pickup truck—as if I have nothing better to do with my Sunday than to sit at his work site and watch grown men play with blocks.

"Have fun," says Mom, as if that were possible. "Don't stay out too late."

My dad smiles at her and waves as we drive off. It's the warmest gesture he can give her, now that they're divorced. Dad shoves a doughnut and a juice box into my hands as a makeshift breakfast, then he spirits me away to his work.

Big walls. That's my father's specialty. He built his first wall when he was nineteen, in the basement of an old house. From what I heard, a mudslide had caved in the weak basement wall, and Dad had gone in with Grandpa to build a strong retaining wall to hold the mud back where it should be. Thing is, Grandpa died halfway through the job, and Dad had to finish it alone. Since then, he hasn't stopped building walls.

As we drive, I can see my father's anticipation building. He likes his work—it invigorates him. You could say he lives for it, as if what he does has an importance beyond what I can measure. I always thought him small-minded to find such pleasure in the placement of stone. But then who am I to talk? I spend hours in front of a TV screen playing video games. I guess the best I can say is that what he does is *constructive*, in the literal sense of the word.

My ears pop, and I realize we are heading out of town, up into the hills. Out of the window, through the early morning haze, I can see our town below us, a grid stretching toward the horizon.

"Nice view from here," he says. "Even better where we're going." He grins at me with a glimmer in his eye. "You'll like this one, Memo."

He's the only one I still let call me Memo, or even Guillermo. To most everyone else, I'm Billy.

"I thought we were going to work on my pitching today."

"This is an important job," he reminds me. "I'm on a tight schedule. We'll do it next week," he says.

Which is what he said last week, and the week before that. I only get to see him on Sundays—you'd think he'd be able to take that day off to spend with me, but instead of making time for me, he just squeezes me into what he's already doing, whether I fit or not.

We head up a dusty dirt path that seems to be made for things with feet rather than wheels. The cab of the pickup bounces, and I can feel the doughnut and juice sloshing around in my stomach like surf in a storm.

Finally we pull off to the side of the dirt road, in the middle of nowhere, with a cliff to the right of us and a steep slope looming above us to the left. "We're here," he tells me.

"Here, where?"

"You'll see," he answers. Then he begins to climb up the side of the slope. I follow, feeling sleep still gnawing at my bones.

As we come over the top of the hill, I can see half a dozen workers—Dad's crew—busying themselves dusting and buffing the large boulders on a plateau. I see no house, no construction site. Nothing but a mountain.

"What's the deal here?" I ask him. "Where's the wall?"

"We're doing boulderscape today," he answers.

I know about boulderscape. No matter how much I've tried to ignore my father's work, some of it sneaks into my head. He's done whole patios and pools that look just like natural rock formations, when in reality it's just mortar over chicken wire.

"Can you tell which is real and which I put in?" he asks me, proud of his accomplishment.

As I look around, I can't tell—but the thing is, what's the sense of putting fake rocks in the middle of real ones? I mean, usually it's rich people who put in boulderscape. They have my dad build pools, and waterfalls, and hot tubs in fake caves to impress their friends and neighbors. But out here, the only things to impress are coyotes and rattlesnakes.

He leads me to a sheer rock face looming above the plateau; a dark granite mountainside that must have been here for eons.

"The real rock starts about ten feet up," Dad tells me.

I stare at him dumbfounded. "You mean . . . ?"

"That's right," he says. "This stone face is a retaining wall. I built it!"

I shake my head, not getting it. "But . . . can't a mountain retain itself?"

Dad raises his eyebrows. "Apparently not," he says, then goes off to discuss the progress with his crew.

As I look around, I find a small spot that hasn't been finished: a patch of gray mortar and chicken wire in the midst of the boulders and evergreens, like a hole in reality.

Humberto, Dad's best craftsman, spreads mortar across the chicken wire, hiding its fine metallic honeycomb.

Now I begin to notice the breeze. It's been chilly, and breezy, but up here, on this strange plateau, it feels different from the dry mountain cold elsewhere. It feels damp—and there's something about the smell. I take a deep breath and have a sudden flashback to a vacation we had years ago, in Florida. I don't understand why at first, but then the reason strikes me. It smells like beach. It smells like the ocean.

I hold out my hand to feel the breeze and notice that it's not blowing down the mountain, but blowing up—as if it's blowing out of the ground—I can feel it against my palm!

I turn to see that the workers all carry caulking guns and are going around the base of the boulders, filling in the cracks with thick cream, the kind of stuff you put around a bathtub to keep it from leaking.

I kneel down next to Humberto, and for an instant I think I see something through the wire framing of the boulder. I see a greenish-blue light. I see mist and clouds. I get dizzy, as if suddenly I'm looking down from a great height.

"Whoa!" I say, grabbing onto a boulder for balance.

"What's the matter?" asks my father, coming up behind me.

"I don't know . . . I think there's a cave down there . . . a pretty deep one."

"Really!" he says.

"Yeah! I tried to look into it but—"

"Did it look back?" my father asks.

"Huh?"

He grins. "Your grandfather used to say that when you look into an abyss, the abyss looks into *you*."

The thought gives me the shivers. I glance back down to peer in the hole, but Humberto has already smeared a thick patch of mortar over the chicken wire.

There are lots of reasons to build a wall, I suppose. To mark off territory; to hide things you don't want to deal with; to keep things in; to keep things out. To repair the damage. There must be an awful lot of damage to repair, because my dad's beeper always goes off, calling him to new jobs—sometimes halfway around the world. That's how good he is.

On Monday morning, I ask my mom about my father, and walls.

Mom doesn't answer right away. She slowly pours herself a cup of black coffee, dumping in a heaping teaspoon of sugar. Then she weighs her response very carefully.

"Your father's walls are special," she says. "Not just his walls, but his patios as well."

"And his boulderscapes?" I add.

She nods. "There are very few masons in the world who can do work like your father," she tells me. "He's a true artist."

"Then why did you divorce him?" I ask her, point-blank. It's a question I've never had the guts to speak aloud before.

Mom takes a long sip of her sweet, steaming coffee. "I don't know if this will make sense to you, Billy, but when someone is as good as your father is . . . sometimes they *become* their work."

"You mean that talking to him is like talking to a wall?" I suggest.

She laughs out loud. "Something like that," she says, although I can tell there is much more to it.

I'm about to tell her about the mountain boulderscape and how strange it all seemed. I open my mouth to talk—but before I can, my hand saves me, by shoving a spoonful of cereal in my mouth and shutting me up.

Next Sunday I'm awake before dawn, waiting for my father to arrive. Until last week, I had never looked closely enough at my dad's work to notice, or care, about what he was doing—but last week's excursion has lingered with me. I can't wait to see what job we're working on today.

He picks me up at the usual time. Six o'clock A.M.

"Are we headed to the mountains today?" I ask.

He shakes his head. "Nope, we're finishing up a wall downtown."

"What kind of wall?" I ask.

"The usual."

Half an hour later, we reach the deserted business district, where nobody in their right mind comes on a Sunday. We enter a twenty-story building. The wall is on the fifteenth floor, in the offices of Moreland and Beck, Attorneys-at-Law.

The second the elevator doors open on fifteen, we

are blasted by a breath of hot air from down the hall. And as we approach the offices of Moreland and Beck, the heat rises a degree with every footfall.

"Haven't they ever heard of an air conditioner?" I say, but even as I say it, I can feel the cooler air blowing from the vents above, fighting a losing battle to control the temperature.

In the law office, a spongy gray carpet has been rolled back, revealing the concrete beneath, and at the far end is a twenty-foot-wide stone-block wall where a window should be.

"That's a weird place for a wall," I tell my father.

"Walls go wherever you need them," says Dad.

As I get closer, the heat becomes more intense. My jacket, which had been protecting me from the cold morning, suddenly seems ridiculous. I take it off and throw it over a chrome-backed chair. Humberto and the others drill holes in the existing cement floor and insert heavy three-quarter-inch rebar—those heavy iron bars that hold walls together. Seems to me that they're spacing those bars closer than they usually do. I can see that they're building a second wall of cinder block, in front of the finished stone one.

"Two walls?" I ask my father. "Isn't that a waste?"

"Believe me, it's not," he says. He puts a mortar trowel into my hand, then brings me a bucket of mortar. "It's about time you started to learn the trade," he tells me. "Our family has been masons for as long as anyone can remember. It would be a shame if that tradition ended with me."

I hold the tool in my hand, feeling clumsy, like I have no right to use it, as if it were a medical instrument and I was about to perform surgery.

"You spread," he tells me. "I'll lay the stone."

And so I join him and his workers building the second wall in the oppressive heat. The sweat beads on my face and rolls down my cheeks. I lick my lips and can taste its saltiness.

"Very good," he tells me as I spread the mortar as smooth as cake icing. "You're a natural. Someday you'll be building walls better than all of us."

The idea doesn't thrill me, but it doesn't sicken me either. Not if the walls I build are like this.

There are a lot of things I should be asking my father now. I should question him about this steaming wall—about the mountainside the week before. But the thing is, communication has never been a family strong point. We've spent most of our lives holding things back and keeping problems out. It's hard to fight a lifetime of training, so I don't ask him the questions I want to. Instead I just spread the gritty gray cement and watch as Dad piles on the heavy blocks.

I keep my eyes focused on that first wall. I can feel the heat pulsing from it, like highway blacktop in summer. I want to know what's behind it. I reach forward to see just how hot it is, touching my fingertips against it.

"Memo! No!"

Too late. I touch it for an instant, and that instant is too long. I draw my hand back reflexively, feeling the shock of the burn even before the pain, and when the pain comes, it flows down from my fingertips in angry waves. I refuse to scream. I grit my teeth, and the scream comes out as a moaning hiss.

Dad grabs me and pulls me away.

"Humberto, the first aid!" he orders.

He leads me to an outer room, which is a bit cooler, but not by much.

As Dad tends to my throbbing fingertips, I can feel

the pain turning into tears, which roll down my face, mixing with my sweat. Hanging on the wall around me, I can see the fire-suits they must have used to put up that first wall. *What's behind there?* I want to ask. *Why did you have to build this wall?* But I don't say a thing. I just look away as my father gently bandages my hand, and I watch as his crew rolls out thick insulation as pink as cotton candy to fill the space between the first and second wall.

Dad keeps me late tonight. Maybe he just doesn't want to face Mom's wrath when he brings me home with bandaged fingers. We grill burgers and I eat with my left hand instead of my right.

Away from his work there isn't much he knows how to say.

"How's school?" he asks. Fine, I tell him.

"How's baseball?" he asks. Fine, I tell him.

And in a few moments, there's nothing he can think of to ask me. But rather than letting the ball drop into an uncomfortable and distant place, I start to mention things I'm sure will keep him talking.

"What's the hardest part about building walls?" I ask.

His ears perk up with the question. "The hardest part is figuring out how to build them strong enough."

"Strong enough for what?"

"So that nothing can ever break through," he answers. "Strong enough so that the wall will last forever and ever."

I grin. "C'mon, Dad," I tell him. "Nothing lasts forever."

He thinks about that. "I guess you're right," he admits. "If things lasted forever, I wouldn't have any work."

He takes a bit of his burger and ponders me while he chews.

"I want to show you something before I take you home," he announces, then he stands up, grabbing his jacket. "Let's go."

I have no idea what he has in mind, but I go along, not daring to ask what it is.

An abandoned house sits at the end of an abandoned road, at the edge of Dad's neighborhood. Broken windows stare at me like eyes, their tattered shades like drooping eyelids. They gaze out with the indifferent look of the dead.

Dad opens his car door and steps out. I follow. The sun is already gone from the horizon, and what little glow remains will fade in a few minutes. I think I know what this house must be—and I have no desire to see it—but I can't tell Dad, so I force my feet to follow him to the front door.

There's a padlock on the termite-gnawed wood of the door, but it's easily kicked in with his strong foot.

Inside the empty dwelling we go, then down a rickety set of basement steps, to the only thing in the house that is sturdy.

The wall.

It's a simple thing, made of red brick, completely out of place in this decaying home. About as out of place as the hot stone slab in the glass office building.

The ground beneath us is covered with two inches of water. A hundred rains from a dozen rainy seasons have taken their toll. Around us are cinder blocks, and bags of old mortar piled on a table, as if more work had been planned but got abandoned like the house.

"Every mason has his first wall," says Dad. "This

was mine. I was nineteen," he reminds me. "I didn't know what I wanted to do with my life. And after seeing how hard my own father worked, I didn't think building walls would be for me—until this one." He touched his hand against a rough brick, feeling the troughs in the crusty mortar. "With each brick I laid in this wall, the clearer it became that this was my calling, too. So I learned to love it."

I can't read the look on his face—which is no surprise. If I could read faces, I probably would have known my parents were getting divorced before they sprang it on me that day.

"It's just a wall," I remind my dad. "There's nothing really special about it."

"Go up and touch it," he says to me, like a challenge. So I take a step closer, and as I do, I begin to feel dizzy. I suddenly reach forward, as if I'm falling down, but I don't hit the ground. Instead my hands slap against the wall, and I feel pain shoot through my burned fingertips. The hard, cold brick seems to have a gravity about it, pulling me closer—and there's a faint vibration in the icy brickwork.

I put my ear against it. They say you can hear the ocean when you put your ear against a seashell, but I've never heard of hearing something when you listen to brick—and yet I do. It's a hollow sound, cold and lonely, punctuated by an occasional rumble that sounds like a growl, and a *pfft-pfft-pfft*, like the flapping of bat wings.

I push myself away from the wall, stepping back until I am far enough away not to feel off balance.

"What's behind that wall, Dad?"

Dad rubs his eyes and bites his lip.

"Your grandfather," he says.

* * *

When I get home that night, I don't tell my mother what happened to my hand. No matter how much she asks, I just tell her it's nothing and yell at her to leave me alone. Eventually she stops asking. I spend the next day out so I don't have to talk to her about it, and then stay late at school through the week so I don't have to answer to her at all. Funny how when you don't talk about things, the easier they are not to deal with. I figure my head is about the best retaining wall there is, when it comes to holding things back . . .

. . . but by the end of the week, my little mental dike has sprung a leak.

Your grandfather's behind that wall.

It's a strange thing to say, even for my father. I had half expected him to laugh after he said it, like it was a joke—but he didn't laugh. He just climbed silently up the steps and out of the old house.

The thing is, my dad's a very literal person—he doesn't think poetically. He thinks in solid chunks of reality. His mind works in brick and concrete—which means that when he says my grandfather is behind that wall, he means that my grandfather *is* behind that wall.

I'm terrified that I might actually ask him about it when I see him again. It will take all my strength to just go on like everything's normal. Whatever work site he brings me to, certainly there'll be more weirdnesses to occupy my imagination. Still, the wall in the abandoned house is like a brick in my head. What's behind that wall? What's behind all of the walls my father builds? It occurs to me that he's never brought me to a wall when he first starts building it—only when the job is almost done. When it's too late to see the other side.

On Saturday night, I get a call from Dad. Apparently he and Mom have been talking in secret—as usual—

making decisions about my life without involving me.

"Memo, your mom and I have decided that it's best if we don't spend Sundays together anymore."

All I can do is stutter and sputter like an idiot.

"My work sites are dangerous. More dangerous than you know," he tells me. "It's not a place for a kid."

"But . . . but I'll be careful!" I insist. "Please! I *want* to come. I want to know about the walls . . . I want to watch you build them." And then, because I have nothing else to lose, I say, "I want to know what you meant about Grandpa . . ."

I hear him take a deep breath on the other end of the line. "I was wrong, Memo," he tells me. "You shouldn't be putting up walls all your life like me. You should find something *you* love!"

"But I want to be with you!" I scream at him, the tears exploding from my eyes like they did the day he moved out. "When will I get to see you now?"

"Vacations," he says. "Summer, maybe."

But the thing is, he doesn't take vacations—and if he won't take me to his sites anymore, then I'll never get to see him again. That's what he means. We both know it.

"Memo, my work is getting harder. More repairs—more emergency work. You understand, don't you?"

"You stink!" I tell him, and I hang up on him before he can say anything else.

From behind me I can hear my mom trying to talk to me gently, like she can wrap her arms around me and make everything all better. She must be crazy to think I have anything to say to her now.

She holds out her arms, but I push my way past her refusing to talk about it. If the only defense I have is closing myself off, I can do that just fine.

I go out to the garage, and there I find a pickax. It's heavy, but there's angry adrenaline rushing through my body now, and I can lift it onto my shoulder. I storm out of the house, ignoring my mother calling behind me. It's a long walk but I know where I'm going.

I push open the ruined door of the abandoned house. The floorboards creak beneath me, and a stair cracks under my weight as I go down into the dank, water-logged basement. A single clouded window sheds a feeble shaft of light upon the brick wall. I waste no time in thinking. If I think, I may find a reason to stop myself.

I swing the pickax high and smash it against the wall. Chunks of brick fly in all directions. It might be solid, but nothing lasts forever. I swing the pickax again, and again, until I've made a crater in its red face.

I *will* know what's behind there. I *will* know what my father has spent his life doing; what he locks behind the walls he builds. I don't care if I have to shatter every single wall to know—and if I come face-to-face with the grandfather I never knew behind this one, then that will be just fine with me.

Another swing, and another. The hollow noises beyond the wall seem to grow louder, until finally the pickax crashes through to the other side. I pull it out and hear a whistling of wind, sucking out through a hole the size of my fist. I swing again, to widen the hole.

The flapping sounds and growls are louder. I hear screeches now, awful high-pitched screeches. Those sounds ought to make me stop, but my mind is like a car speeding off a cliff. I can't stop my hand from swinging the ax.

"Memo! Memo, don't!"

It's my father. Mom must have called him and told

him I ran out with the ax. It didn't take a genius to figure out where I had gone. I can hear him leaping down the stairs behind me, and I know he'll stop me. He'll patch up the hole and never talk about it, like it never happened. But I can't let him do that!

I raise the ax and give one final, powerful swing.

And the solid brick wall shatters like glass.

I can see the fracture lines spreading through the brick in all directions. Then the whistling wind becomes a gale, and I feel myself being dragged forward toward a gaping hole six feet wide.

At the lip of the hole, I feel something sharp against my gut. I've been snagged by a piece of the reinforcing steel bar, sticking out from the brickwork. I grab onto it, to keep myself from falling into the hole.

"Memo, give me your hand."

My father reaches for me desperately, his sturdy hand stretching out for my madly wriggling fingers until he clasps them—but at that same moment I feel something at my feet, and I look into the pit.

In the cold, murky darkness, some creature is moving—a terrible living unknown, with beady, hungry eyes, and reptilian wings. It opens a tooth-filled mouth and nips off the rubber tip of my running shoe, just missing my toes. Then it disappears with a flap of its veiny wings into the darkness, like a great white shark testing its prey before the kill. For an instant, as the mist is torn by its wake, I see a tortured landscape of nightmare trees and screaming skies of black ice. I feel my grip beginning to slip.

"Don't look, Memo!" warns my father. In an instant he is there with me, clinging onto the heavy steel bar, which suddenly seems as frail as wire—just as the unknown beast returns, its jaws spread wide.

My father swings his fist at it, but the thing clamps

down on his wrist. I can feel his pain as he screams. Clinging to the rebar, I kick the creature over and over in its awful eye, jamming it with my heel, until it finally lets my father go and flaps away into deeper, colder regions of miscreation.

We pull ourselves out of the hole, tumbling onto the wet floor of the old basement.

Behind us is the wall—or what's left of it—and beyond the hole, the awful landscape swarms with things too strange and savage to be named.

I take off my jacket and wrap it tightly around my father's mangled hand.

"The hole . . ." he hisses. "We can't leave the hole."

On the table rest the old, forgotten bags of mortar. I hurry to them, tearing them open and letting the dusty mixture pour into the ankle-deep water at our feet. Then I grab the abandoned cinder blocks one by one and move them toward the hole.

My father, unable to help, can only watch as I spread the mortar on thick with my hands and lay the cinder blocks on one by one.

There are no creatures near us now, but still I won't look into the hole again.

When you stare into an abyss, I think, *the abyss stares into you.*

"Your grandfather was working on this wall when he died," Dad says as I pile on another cinder block. "He had brought me here—to show me just what kind of work he did . . . but he looked too deeply into that place . . . and it swallowed him. I watched him fall, but there was nothing I could do. In the end, all I could do was finish the wall that he started."

I spread the mortar thick and slam down another block. In spite of the terror I know I should feel, something about laying those blocks calms me.

"I'm not living with Mom anymore," I tell Dad as I close off one world from another with the last heavy block. "I'm living with you."

My father nods, realizing my decision is final. "If that's what you want," he says.

I smooth the mortar between the blocks. I know that I won't speak of this night again. Not to Mom, not to Dad, not to anyone. I will hold it back. I will keep it in the dark—as Dad has kept dark the many strange places he's seen through the holes of the world.

And I, too, will build walls.

After seeing that other side, there's an acceptance and understanding in me now. I know what my life has to be.

I suppose there are three kinds of people in this world. Some people live their lives *around* the holes—never finding them, never even worrying about them. Their lives are full and happy. Then there are others who keep falling through those hidden gaps, into nightmares they never knew existed. I wouldn't want to be one of them.

And then there's a few like my dad and me; restless people who spend our lives plugging holes in the unfinished corners of creation and building walls to hold back all the things that must never be seen.

Perhaps there's more holes than can be patched in a lifetime. But I've got to live on the hope that maybe, just maybe, we'll get them all . . . and the abyss will never look into us again.

DARK ALLEY

••••••••••••••••••••••••••••••••••••••

A rainy Friday afternoon. My bowling bag pulls down on my arm. If my arms were rubber, my knuckles would be dragging on the ground from all those Friday afternoons lugging my ball to Grimdale Lanes. But it's something I have to do. Something I *want* to do.

"Do we have to bowl today, Henry?" my sister Greta asks as we get off the bus. "My thumb hurts."

"Maybe it wouldn't hurt if you didn't suck it."

She pulls her thumb out of her mouth, and hands me her bowling bag. "Then you carry my ball," she says. "It's too heavy." Greta's six, although sometimes you'd think she was younger. Usually Mom is home when Greta comes home from school, but she works late on Friday's—the only weekday I get to go bowling after school.

The skies let loose as if the rain has waited for us to get off the bus. My waterproof jacket isn't that water-proof. Greta's bright orange poncho makes her look like a walking traffic cone, but at least she's dry. Finally we reach the double glass doors of the bowling alley, and they slide open automatically to admit us.

Instantly we are hit by the familiar smell of greasy pizza and floor wax. It's a madhouse. The high school has leagues at five, and it's already after four, so most of the lanes are taken up by big kids warming up. We wait in a slow-moving line in front of the counter until we reach the attendant—a fat man with a stubbly beard, and suspicious eyes.

"Size?" snaps the fat man.

"We have our own shoes," I tell him. "We just need a lane." I wonder how many years I have to keep coming here for him to know me by name. But then again, I don't know his name either. To me, he's just "the fat guy who gives out lanes."

"Sorry, all the lanes are full," says the fat guy. "I just gave out the last one."

I take a look down the alleys. Movie theaters and bowling alleys really clean up on days like this . . . a rainy afternoon can do that. But then I notice that there's a single dark alley, right next to lane 24.

"What about lane 25?" I ask.

"We ain't got no lane 25," says the fat man. "It only goes up to 24."

"But—"

"Look kid, it's been a long day. All right? Why don't you give me a break, huh? You want a lane, come back tomorrow."

Greta twirls her finger in her hair and grins at me. "Oh well, I guess we'll have to go home. Too bad," I say.

But then a high school guy and his girlfriend—the ones who were in front of us and got the last lane—turn to us. "Why don't you bowl with us," offers the girl.

The fat man grabs my money, and we go off with the high school couple. They've been assigned to lane 24.

The high school guy goes first. He sticks his butt out, holds the ball against the tip of his pointy nose, and launches himself down the approach for his first throw. Not interested, my eyes wonder to the lane beside us. It should be lane 25, but unlike the other lanes, it has no number, and unlike the others, it doesn't share a ball return with another lane—it has its own ball return. The lane is dark, and its pins are in shadows.

The high school couple have thrown their first frames, and since I'm not paying attention, Greta seizes the opportunity to pull her light-weight pink ball out of her bag, and go ahead of me. She plods up to the foul line, drops the ball with a heavy thud, and it meanders its way down the alley, lazily taking down three pins.

"Yaay!" she cries. On her second shot, she knocks down another one.

The pins are reset, and I step up to the lane carrying my personalized deep green ball. As soon as I'm in place, my mind begins to clear. It's always like that. I forget the rainy day. I forget school, I forget home; I just think of the pins and my ball. My dad was a great bowler. He tried to teach me, but I was too young, and then one night, after a long day at his construction site, he fell asleep at the wheel of his car. I think about him sometimes. I think about how I could have saved his life if I had been there, because I'm always alert in the car. But mostly I think good thoughts about him. Especially when I bowl. I imagine the way he bowled, how his ball never made a sound when it left his hand, and touched the lane, gentle as a kiss. Each time I bowl, I try to do the same.

With the high school couple and Greta behind me, I focus all of my attention to a pinpoint, lean forward, and begin my approach. At the perfect moment, I release the ball . . . and it clunks down hard on the wood, careens a crooked path toward the pins, and plops into the gutter before it can take down a single pin.

"Guttrrrr Balllll," says Greta, like an baseball umpire would say, "Steeeerrrrrike!"

"Tough break, dude," says the high school guy.

I don't look at anyone. I put my hands over the little air blower to keep myself busy until the ball return spits my ball back to me. I take it and go for the second shot.

Again I prepare to imitate my Dad's bowling form. I inherited my dad's big feet, and his bad teeth—you'd figure I might have inherited his bowling skills, too. Right? I throw the ball with all the heart and guts I can spare . . . and again it rolls diagonally down the alley, this time tapping the ten-pin enough to make it wobble, but not fall down.

I stare at the pins grinning at me—like a full set of mockingly perfect teeth, before the bar comes down, and sweeps them away.

The high school kid snickers, flipping back a lock of tatted hair. "Not very good, are ya?"

His girlfriend raps him in the stomach. "Shut up. You'll hurt his feelings."

But the fact is, he's right. I'm not very good. And how can I get any better if I can only afford to bowl once a week? I look around at the expert bowlers hurling strikes and spares in every frame. Then I turn to look at the dark lane beside us. I know why the attendant wouldn't give me the last lane: he didn't think I deserved it. He might be just "the fat guy who gives out lanes" to me, but to him, I'm probably just "that kid who can't bowl."

Suddenly the lights flicker on, on the mysterious extra lane. I hear the ball return crank into action. I look back to see if the attendant switched it on from behind his counter, but he's not even at his station. And no one is coming this way to claim the lane.

"Thanks," I say to the high school guy. "But we'll bowl over here now. C'mon Greta."

Greta dutifully grabs her ball, and brings it over to the empty ball stand of the numberless lane. I figure someone will eventually kick us off, but until then, I'll bowl all I want to bowl!

As I put my ball down, I begin to feel uneasy, and I don't know why. It seems a degree or two warmer over here in this lane, and yet I feel a chill set in. There's a smell here, too. An earthy, organic smell, like a wet pile of November leaves. And there's a sound—a whooshing, whispering sound. I turn my head from side to side, until I zero in on where the sound is coming from. It's the ball return.

"Can I go first?" asks Greta.

"Shhh!" I get down on my knees, and lean closer to the dark opening of the ball return. Deep within, I can hear the groaning of belts, pulleys, and rollers, but beneath all that noise there's something else; A sound just at the edge of my hearing. I put my ear closer to it, and feel against the side of my face a warm wind flowing out of it. That wet-leaf smell is stronger here, and as I take a breath of it, that air feels strange. It feels thin and . . . well . . . unfulfilling—like the air you get when you keep your head under your covers too long.

Then the sound suddenly changes, and the air pressure flowing from the ball return seems to change, too. There's a sudden mechanical rumble, and for an instant I see something large and white eclipsing the dark hole.

Instinctively I launch myself back, away from the ball return—and its a good thing I have fast reflexes, because the second my head is out of the way, a bowling ball blasts out of the ball return, flies down the ball stand, and smashes into Greta's bowling ball with bone-crushing velocity.

"Close one, huh kid?" says the high school guy with a smirk. I ignore him, and look at the ball. It's not my green ball. This one is shiny white—but not just shiny. It's wet, dripping with a clear, slippery slime that puddles on the floor beneath the ball stand.

"Gross!" says Greta. "A bowling-booger."

I approach it, not sure what to make of it . . . and that's when I notice that the force of its impact has cracked Greta's ballin half.

As soon as Greta notices, tears begin to pool in her eyes. She can't stand bowling, but that doesn't matter right now—all that matters is that something of hers has been broken. That always calls for tears.

"It's okay, Greta. It's all right, we'll get you a new one," I say, even though I'm sure a new bowling ball won't be in the family budget until her birthday, which is a long way off.

I turn to look down the silent, well-waxed lane, just waiting to be bowled on, then I look at the slimy white ball one more time. Suddenly I don't feel like bowling today.

"C'mon, Greta, let's go home."

"Can we play Barbies?" she asks.

"Yeah, sure, whatever, lets just go."

I put my own ball back into the bag, and leave Greta's ruined one where it is. Then I take my sister's hand, and we head out into the rain.

* * *

When we get home, Phil is on the couch, watching the sports channel.

"Hi squirts," he says as we enter. Phil is Mom's current boyfriend. Lately we find him over even when Mom isn't home. Phil eats our food, puffs cigarettes in our air space, and spends Mom's money whenever he can. I'd call him a sponge to his face, if I didn't think he'd punch my head in for it.

"You oughta get your TV fixed, everyone looks purple," he tells me, then blows a big cloud of Camel breath in my face. I cough from the stench of the smoke. He laughs.

"Your lungs are too sensitive, just like the rest of you," he says. "We gotta toughen you up, kiddo!"

"Yeah, sure, toughen me up."

Greta has already slipped off to her room to play, and since I promised I'd play with her, I follow her, prepared to endure whatever girlie nightmare she has planned. Anyway, it's better than being put down by Phil. Since he works a swing shift, he's always gone by five—just long enough to steal a kiss and twenty bucks from Mom, before he saunters out the door.

That night long after he's gone, and Greta's gone off to bed, I sit with Mom over hot chocolate, and ask her something I've been afraid to ask, because I've been afraid of the answer. "What do you see in Phil, anyway," I ask her. "Do you love him or something?"

She chooses not to answer that question. Instead she says, "He makes me laugh."

"Yeah," I tell her. "So does Bozo the Clown but I don't see you dating him."

Mom chuckles. We're both quiet for a moment, and I can hear the rain lightly hitting the rain gutters. *Gut-*

ters. It reminds me of my miserable performance today at the bowling alley. And it reminds me of the strange lane with no number, and its mean ball return. I'm about to tell Mom what happened, but think better of it. *They grease those ball returns don't they? Sure they do—that's why the ball was so slimy. That's why it shot out so fast.* Suddenly I feel mad at myself for giving up a lane that I could have bowled on all afternoon.

Instead I say, "Mom, can I have a couple of dollars to go bowling tomorrow?"

She sees how much I want it, and so she agrees. That night I go to sleep dreaming of perfect strikes down midnight alleys.

"I'll take lane 25."

"We only got twenty-four lanes, kid," says the fat guy. Here, take lane three."

It's Saturday morning at 8:15. The weekend leagues don't start for two hours, and only a few people are bowling this early. Lane 3 would be just fine, but instead, I head in the other direction, all the way down to the end, to the numberless lane, next to lane 24.

Again it's dark, but then many lanes are dark, because no one is on them yet. As I sit down and put on my shoes, the lane comes on by itself. I can hear the rumbling whisper of the ball return again. Nothing wrong here.

I stand alone on the approach, and hurl my ball down the alley, for once, hitting the head pin exactly the way I meant to hit it. Six pins go down. Not a strike, but not a gutter ball either. Practice makes perfect. I anxiously wait for my ball to come back.

I throw one frame after another, some good some bad, and even manage to get a spare in the ninth frame. The score for my first game: a 74, which is pretty good for me. I mark the final score down, then get ready to bowl a second game, hopefully even better than the first.

The pins reset, and wait for me with a toothy grin. The ball return hums and groans but my ball doesn't come back. I hit the pin-reset button again—sometimes the ball gets stuck back there, and it takes an avalanche of falling pins to jar it free. The bar comes down, sweeps away the pins, new pins descend from above, and as I expected, I hear my ball rolling back toward me underground. I wait for it to shoot out of the ball return. As it does, I reach for it . . . and my hand gets covered in warm slime. I look down to see a white slimy ball, just like the ball from yesterday. Quickly I pull my hand back and wipe it on my pants. The slimy white ball sits there, alone on the ball stand, and my ball never makes an appearance. Finally I hit the service button.

"What's the problem?" asks the fat guy, as he saunters over. "Aren't you supposed to be on lane three?"

"I liked this one better," I tell him, "but it ate my ball." I don't bother to mention that this is the very lane he insisted didn't exist.

"Lousy stupid machine." He glances back at the counter, where a couple of pretty girls are waiting for a lane. "Why don't you use one of our balls until I can go back there and check it out?" He gestures to a rack against the wall full of balls. "You can even keep it, for all I care."

Usually the racks are filled with scarred black balls, but on the rack behind lane twenty-five, all the balls are white. I go over to examine them. They look exactly like the ball sitting in the ball stand—exactly like the one that shattered Greta's ball yesterday, only these are dry. I touch one. It's smooth, and its surface glistens like a pearl. I roll it over, then roll it over again, and realize something very peculiar about it, and the rest of the balls on the rack.

None of these balls have finger holes.

I tell the fat guy and he throws me a burning glance. "You're a real pain in the neck, you know that, kid?" Then he goes to the walkway alongside the lanes, and disappears through a back door. In a few moments, I can see glimpses of him through the pins, as he pokes around behind the pin-setting mechanism, in search of my ball.

I wait, and watch. Then suddenly, the sweeper bar comes down, and the pins reset themselves.

"Hey, what the—" I hear the fat man grumble, then a jawful of fresh pins comes down. I hear a brief yelp from behind the machine, the pin setter raises leaving ten fresh pins, and I can't see the fat man anymore.

I wait. I wait some more, but he doesn't come back. Soon there's an irritated line of people at the counter. Suddenly I get scared. I mean really scared—like maybe he's had a heart attack or something.

I run to tell the snack bar attendant, who gets the janitor to go look, but he finds nothing. Not a trace.

I don't tell them about my missing ball—suddenly it doesn't seem important. Instead, I decide to take the fat man up on his offer. I go to the rack of hole-less white balls, and shove one into my bowling bag. I can always get holes drilled into it. I leave, but as I stand near the exit, I steal a glance back at lane 25. Its lights go out, leaving it dark again as I leave.

When I get home, Mom's out somewhere with Greta, but Phil is there, lounging on the couch, and watching reruns of Gilligan's Island. Stale cigarette smoke hangs in the air like dirty layers of floating silk.

"How's life treatin' ya, Hank?" he asks.

"The name's Henry," I remind him. "Like my father."

He takes a swig from his beer, and glances at my bowling bag. "You know bowling's not a real sport," he says. "Throwing a ball down an alley—it's a no-brainer."

"Then you should be real good at it," I tell him.

He glares at me, but doesn't get off the couch. "Some day, kiddo, that wise mouth of yours'll shoot off one too many times, and someone'll clean your clock real good."

I grit my teeth every time he calls me "kiddo", but I let it slide like a bad gutter ball. He's not worth the effort, I tell myself. "Thanks for the advice, Phil," I say, and go down into the basement.

Our basement is a cold, dim place where we put things we'll probably never see again. I find a clean corner for my bowling bag. After today, I don't know when I'll want to bowl again. And that pearly-white bowling ball is too heavy for me anyway—it practically ripped my arm off getting it home. I take a long sorrowful look at my bowling bag, before heading upstairs, and turning off the light.

The fat man never turns up. People figure he got bored of his job and moved on. I don't have my own theory, because if I tried to come up with one, I know I wouldn't like it. I just go about my business, go about my life, and pretend like it never happened.

The bowling urge doesn't return to me for more than a month, but when it comes back, it comes back in full force. Maybe it's that my arm muscle feels like it needs to be used. Maybe it's that sound of tumbling pins I hear every time I walk past Grimdale Lanes that makes me want to bowl again . . . or maybe, it's because one of my friends mentioned that there are 27 lanes now and no one can remember the extra ones being built.

It's after school on Friday. Greta's at a friend's house, which means I can bowl by myself, and I can't wait! I race into the house—I've saved enough money to get the new ball drilled, and even it it's too heavy I know I can get used to it. It's 3:30 when I clatter down the rickety basement steps, and turn on the light.

It takes me a few seconds to come to terms with what I see, and it comes to me in stages. First I notice that the floor beneath me isn't concrete, but it's wood. And the smell—it's not dry and musty, but wet, and earthy. Suddenly another light comes on to my right, and I hear the soft groaning of some mechanism. I spin around to see . . .

. . . a bowling alley.

It extends through the edge of our basement, out past the foundation of our house. Past that foundation, I can see tree roots, poking through dirt above the alley, and the red, exposed edges of sewer pipes. Someone's dug a tunnel under our street, just to fit a bowling alley in our basement. But who would have done this? And why?

Everything that had filled our basement is now pushed back into the far corner. Suddenly I feel light-headed, and realize that I'm hyperventilating. I have to sit down, and like any bowling alley, there's a little row of plastic seats behind the scoring table. I sit down to catch my breath, and stare toward the end of the alley, where ten pins wait in silence for a ball to take them down.

A ball!

I get up as quickly as I sat down, and search for the hole-less white ball. I leap over boxes, and other junk

in search of my bowling bag, but everything's piled so
high now, I have to dig through everything just to find
it. When I finally do find it, I realize that the bag's been
torn open. I reach inside to get out the pearl bowling
ball, but instead I find it cracked in half, its edges
jagged and sharp. It's not at all like Greta's broken
ball— *this one is hollow*, with a shell only a quarter-
inch thick. I run my fingers along its curved surface
inside, which is just as smooth and pearly white as the
outside. It reminds me of something, but my mind
doesn't make the connection. Not yet.

That's when I hear a voice. A deep, disdainful voice.
"What the heck is this?!"

I peer out over the stacks of boxes to see Phil standing beside the ball return, gawking at the underground
alley. Quickly I climb over the boxes, trying to keep
calm and rational. Trying not to sound as frightened as
I really am.

"Hey, Phil," I say. "How's life treatin' ya?"

"Since when do you have a bowling alley down
here?"

I wrinkle my eyebrows, and look at him as if there's
something wrong with him. "Haven't you ever been in
our basement before?"

"No . . ."

"It's always been here," I lie. "My dad built it years
back. Got permits from the city, and everything."

And since Phil knows that my dad was a construction worker, he falls for it, never doubting me. "So how
come you always go out to bowl if you got an alley
right here?"

"Oh . . . uh . . . it's been broken. We just had it
fixed."

Phil puffs on his "cancer stick," and blows a cloud of
foul smoke into my face. "Waste of money if you ask

me. What lame-brained father builds his kid a bowling alley?"

Then he turns to head back upstairs.

I don't know what comes over me then. Or maybe I do know. Maybe suddenly I don't care what Phil does to me, because nobody says things like that about my father.

"You don't deserve my mother, Phil."

Phil hears me, stops dead in his tracks, and does a slow about-face. "What did you say?"

Standing on my new alley, I suddenly feel courage backing up my anger. "You heard what I said. You're a miserable low-life who sponges off our family. You're a turd on a couch, that's all you are."

His fingers begin to pump into fists, and his voice comes out low and gutteral, like a growling pit bull. "You're in deep trouble little man. You're gonna get yourself a lesson now."

"Go ahead, Kiddo, teach me a lesson," I say, figuring maybe after Mom sees the kind of lessons Phil teaches, she'll throw him out of her life for good.

He lunges at me, and I reflexively dodge out of his way. His momentum carries him past the foul line, onto the shiny waxed surface of the alley, and suddenly he loses his balance. His feet fly out from under him and he lands on his butt.

He tries to grab at me, but his momentum is too great, and the alley too slippery. He continues sliding toward the pins, almost seeming to accelerate on his way down the alley. I begin laughing.

Phil is frothing mad. "Why you . . . I'm gonna get you, you little—" but he never gets to finish. Instead he bowls right into the pins, taking them all down with a wooden crash. I laugh so hard my sides ache.

"A strike, Phil! See, I told you you'd be good at bowling!"

I'd keep on laughing. I could laugh forever . . . but something happens. Something I could have predicted, if I had had the time to really think things through. If I had the time to figure out that the broken white bowling ball didn't look like a bowling ball at all.

It looked like an egg.

Suddenly the sweeper bar drops in front of Phil, blocking my view, and behind it, the heavy pin setter comes smashing down on him like the jaws of a shark. Phil doesn't have a chance to say another word, and my own words become choked in my throat. I can't see everything, but I see enough to know what's going on. The silver pin setter slams down again, and again, more powerful each time. I can feel the ground shake with the force of it. Then finally the pin setter raises up, and the sweeper bar brushes in, and brushes out, leaving a perfectly clean, pinless lane. Finally the pin setter descends again, gently this time, depositing ten fresh pins, patiently waiting for a bowler. There's no sign of Phil anywhere.

"Phil?" I call, desperately hoping for an answer. "Phil?" But I hear no sound. Only the hollow breathing of the ball return.

I leave the basement in a daze, not ready to think about it, and not really knowing where I'm going until I get there. Finally I find myself in my mom's closet. Way in the corner there are a few sets of men's clothes—my dad's clothes because, after all, there are just some things you can't bear to part with. I get on my knees, and beneath the dangling pairs of pants, I find what I'm looking for. A black leather bag, with the name Henry Waldron stamped on it in gold. That's my name, too. I reach inside, and pull out a marbled gold bowling ball, as shiney and smooth as the day it was made. It's heavy, and my fingers don't quite fit in the holes, but I could get used to it. I gently remove it from the bag, and carry it down into the basement, where the living alley awaits, its pins grinning at me, the way my father grinned at me so many years ago, each time I threw a ball down a lane.

I stand far back, focus my attention on the pins, and with my father's ball I begin my approach. My arm swoops down, and the ball kisses the wood without a sound as I release it. I watch as the ball curves to the right, then just as it begins to curve back to the head pin, I turn my back, and strut to the scoring console, just like my father used to do. I hear the smash of pins, and the heavy clatter as they fly in all directions. I don't even have to look to know that it's a strike.

Two months later. It's a cold, windy day, but that doesn't matter in my basement.

"One seventy-eight," says Greta, reading my final score. "Is that good?"

"Yeah," I tell her, "but it could still be better." My mouth begins to ache, and I try to ignore it.

Greta picks up her new bowling ball from the ball stand. She's had it for several weeks now and likes it even better than her old one. "Can we play another game?"

"Tomorrow," I tell her. "Mom'll be home soon."

"No she won't," says Greta coyly. "Robert's picking her up at work tonight. They're going to the theater."

As we head up the stairs, I have to smile. Mom missed Phil for about three minutes, and she didn't really question where he went. She figured he just moved on. Then she met Robert. I don't mind babysitting Greta when Mom's out with Robert.

"Do you think Robert will give me braces, too, when I'm old enough?"

"You've got Mom's teeth," I tell her. "You probably won't need braces. But, yeah, if you need them, I'm sure he'll give them to you, too."

Greta thinks for a moment. "An orthodontist is a lot like a construction worker, isn't it? she says. A construction worker in the mouth."

I laugh at that. "Yeah, I guess so."

Greta heads off into her room, and I take a few moments to relax in the living room, almost enjoying the ache in my teeth, the way I enjoy the ache in my shoulder after a good day of bowling. We haven't told Mom about the alley yet, but between work, and Robert and us, she doesn't have the time or the need to go down into the basement. It could be many months until she goes down there, and when she does, I'm sure I'll come up with an explanation that she'll believe.

As for the alley—it's behaved far better than that nasty one in Grimdale Lanes. It always returns our balls, and never sends them out of the ball return too fast. Like everything else, you get what you give, and we treat it very, very well. Just last week it started producing eggs, but we know what to do with those. After all, Christmas is coming, and we have lots of friends and relatives who bowl. The only problem is feeding it—but I've got that one solved, too.

The doorbell rings, and I open the door to a grungy-looking, scowling slacker-dude. He's nineteen, maybe twenty. "Yeah, I'm looking for Henry Waldron Jr.," he says, clutching a torn slip of paper in his hand.

"That's me," I say cheerfully.

"You?" he sneers. "You put this ad in the paper?"

"That's right. Do you have the qualifications for the job?"

He looks down at the classified ad in his hands. "Let's see. 'SEEKING LAZY INDIVIDUAL FOR THE JOB OF A LIFETIME. MUST BE DIFFICULT TO WORK WITH, BE DISLIKED BY EVERYONE, AND HAVE A BAD ATTITUDE.' Yeah that's me all right. So what kind of work is it?"

"We have a basement bowling alley," I explain. "We need someone to . . . uh . . . service it once a month."

"Sounds like a lot of work, man."

"Naah, It'll only take a few minutes."

"Cool. The job sounds better all the time." He reaches into his pocket. "But if it's bowling alley work, why'd you have it listed under 'Food Service'?"

I offer him a shrug and open the basement door, but just before we go down, he reaches into his pocket to pull something out.

"By the way, I smoke," he says. Then without warning, he lights up, takes a drag, and blows the smoke in my face. "You got a problem with that . . . kiddo?"

I slowly lead him down the basement stairs. "You know what?" I tell him, and I can't help but smile, "I think this job is right up your alley."

THE IN CROWD

·······································

Alana was a boomerang, flying through her sixth foster home, doing maximum damage, and then heading right back to Harmony Home for Children—where she had spent most of her life.

"Why, Alana?" the therapist would ask. "Why is it always the same with you?"

Alana could not—would not—look her in the eye. She could hear the stabbing anger and accusations in the woman's voice—she didn't have to see it in her face as well.

"The Astons are good people—but you just had to lose your temper, didn't you. You couldn't control it just this once. Didn't you even try?"

The fact was, Alana had tried. She had tried for three whole weeks, accepting the pitying way her new foster parents spoke to her. Enduring all those overly kind, bend-over-backward sort of gestures. She lived with the way they whispered about her at night, as if she was a pet that had to be house-trained, and she pretended to "belong," when all the while she felt outside of their double-paned windows, even though she stood inside their house. Then that morning, she just snapped. She couldn't say what caused her rage, but when it was over, everything that could break in the Aston household had been broken. The gentle couple wasn't too gentle when they hauled her back to Harmony Home and washed their hands of her.

"You're like a land mine," said the therapist. "Someone treads too close to you, and you detonate."

Still not looking up, Alana heaved a shrug. "I guess I kinda push people away from me."

"Yes, Alana, you do."

Dinner in the cafeteria. Silly gossip, petty cliques scheming against one another. Kids either preening, posturing, or fighting. It was like any other prison. Yes, Alana had come to think of Harmony Home as a prison, for although the halls and grounds of the old converted mansion were more inviting than many other homes for "wards of the state," it wasn't a place she was free to leave. At least not until she was eighteen, and that was four long years away. She and at least fifty others lived in its overcrowded rooms, went to school there, suffered through adolescence there. Now as she sat with her regular friends, it felt to Alana as if she hadn't been gone for a month. It was as if she never left—and that wasn't a good feeling.

"You mean you haven't met the new boy?" Linda was saying over dinner.

"Of course she hasn't met him," said Gina. "She hasn't been here to meet him." Gina and Linda were permanent fixtures at Harmony Home. For whatever reason, the powers that be had deemed them "unplaceable." Alana could never understand what made her friends less placeable than herself, and she never asked because she really didn't want to know.

"I don't care about any 'new boy,' " Alana told them. She had seen her share of new boys come into Harmony Home, and they were nothing to shout about. They bragged about the cruel and awful things they did, they wore their body odor like a fine cologne, and they treated girls with disrespect and contempt. No. Alana wasn't interested.

"But this boy's different," insisted Linda.

"And he's good-looking," added Gina.

"And he's smart, too," offered Linda.

Alana gave her dry pork chop a decent burial beneath her mashed potatoes. "So if he's, like, heaven on wheels, what's he doing here?"

"Why should that matter?" snapped Gina. "The fact is, he *is* here."

Linda grinned. "And he likes us."

"He likes *me*," corrected Gina.

"Dream on, Cinderella," Linda grunted.

Alana looked around, trying to spot this new kid, but no one in the cafeteria seemed to fit the description. "Where is he?" she asked.

"Psychological testing," Linda explained. "They've been shrinking his head for weeks now."

"Why?"

Then Linda leaned in close enough for her hair to dangle into the motley mess of Alana's lunch tray. "They say he killed his family."

"Not just his family," added Gina, "but his entire neighborhood."

There was a windstorm that night. The kind that blew hot through the canyons, rattling windows, uprooting trees, and tearing up the roof. Alana could hear those orphaned shingles bouncing helplessly above her. When she was younger, she would hear the shingles and tar paper scraping past, and would think the sky was falling. She heard the phantom sounds of the wind in her dreams that night, jolting awake to flashes of heat lightning. Then when morning came, she awoke to find herself alone in the oversized bedroom she shared with five other girls—Linda and Gina included.

"Rise and shine," said Mrs. Mallard, the social worker assigned to their wing—but as she stepped into the room, there was only Alana to coax out of bed.

"Where are the others?" Mrs. Mallard asked.

"Beats me."

Alana quickly dressed, figuring she would meet her friends at breakfast. Maybe they were waking up earlier these days. But they weren't at breakfast. In fact, a good twenty kids didn't show up for breakfast that day, and through Alana's classes, the empty seats screamed out in their silence. Every corner of the grounds was searched, from the furnace-blackened basement to the creepy old storm cellar by the edge of the woods. All searches came up dry—but rumors ran rampant. According to what she had overheard from the teachers, the kids had conspired to run away—in fact, they had been planning it for weeks—and since teen conspiracy theories were big among the adults who ran Harmony Home, everyone figured that's what happened. Authorities were notified, and it was left in the hands of the police. Alana had to admit they were probably right. She had run off with various groups of friends many times before. But her boomerang spirit always brought her back. Perhaps Linda and Gina would be the same. Still, it troubled her that they hadn't told her what they were up to.

It was that afternoon, when she passed one of the private bedrooms reserved for special cases, that she heard someone crying. Alana stood outside the unlabeled door, listening for a full five minutes to a boy whose sobs sounded so agonizingly genuine that Alana wanted to cry as well. The sobbing didn't stop. It was as if his grief knew no bottom. To Alana he sounded like an endless well of sorrow. What could possibly make someone cry like that?

Alana never looked into the room, but she instinctively knew that he was the new boy.

"You don't look so smart."

For Alana, first contacts were more like pokes with a stick, but at least it got his attention. It was two days later. The afternoon was bright and clear, and those who didn't have some trouble to tend to were out in the rec yard after classes. Alana found him sitting against a tree, alone, watching some other kids shoot some particularly brutal hoops.

"Who said I was smart?" he said, only throwing her the slightest of glances. Alana stood above him, arms folded. "My friends did. Gina and Linda."

"Oh. Them."

"Don't you want to know my name?" prompted Alana.

"You'd be better off if I didn't."

"It's Alana. An *a* at the beginning, middle, and end."

The boy stood up, but not to greet her. Instead, he turned his back to her, pushing more of his attention onto the basketball game he was watching. It annoyed Alana to no end, but she fought the urge to say something rude.

"If you're so interested in the game, why don't you go play?"

The boy took a few moments before answering. "I don't know any of those guys."

Alana snickered. "How long have you been here? A month or something? And you don't know any of them?"

"That's right."

"What are you, the kind of guy who doesn't have friends?"

He turned to her sharply, stung by her words. "I have friends. They're just not here right now. That's all. Okay?"

Finally Alana understood. "So the friends you made here all ran away the other day, huh? Is that why you were crying?"

His expression hardened. He became guarded. Suspicious. But he didn't deny that those tears had been his.

"There can't be anything so bad that you have to cry like that," said Alana. "I don't even cry like that, and believe me, I've got plenty of reasons to." He regarded her, stone-faced. It was strange—she felt as if his eyes were somehow invading her. Picking her like a lock. "Anyway," continued Alana, "someone'll catch those guys that left and bring them back, so you won't be friendless for long."

He continued to regard her with that lock-picking gaze, and Alana refused to look away. If he was trying to intimidate her, she wouldn't give him the satisfaction. That's when he said something that chilled her in spite of the heat of the day.

"They're never coming back," he said, speaking so matter-of-factly it was all the more disturbing. "And if you're not careful, *you* won't be coming back either."

Alana felt anger rising to her face in a bright red flush. "Are you threatening me?"

"No," he said, not an ounce of anger in his own voice. "It's a warning."

His name was Garrett. Garrett LeBlanc. Linda and Gina were right—he *was* different. He didn't hang around with the other kids, and although Harmony Home was famous for its loners, he wasn't your run-of-the-mill loner. Most loners insisted on distance, and usually got it. No one much cared that they kept to themselves. They'd sit by themselves at a table, or wander off to a quiet corner, and they'd be out of sight, out of mind. But Garrett was never out of mind. When he was in a room, you could feel him there. You could feel his eyes boring into you, even when he was looking in the opposite direction. And it wasn't just Alana—other kids could feel it, too. Too many conversations seemed to be about Garrett. Who was he? Why was he here? Why, once you started thinking about him, couldn't you get him out of your mind?

Garrett was right about one thing: Those other kids didn't come back. Not one of them. They had made good with their escape. With her closest friends gone, Garrett became a project for Alana. She would systematically break down his layers of defenses, and find out what made him tick. And then she would find out if any of the dark rumors about him were true.

Day after day she forced herself to treat him decently, which proved to be a chore. Even though he excelled at ignoring people, she would talk to him until finally the cold reception he always gave her heated to lukewarm.

It was on a rainy Saturday that she found him in the Multiuseless Room, which was really called the Multi-purpose Room, but most of the kids had concluded that it was purposeless. In an attempt to "socialize" him, Garrett had been taken from his secluded little bedroom and forced to share a larger room with five other boys. Apparently it hadn't worked. Garrett was sitting alone playing solitaire.

Alana slid in across from him, pushed all the cards together, and began to shuffle them.

"I was winning," complained Garrett. "What are you doing?"

"No one wins at solitaire, you moron," she told him, "because even when you do, you just end up dealing the cards again until you get even more bored. You play blackjack?"

"No."

"I'll teach you, so we can run away together and take Las Vegas for millions." He just stared at her again with that lock-picking gaze. Alana ignored it and continued to shuffle. When she heard the Ping-Pong ball behind her stop bouncing, she looked up to notice that most everyone else in the room was looking at them. Perhaps because no one had kept Garrett this close to them for this long. It was a grand victory for a girl who was famous for pushing people away, and she was happy to flaunt that in front of everyone.

"You get dealt two cards, one up, one down. Dealer has to hit to seventeen. You don't."

"This is twenty-one. I know how to play this."

"Good for you." She dealt him his second card faceup. A one-eyed Jack. Alana always found one-eyed Jacks mysterious. Like Garrett.

"You know," she offered, "if you ever feel like talking with someone who doesn't have a Ph.D. at the end of their name, I'm sure I can find the time in my busy schedule."

Garrett leaned away from the cards, obviously realizing this was just another ruse to get inside his head. "Suddenly I don't feel like playing," he said, then stood up and breezed out of the room. Alana tossed the deck on the table and followed closely in his wake, undaunted. In a way, he was like a game of solitaire himself. Alana's game, and she was determined to deal again and again.

"Don't you know when to quit?"

"No," answered Alana. "That's why I'm stuck in this place. How about you?"

She followed him up the stairs and through the door to the roof, which was supposed to be alarmed but never was. The roof was strewn with dead leaves and other debris, waterlogging in the rain. If Garrett thought coming to this uninviting spot would deter Alana, he was wrong. In fact, she decided to call his bluff in a major way. The door to the roof didn't close all the way unless you really closed it tightly, which was exactly what Alana did. Until someone noticed, they were locked up there. Garrett had no way out—no path away from her. *Fine,* she told herself. *If he wants to be out on the roof in the rain, he will be. For a good, long time.*

"Oh, that was just brilliant," snapped Garrett.

There was a warped plywood shelter in the corner built to protect a bird hutch—but like so many residents of Harmony Home, the pigeons had flown the coop years ago, and the hutch had been scavenged for various arts and crafts projects. It was beneath the low shelter that Garrett and Alana waited out the rain.

He could just scream like hell until someone came up here to let us in, thought Alana, *but he's not doing that. Perhaps he isn't as anxious to be free of me as he seems.* Knowing that made Alana even more bold. They sat watching the torrents pummel the roof.

"What really happened to your family?" Alana asked. "I promise I won't hate you—whatever you tell me."

Garrett laughed. It wasn't the response Alana expected. Anger, maybe, but she didn't expect to be laughed at. He brought up his knees, to tie his drenched laces. "I didn't kill them, if that's what you're asking."

Alana tried not so show her relief, but she knew it could be read in her body language. "That's good," she said, which she thought might have been the dumbest thing she had ever uttered in her life.

But Garrett didn't laugh again. He kept his eyes focused on his own shoes. "Do you ever get . . . close to people?" asked Garrett. "So close that you can't let them go, no matter how hard you try?"

Alana looked away from him. She knew what he meant, and just the thought of it made her suddenly feel that disconnection—that unbearable loneliness that all too often sent her into a rage.

"No," she answered. "No, I've never really felt close to anyone."

"I might not seem like it now . . . but I get very close to people. I've always had lots of friends. People always like me—they want to get to know me. Just like you."

"So . . . you're saying I'm just like everyone else."

The corner of his mouth turned up in a grin. "No— you try harder." And then the grin faded. "You know . . . they say you carry with you all the things that ever happened to you in your life—even the things you don't remember. They're all inside your head some-where. It's like that with people, too. All the people you know—they're all rattling around inside your skull. You know what I mean?"

Yes, Alana did know. Her own father had vanished

from her life when she was five—but she still heard his voice yelling at her. She still felt the slap of his hand on her face. Yeah, you do carry people with you.

"There are some people," Garrett continued, "who go crazy from all those people telling them things in their heads. All those voices screaming at once, all out of control . . ." Until now, Garret had kept his knees pulled up to his chin, but now he relaxed a bit, lowering one knee to the ground and turning his shoulders to face her. "I don't go crazy," he said. "But I do have seizures."

"Seizures? What do you mean seizures?"

Doctors say it's a brain thing. Like epilepsy or something—only instead of my head getting all fuzzy inside, everything becomes superclear. Suddenly I see the faces of the people I know—the people I've gotten close to. I hear their voices, I sense their thoughts . . . until *their* thoughts are *my* thoughts."

A sudden gust of wind blew a spray of rain across their faces, and Alana couldn't tell if the wetness on Garrett's cheek was rain or tears.

"See, I have these seizures," Garrett repeated. "And when I come out of them . . . the people I know are gone. . . ."

Above them, the bowed plywood creaked from the weight of the rain—but Alana didn't care about that. She was locked on Garrett's eyes—those eyes that seemed so invasive, as if they could decode every ounce of her being. He was trying to tell her something major—something terrible—but her mind felt like a brick, unable to absorb what he was saying. She could only stare at him, her mind a blank. And then what few coherent thoughts Alana had in that moment were extinguished when he leaned forward and kissed her.

There had been other boys who kissed her before. Usually they forced their lips against hers when she wasn't expecting it, stealing the kiss rather than offering it. Usually she swatted those boys away like mosquitoes, flattening them against the wall. But this was different. The kiss felt huge and overwhelming, as if it would swallow her whole . . . as if she could disappear inside of it. But then he pulled away, and she was left looking into his eyes once more, feeling as if the rain would melt her like the Wicked Witch of the West.

"I really like you, Alana. And so I tried to stay away from you. Do you see, now, why I told you about the seizures? I've gotten too close to you . . . and now you've got to get away from here—away from *me*— before it's too late."

Suddenly the plywood above gave way, dumping on them its heavy load of rainwater. The deluge snapped Alana out of her trance. Surrounded by the here and now once more, she let the world around her take hold . . . and a familiar reflex took hold as well. The reflex to push away. The urge to put everyone and everything at arm's distance. She felt the rage build in her, like her own peculiar seizure, and rather than spewing her fury at Garrett, she hurried to the door, pounding it, kicking it, bashing it until the metal dented, until the doorjamb fractured and the lock sprung open, letting her back into the stuffy air of the stairwell.

"Hate me, Alana," she heard Garrett call after her. "Hate me and run away. Get out of this place! Go as far and as fast as you can. Maybe that way it won't happen to you . . . the way it happened to the others. . . ."

Alana didn't run away . . . but she didn't seek out Garrett's company the next day either. Instead, on that black-clouded Sunday, she snuck into the computer room, for although Harmony Home didn't have much contact with the outside world, it did have the Internet.

Alana spent the day running search engines, scouring articles, and probing databases. She had already snuck an unathorized peek at Garrett's file in the main office—and although several key pages were missing, she knew he had come from the town of Cranston, which was clear across the state.

Finally she found the article she was looking for. It didn't have any direct links in the Net, or any other references. In fact, every other reference to the town of Cranston on that particular day had been systematically deleted from the Net, as if someone had done it intentionally. But this one article, from the *Cranston Sun-Bee*, had slipped through the cracks.

BLOOM STREET MYSTERY, the headline read. The story was more like the kind of thing you read in the cheap tabloids, next to stories of Elvis sightings and three-headed babies. Only difference was, this story was real.

Apparently, eighteen people on a place called Bloom Street had vanished without a trace. All of them were neighbors. All friends. Even their pets were gone. In fact, only one person was left: a fourteen-year-old boy, smack in the middle of the circle of missing people. Although the article didn't print the name, Alana knew who it had to be. She reached over to turn on the printer, but a hand grabbed hers before she could touch it.

"What are you still doing here? Didn't I tell you to go?" It was Garrett. The expression on his face was between anger and a desperate fear, but there was something else there as well. He was sweating something terrible, and his eyes kept trying to roll back into his head, as if he was fighting to keep control over something. *Over his seizures*, thought Alana. *He's about to have one of those seizures.*

Alana was caught off-guard. Her voice quivered. "The gates are locked ever since those other kids ran away—"

"You're smart, you can find a way out!" he insisted.

"Maybe I don't want to go!"

He grabbed her other arm, pulling her out of the chair so hard the chair fell to the ground behind her with a crack. In turn, she wrenched herself free and pushed him as hard as she could. "Get your hands off me!"

He hit a bookshelf, jostling a set of encyclopedias that toppled and cascaded down around him. The books pounded on his shoulders and lay sprawled at his feet. To Alana he looked worn and beaten. He kept his distance. He didn't apologize, and neither did she.

"What happened on Bloom Street?" Alana asked.

"I don't want you to get hurt!"

"What happened on Bloom Street?" Alana demanded.

"I can't protect you from it!"

"WHAT HAPPENED ON BLOOM STREET?"

Silence from Garrett. He stared at Alana, reading her, grimacing as the sweat poured down his forehead. She swore she could see his temples pulse. And then he finally spoke. "When you were nine," he told her, "you snuck out of here late at night and went to see a movie."

Alana shook her head, trying to hitch herself onto whatever train of thought he had just begun. She swallowed hard when she remembered that she had never told anyone about the midnight movie trip. "How did you know that?"

"I know because Gina was with you that night."

"She told you?"

"She didn't have to. Just like Linda didn't have to tell me about the time she was six and got hit by a car.

Or the time she and Gina hid in the old storm cellar so that everyone would think they were missing—but nobody noticed. Not even you. I could tell you a million things about a hundred different people, Alana. Things that no one knows but them."

"You read their minds?"

"No, I *have* their minds!" Garrett blinked hard to keep his eyes from doing those flip-turns in his skull. Then he took a step toward her. "I get too close to people, Alana. I get too close, and somehow they get pulled inside. They're not dead, but they're not really alive either. My parents, my neighbors, all my friends from the last place I was at, and the first twenty-three people I met here. I got too close to them . . . and now I carry them with me."

Alana could only shake her head dumbly, then her wall of resistance came crashing down like the plywood on the roof. She was suddenly flooded by everything he was trying to tell her. Still, she couldn't accept it. She would rather have heard that he had killed them all—that he was a psycho freak who did away with people. But to think that his mind had latched on to the people it knew—on to Gina and Linda and the others. To think that his mind was powerful enough to wrap around them . . . and swallow them whole. . . .

The door flung open, to reveal two men in dark suits, and two others behind them. They wasted no time. "That's him," one of them said. Then they grabbed Garrett. "Garrett LeBlanc, you're going to have to come with us."

All of a sudden it became clear to Alana. Why all the articles were missing about the people who had disappeared. Why Garrett's file was incomplete. He was under surveillance all this time. There were people watching, and waiting. Trying to piece together what he had done and how he had done it.

So that they could use him.

"No, you can't have him!" yelled Alana.

One of the men flashed a badge, as if she cared. "This is official business, little missy, so why don't you let us do our job."

"Yes," said Garrett. "Take me away from here. Put me someplace that's safe."

One of the men laughed. "Oh, don't worry. We got a nice cozy place for you, don't we?"

The others mumbled their affirmation. But Alana knew as well as Garrett what would lay in store for him. Where would they put him? A chrome lab where they could run test after test after test? Even life at Harmony Home was better than that.

She kicked one of them in the kneecap and grabbed Garrett. One of the others pulled a gun. *Fine,* thought Alana. *I dare them to shoot.* They didn't, of course, and her momentum pulled Garrett out the door, with the agents right behind, one of whom was limping.

But halfway down the hall, Garrett dug in his heels and stopped. "It's too late," he whispered desperately. "It's happening."

Now Alana was certain she could see his temple throbbing. His teeth locked, his eyes began to roll, and he forced his head to turn away from her to the four men, whom he had only just met. His body jerked once, as if he had been hit with an electric shock, there was a flash of light, like a camera flashbulb . . . and the four men were gone, leaving nothing but a pop as the air rushed to fill the space they had been.

Alana could have stared in shock for a good hour, but there wasn't time. Not now.

Garrett fell to his knees. "It's going to get worse before it gets better."

"What do you want me to do?"

"Run!" he said. But Alana still wouldn't do it. There had been so many things she ran from. So many people. And here, finally, was someone she didn't want to leave. No matter what happened to her. Even if his gaze turned her into little more than a snapshot in his mind, she would not leave. He was too close to her heart now. Too close to run.

"Quickly," she said to him, helping him up and moving down the hall with him again. Several people stopped to look at them suspiciously. Alana ignored them. "Quickly—tell me how it works. Do you have to be looking at them? Do they have to be in the room with you?"

"No. They can be anywhere nearby. I just have to *know* them. To have seen them, or heard them, or smelled them, or—"

Garrett groaned, his body jolted, there was a snap of light and a series of pops. A few of the people in the hallway disappeared, followed by the sudden pops of air. The others who hadn't vanished stood dumbfounded, voicing their shock at what they had just seen. Alana had to bite her own lip to make sure that she was still there.

"Okay," she said, keeping herself under control. "We just learned something. We just learned that it's random. And that it doesn't take everyone at once. Just a few at a time."

"They're so frightened," wailed Garrett, and it took a second for Alana to realize that he wasn't talking about the people around them; he was talking about the people who were gone. The ones he had just pulled *inside*.

"They don't know how they got here. They don't under-stand where they are. They're so afraid. . . ."

"Don't think about that now!"

Another body jolt and another set of flashes. They were coming more quickly now, building in intensity. *Would it take over his whole body?* wondered Alana. *Would he start convulsing right here on the floor, the air strobing around them in bright flashes until they were all gone?* By now Garrett had met everyone at the home. When his seizures were done, no one would be left.

"What's its range?" she asked him. "If it only took eighteen people from your neighborhood, then maybe it only reaches a few hundred yards or so, right?"

"I don't know."

"Maybe if we got you out onto the street, away from here."

"No time."

Flash! Flash! Flash! Trays dropped to the ground in the cafeteria as the people holding them were drawn from their lives, sucked through the walls, captured by Garrett, for all time.

They paused for a brief moment, and something finally clicked in Alana's mind. *Through walls . . .* The walls at Harmony house were practically paper-thin—but there *were* thicker walls nearby. Although Alana didn't know the strength of Garrett's soul-snatching seizures, she did know that the storm cellar had been turned into a bomb shelter many years ago, by the pre-vious owner, long before the mansion became Har-mony Home. The old man was a nut, and had lined the small underground bunker in lead. If lead could block radiation, maybe it could block other unseen forces as well. All at once Alana knew where Garrett had to go.

"Let's go!" She pulled Garrett down the stairs. He

didn't ask where he was going—perhaps he already knew. If it was true that he now owned Gina and Linda's memories, he would know all about the lead-lined shelter.

She struggled with him out the back door, his body becoming stiff and rigid with each flash of hot, searing light. A basketball bounced on the court nearby. Instinctively Garrett looked over. A bunch of kids were playing a half-court game. Too late. The players and spectators were already beginning to vanish.

"Marco . . . Peter . . . Evan . . . Rachel . . ." Garrett could only recite their names helplessly as they passed that barrier between matter and thought, becoming permanent residents of Garrett's mind. "I won't think about you, Alana . . . I won't think about you . . ." But Alana knew it was only a matter of time until he flashed a thought of her as well, and she became a memory, like the others.

Garrett fell to his knees, and a security guard took notice of their panicked activity. Alana tried to drag Garrett through the thick, muddy grass. She was strong, but she couldn't move him fast enough. The storm cellar was still a dozen yards away, on the other side of the basketball court.

"Get away from me!" Garrett gasped. "You have to go! Now!"

The burning flashes of light came one after another now, like a strobe, as Garrett fell to the ground, his limbs jolting, his back arching, and only the whites of his eyes showing through his fluttering eyelids.

She couldn't get him to the shelter, she couldn't stop his seizures . . . but there was something she *could* do. She could leave him. She could push herself away, as he had begged her to do. In so doing, maybe she could save the others.

She turned from Garrett just as the security guard approached. For an instant he stood in her way, but then he dissolved in midstride, and Alana could swear she felt him pass through her as he was sucked into Garrett's mind. She couldn't think about that now. She had a mission to accomplish.

She raced onto the basketball court, where kids were still reeling from the random disappearances. They all looked around, not sure what to think, not sure what to do. The younger kids who were watching the game all began to stand, confused and terrified, searching for someone older to explain what had happened. It was Alana who took charge.

"This way," she yelled, grabbing them, pushing them. "The shelter! Now!"

She managed to get nine of them moving, but there were only seven left by the time they made it down the leaf-strewn steps of the shelter. She herded them into the dark, musty room and slammed the lead-lined door, shutting out the outside world, and Garrett's inside world.

"What's happening?" one kid asked. But Alana did not answer. Instead she held the door closed, as if an invisible hand might tear it from its hinges.

Then, as she stood there, she felt it. The room was dead dark, but tiny points of light came in from around the doorframe, which wasn't a perfect seal. One of those points of light had come for Alana. It latched on to her, tried to swallow her; she could feel her whole self being drawn through that tiny gap in the door, smaller than a keyhole. A part of her wanted to go—to be with Garrett—to be part of his crowded mind. But she fought it, asserting her will to be separate and apart, to be—as she always was—alone. Garrett's capturing light, robbed of its strength by the lead-lined room, lost the battle, and in a few moments the flashes of light shooting through the cracks came less and less frequently. Alana held the door closed for several minutes longer, gripping the handle tight, feeling her knuckles grow numb and cold. Then, when she was absolutely certain it was over—long after the last flash—she released her grip.

The world had not changed. The trees were still there, the basketball court was still there. But the people weren't. The kids Alana had saved filed out of the shelter, not sure what to make of the silence, and for a long, terrifying moment, Alana thought that perhaps Garrett had pulled in the whole world. But no. She could hear the traffic on the highway, full of cars and trucks between destinations. People whom Garrett had never met. No, everyone was still there. Everyone, that is, but the souls of Harmony Home.

Garrett was gone, too. She found his muddy footprints leading away from the spot where she had left him—a random, haphazard set of prints, as if he had stumbled away into the woods in agony. She wanted to go after him, but realized that he didn't want her to find him. The one thing he needed more than anything else in this world was distance from those around him—for he could only be happy if somehow he found his way, alone. And so Alana finally gave in to his lonely desire, allowing him the distance he so desperately needed.

She tried to imagine what it must be like, inside his thoughts right now, where a crowd of frightened, furious people, crammed like sardines in a can, all fought to retain something of themselves. She could almost hear the dozens of individual voices struggling for the right to exist. How long would it be until they accepted their fate? How long until they all dissolved into one another, their thoughts, feelings, and memories becoming part of Garrett's? She supposed no one but Garrett and the people in his overcrowded mind would ever know.

As she stood there, looking down at Garrett's footprints in the mud, one of the younger children she saved—a girl about eight years old—came up to her.

"Where is everyone?" she asked, fear painted pale on her face. "Why did they leave without us?"

Alana felt the urge to ignore her—to just walk away and not deal with it. But she swallowed that urge, and offered the girl a slim smile instead. It occurred to Alana that she did not know this girl. In fact, aside from her own close circle of friends, she had known very few of the kids at Harmony Home. "What's you're name?" she asked.

"Cindy."

"Well, Cindy, we're going to have to get along without the others."

Emotion welled up in the girl's eyes and she began a steady flow of tears. Alana opened up her arms and folded her in, holding her, comforting her, and feeling a sense of compassion in herself that had always been absent from her heart . . . and she realized that Garrett had, in his own way, left her with a very precious gift.

I get too close to people, Garrett had told her—and here in his wake, Alana had somehow been given an ounce of that closeness as well. Nothing like Garrett's capturing light, but a warm glow that filled her own darkest corners. A blessing rather than a curse. For the first time in her life, Alana could feel herself caring, and it was a wonderful thing.

The next few days would be rough. The confusion, the questions from police and reporters. But eventually all that would fade away into memory, just as the strange passage of Garrett LeBlanc would fade into rumor.

I hope you find your peace, Garrett. I hope you find some far-off place where you can live your life alone with the crowds in your head, and in your heart.

Alana slowly rocked back and forth, feeling the child in her arms begin to breathe just a little bit easier.

"We're all going to be okay," Alana said, knowing that if she could only hold on to this gift of closeness Garrett had given her, she truly would be okay, and her life would no longer be a boomerang.

SPECIAL DELIVERANCE

....

He walks toward the towering apartment building, his heavy package clumsily balanced on his shoulder. It is dusk, and the sky burns a smoggy orange as he makes his way across the deserted square, where weeds squeeze between blocks of pavement, turning the concrete expanse into a giant checkerboard. Shredded newspapers, yellow with age, blow past and gather in the sieve of a chain-link fence. He zips his coat against the cold.

As he approaches the central apartment building, he spots a row of mailboxes, all pried open and rusted, but this doesn't deter him. The package he must deliver is of a completely different nature. He checks the address on his small slip of paper, then continues on.

As the twilight dies, losing itself to a starless night, he realizes that the desolation around him is more than imagined. This apartment building—the entire complex—has been abandoned by most of its residents. It's an oasis of sorrow in the midst of a thriving city. Just a few streets away, crowds of people go about their business, thinking of the night ahead and what tomorrow will bring . . . but here stand dozens of buildings filled with nothing but the hollow tones of the wind blowing across broken windows, like slow breath across the lip of an empty bottle.

The heavy glass door of the entryway creaks open as he leans on it, its hinges shrieking with bitter complaint. The glass door itself is clouded with layer upon layer of graffiti, etched into the glass with blade points. But it's more than mere graffiti—these scrawlings are runes. Perhaps not as ancient as some, but these runes are full of potent warnings.

Suffer eternity, reads one. *Don't be caught dead here,* reads another.

He takes a deep breath, shaking off the growing sense of dread, and heads for the elevators.

An elevator arrives in moments, its dented metal door struggling open to reveal the bleak gray box within. Like the glass doors of the apartment building, the elevator is covered in uniquely American hieroglyphics. Some are rude, some are terrifying, but all are void of hope.

There is also a man in the elevator.

Shifting the awkward bundle in his arms, the delivery boy enters the elevator and turns to face the closing doors.

"A bit young for this kind of work, aren't you?" comments the man.

The boy shrugs. "I do a good job."

He looks at his slip of paper in the dim fluorescent light, and realizes the apartment number cannot be read. Too late. The elevator begins to move before he can push the button. It starts downward. The floor counter registers the basement, and continues past it.

"Aren't we supposed to be going up?" asks the man, wringing his hands, just the tiniest bit worried.

"Beats me. Which way were you going when I got in?"

"I can't remember."

The elevator passes the subbasement and continues down through the three parking levels. The man looks at the padded package the boy carries, and wrinkles his nose. "Smells like dead fish."

The boy shrugs. "It's not for you."

The elevator reaches parking level three. The last floor. Instead of stopping, it continues its descent. The delivery boy begins to feel light on his feet, and senses the package lighten in his grip. *We're accelerating,* he thinks.

The man's eyes begin to dart around. He backs up into a corner. "Wait a second. Wait a second, this isn't right!"

It is then that the delivery boy notices that the man, pale and gaunt, is not entirely there. He seems only the shadow of a man. The boy gasps. He can see right through this man to the graffiti scratched into the wall behind him! It reads, *Abandon all hope.*

"This is all wrong!" wails the ghost huddled in the corner of the elevator. "I'm supposed to be going somewhere else! I did everything right, didn't I? I'm not supposed to be here!"

Deeper and deeper. The elevator rattles back and forth in the seemingly bottomless shaft. Inside the elevator the boy notices the temperature rise. It's a dense, humid heat, a soggy heat that makes it very hard to breathe. His heart begins racing. The delivery boy balances his package on one hand, being sure to keep it flat, and with his other hand pounds on the buttons that would send the elevator back up. But none of those buttons work, and suddenly it occurs to him that this elevator doesn't go to any upper floors. There's only one place it goes. Down.

"Stop the elevator! Do something!" yells his ghostly companion, but the boy can do nothing but feel his ears pop as the air pressure increases as they plummet through the earth.

Finally comes the telltale heaviness—sudden weight as the elevator slows. They have arrived.

The man flings himself against the doors. "No! No!" he cries as he tries to hold the doors together. But his hands have no more substance than vapor. Gears grind, the doors whoosh open, and a ferocious blast of hot wind catches the delivery boy in the face. He has to turn away. When he dares to look again, the ghost-man is gone. But his wails can be heard echoing down a jagged stone corridor down which he had been dragged. A corridor that is angry red and lava-hot.

Someone is standing just outside the elevator door. A dark specter who seems coolly at home in this furnace of a place. "I am the Gatekeeper," the creature announces.

The delivery boy swallows his fear, takes a deep breath of the hot air, and holds up his package.

"You ordered a pizza?"

The Gatekeeper smiles, showing a set of sharpened teeth. "Yes! And you're on time, too."

"We guarantee delivery in thirty minutes or less." The boy slips the box from its thermal hot pack, which suddenly strikes him as pointless, and the Gatekeeper reads the words printed on the pizza box.

" 'You've tried the rest, now try the best.' " The Gatekeeper smiles smugly. "How droll."

As is his custom, the delivery boy opens the box for inspection. "Here you go—double onions and triple anchovies. Is that what you ordered?"

"Yes. Yes!"

"That'll be fifteen ninety-five."

The Gatekeeper pulls out a pen and a checkbook.

"I'm sorry, we don't accept checks," says the delivery boy.

The Gatekeeper is not pleased, but forces a pleasant smile. It comes out conniving and sinister. "I'm a little short today. Couldn't you make an exception?"

"Not a chance. But we do take all major credit cards," suggests the delivery boy.

This time the dark customer flashes his teeth in a threatening grimace. "They won't give me credit cards!" he bellows. "None of the banks trust me."

The delivery boy shrugs. "Not my problem." Then he pulls the pizza back from the Gatekeeper's long, bony fingers.

"I want that pizza!" growls the Gatekeeper, eyeing the delivery boy as if he might be dinner instead. But the delivery boy does not show fear. Instead he says, "Perhaps we could work something out."

The gatekeeper folds his arms. "I'm listening."

"That man who was in the elevator with me . . ."

"Yes, that was Mr. Pratly. What about him?"

"Send him back with me, and you can have your pizza, anchovies and all."

The Gatekeeper's expression changes. He thrusts his chin forward, insulted and indignant. "Out of the question. But perhaps I can offer you something else you desire. Power? Fame?"

"Not interested." Quickly the delivery boy backsteps into the elevator. "No Pratly, no pizza," he says. "That's my final offer, take it or leave it."

The Gatekeeper folds his fingers into tight fists and raises them above his head in anguished fury. "Blast!" he screams to the steaming walls, and the stone itself recoils at the sound of his voice. There comes a rush of boiling wind, and suddenly there, beside the delivery boy, is Mr. Pratly once more, not a happy camper, but much happier now that he's back in the elevator.

The Gatekeeper snatches the pizza from the delivery boy. "Get out," he says with a wave of his hand. He begins devouring a slice of pizza.

But the delivery boy wedges his foot in the elevator door. "What? No tip?"

The Gatekeeper swallows hard, then leans into the elevator. "All right then," he whispers into the boy's ear with his onion-and-anchovy-tainted breath. "Here's your tip: Stay off of airplanes next Tuesday."

Then the elevator door slides closed and the car begins its ascent to higher ground. Slowly the temperature begins to cool, and Mr. Pratly's relief is more powerful than the leftover aroma of the pizza. He takes a transparent handkerchief and blots it against his translucent forehead.

"I don't know how to thank you," he says.

"No biggie," says the delivery boy. "Hey—if I were you, I think I'd get out of this neighborhood and take a train uptown. *Way* uptown."

"Yes," says Mr. Pratly. "Yes, that's exactly what I'll do."

As the elevator reaches the parking levels and continues up toward the lobby, the boy can't help but smile. There might be better jobs out there, but he can't complain. After all, who doesn't love a delivery boy?

MR. VANDERMEER'S ATTIC OF SHAME

....

I could tell you about time and space and fill your head with all of that strange scientific stuff that scrambles your brain. I could try to tell you exactly how the attic came to be the strange and terrible place that it was, but to be honest, I don't understand that myself. All I know is that our neighbor Mr. Vandermeer built a place that was half magic and half science, and then filled it with the dark corners of his own soul.

My name is Lien. I'm thirteen, and live in a small house on a small street in an old neighborhood that's changing. More and more stores are opening up in our neighborhood where the Vietnamese lettering is just as prominent as the English or Spanish. I suppose it makes my parents happy to see their native language. It must make them feel at home—but I was born here, and my English is far better than any Vietnamese I might speak. But Mr. Vandermeer spoke fluent Vietnamese, Korean, Spanish, and just about every other language you could name. I always wondered why a man who never seemed to go anywhere, would want to learn so many languages. Turns out, he had his reasons.

I don't know when it first started—all I remember is the night I first noticed that something was strange. It was at three in the morning, on the night of a new moon. The sky was as nightmare dark as it could get, and somewhere beneath that cloak of darkness, I heard a deep, far-off rumble. At first, I thought it was the paperboy in his old pick-up truck. There were many times I'd been up to hear the whap of the paper against the concrete driveway, but this sound was deeper, resonating through the night, like a heavy, hungry beast. I wrapped my blanket around myself as I stepped out of bed, because my nightgown was too thin to keep me warm, then I peeled back the curtain and looked out the window to see the nature of this beast. A truck. A big one. Eighteen wheeler—the kind you could fit a whole house in, with room left over. It came down our block with its headlights off, barely able to squeeze beneath the heavy boughs of our tree-lined street. Its engine was a muffled whisper—you could tell that the engine had something on it to keep it from making noise, like the silencer of a gun. I kept my eyes on it as it slowly rolled down towards our house, its smokestack belching hot diesel fumes into the cold night. I heard the squeal and hiss of the airbrakes, as it pulled to a stop right in front of Mr. Vandermeer's house, right across the street from ours.

Mr. Vandermeer stood on his porch in a long overcoat, arms folded. "You're late," I heard him say to the driver, as he got out of the truck. "Just like last month."

"Couldn't be avoided," answered the driver, then he went around to the back of the truck, and swung open the big double doors.

I brushed my long hair out of my eyes, and squinted

to get a better look. At first, I thought that perhaps this was a moving van, and Mr. Vandermeer was making a late-night departure. He was always a strange bird; very solitary, the type of guy who would grunt at you, or mumble something under his breath if you said hello, or throw you a rapid wave of his hand, and then run inside, as if he was too busy to engage a neighbor in conversation. I wouldn't put it past him to pack up and leave, without saying good-bye. That's when I heard voices . . . a number of them, speaking in hushed whispers. I tried to pick out what they were saying, but it sounded to me like a foreign language . . . Asian, perhaps Vietnamese, or Indonesian. I heard footsteps on concrete, but the open rear door of the giant truck blocked my view.

I thought I might wake up my parents, and see if they could pick out some of the whispered foreign words, but before I could wake them, the voices were gone. The truck was closed back up, and in a few moments it left, the throaty sound of its muffled engine trailing off as it turned the corner.

The lights stayed on in Mr. Vandermeer's house for about half an hour—but the curtains were pulled, and I couldn't see what went on inside. Finally the lights went off, and I drifted off to sleep.

There's a trick your mind plays when you look at an empty room. When your brain just sees a floor, and a wall and four corners, it makes you see the place as something small and unpleasant; perhaps that's where claustrophobia starts. But add some furniture, and it all changes. The empty space becomes warm and homey, it becomes a room instead of a box. If you furnish it just right, you can even learn to feel comfortable living in a closet if you had to.

I know all about that, because, between my parents and my brothers, there're six of us living in a tiny, two-bedroom house. I share a bedroom with my three brothers, which is kind of hard when you're the only daughter in the family. At night I have to close my eyes and imagine myself in my own room, where the posters on the wall are ones that I want, and there aren't always dirty socks and underwear strewn around the floor. My parents say that someday we'll have a bigger house, although they've been saying that for years.

But not all the homes in this neighborhood are like ours. Mr. Vandermeer's home was one of the larger ones, set on a double plot of land. An old two-story Victorian house filled with rooms, and very well kept. Did I say *well* kept? I mean *perfectly* kept.

For instance, Mr. Vandermeer always had a perfect lawn, manicured as well as his fingernails and trimmed as closely as his short gray beard. His planters were kept full of winter-blooming plants in the chiller months, and replaced in the summer with the more delicate warm-weather flowers. And in the fall there was not a leaf to be found on the lawn.

"The leaves wouldn't dare to fall on his lawn," my Mom would joke. "That man keeps everything in order. Everything in control."

I never thought much of it until I began to notice those late night delivery trucks, and the strange voices. The fact was, now that I took the time to notice . . . there was always someone working on Mr. Vandermeer's house. When I went off to school, a gardener would be slaving over his tulip bulbs, sweaty even in the chilly air. In the afternoon, someone else would be cleaning the drainpipes, or washing the windows, or painting. And each day, I began to notice that it was someone different. It was the same inside. He had a housekeeper who would take out the trash, and beat out the rugs every day . . . but each day the face I saw carrying those heavy, heavy trash bags to the curb was different. One day it would be a Hispanic woman, with sun-leathered skin, and eyes wizened from a life of labor. The next day it would be a young Chinese girl.

"He goes through housekeepers like I go through stockings," my mother said when I mentioned it to her. "Some people are like that. Never satisfied by anyone's work."

And the fact that his workers were always of different nationalities didn't seem odd to me, because I was used to living in this neighborhood. You see, our neighborhood is like a melting pot that never boiled, so nothing ever melted. Vietnamese families live among Hispanics, among Korean, among Armenians. While there's never any major battles between the groups here, there aren't many friendships either. We live side by side, but our circles never cross.

Still as I watched that melting pot of workers silently going about their business at Mr. Vandermeer's house, I knew there was something not quite right about it, but I couldn't say what it was.

There are times that a mystery begins to feel like a mosquito bite, irritating you in a place you can't scratch, until it seems there's nothing left of you but that nagging bite, screaming for relief. That's how it was with me and Mr. Vandermeer's house.

The next late-night delivery came in the rain. Again I heard the voices, and I snuck out to watch. Just as before, the voices disappeared into the house, the truck drove off, and the lights went out in half an hour. I just had to know what was going on in there. And so, the next Saturday morning, when Mr. Vandermeer went out for his morning walk—which he did like clockwork—I ventured across the street, where three gardeners pruned the bushes, and someone else detailed his spotless Mercedes on the driveway. So busy were they in their work, that they didn't notice me stepping onto the property. I suppose they weren't used to visitors, because no one ever visited Mr. Vandermeer, except for the people who worked there.

Unobserved, I made my way down the side of his house to the backyard, where I found one more worker. It was a man. No, a boy. He couldn't have been any older than I was. He was thin, frail, dressed in fading, frayed clothes. There in the center of the backyard lawn, he labored over a brown patch in the grass, carefully pulling up the dead grass, and planting new seeds. Only, as I got closer, I could see he wasn't planting the seeds the way a regular person might plant them. He wasn't spreading them out to cover the dead spot. Instead, he picked up each individual seed, and, with a pair of tweezers, placed it perfectly in the grass. Then he went back for another.

He's nuts, I thought to myself. *Mr. Vandermeer will see that, and he'll fire him for sure.*

"Hey," I called out, "That's not the way you plant grass."

He spun his head to me, and locked eyes on mine. They were Asian eyes, like mine, but there was something different about them. Different from me, that is. The way he held himself, the expression on his face . . . It wasn't . . . American. Even without hearing him speak, I knew that he hadn't been in this country long.

"Do you speak English?" I asked.

He bolted, heading straight for Mr. Vandermeer's back door, not looking back.

"Hey wait!"

I grabbed for him but he was too fast. Instead, my hand fell on his back pocket, dislodging something there. It was a book.

"Hey, you dropped this!" I picked up the book, and dared to do something that I never thought I actually would. I followed him right into Mr. Vandermeer's house.

The smell hit me right away. The wonderful smell of Christmas and Thanksgiving all rolled into one. A turkey cooking in the oven; vegetables baking; spices and sauce cooking. It almost whisked me off my feet.

The gardener boy spun around the banister post, and sped up the stairs, turning back once to look at me. The expression on his face now was clear. It was fear. Terror. He was terrified of me, but why?

Then as I looked around I could see that he wasn't the only one. There was a housekeeper polishing the brass fixtures of an oversized fireplace. She had stopped in mid-stroke when she saw me barge into the house. Another maid was polishing the already spotless wood floor. She saw me, and her eyes registered even more fear than the boy's. She whispered an exclamation in some language I didn't know, and hurried to leave the room, as if it was a crime to be seen by me. Through the swinging door of the kitchen, I saw a chef slink quickly out of view.

I tried to ignore their strange behavior and hurried up the wide staircase, to the second floor, holding the boy's worn book in my hand—but by the time I got there he was gone.

It felt strange to be trespassing like this, but I did have an excuse. I had to return the book. I clutched the book tighter, and slowly walked down the hall.

Hello? I peered into the open bedroom doors. No

one there. Not in the master bedroom, or in the two other bedrooms. I even pushed open the door to the bathroom, but it was empty.

Only one door remained for me to check now. It was slightly ajar, and I couldn't see anything through the crack. At first, I thought it was a closet—that for some strange reason, this foreign boy had decided I was such a threat, he had to hide in a closet—but when I opened the door, I saw steep stairs, leading into darkness. It was an attic.

Suddenly a hand grabbed me firmly by the wrist, and yanked me around. "What are you doing wasting time? Get back to work!" It was Mr. Vandermeer. He stared a me with cold gray eyes.

"I'm . . . I'm Lien from across the street," I said.

It took a moment to register, then his hard expression softened. "Of course you are. I'm sorry, I didn't recognize you." He let go of my wrist. "How can I help you?"

"There . . . there was this boy . . ."

Mr. Vandermeer smoothly pushed the attic door closed. "Yes?"

I still held the book, but suddenly I didn't want to give it to Mr. Vandermeer. I didn't want to give him anything. "Well . . . I . . . I just wanted to show him how to plant grass."

Mr. Vandermeer's smile left his face. He became just the slightest bit worried. "Was he doing a poor job?"

"No," I said, not wanting to get the boy in trouble. "I'm sure he was trying to do the right thing. It's just that he was using tweezers."

And then Mr. Vandermeer threw his head back and laughed. "Well, of course he was," Mr. Vandermeer said, putting a firm hand on my shoulder, and guiding me back down to the first floor. "That's what I asked him to do."

"What?"

"How do you think I get my grass to grow so neatly? Every seed is hand placed."

I thought about the size of his front and back yards. "But . . . how can that be . . . it must take months to hand plant a lawn that way. . . ."

"And that's what his job is. Believe me, there are millions of people who would beg for a job like that."

I shrugged. I didn't know anyone who would. "I guess you must be rich to have all of these people working for you."

"I'm an importer," he explained. "It affords me a nice income."

"What do you import?"

"Oh, this and that. If you'd like I could explain it all to you another time."

As we reached the first floor the smell of dinner hit me again. "Big party tonight?"

"Yes," he said gently, as he led me to the front door. "Please stop by again. It's always good getting to know my neighbors."

Before I knew it, I was out on the porch, and the door had shut behind me. As I was crossing the street I realized that Mr. Vandermeer's big turkey dinner couldn't be for many people. Because his dinner table was only set for one.

No sky today. We stay below deck. Rough sea makes my father sick. Captain says we will eat soon, but we still wait for the food. My mother says travelling to America is like being born. We must suffer the pains before we see the light of day.

"It's a diary," my brother Ran explained. Unlike me, he could read Vietnamese.

I closed the door to the bedroom, worried that our

parents might discover we're snooping into someone else's business. With my two younger brothers off at soccer practice, it gave Ran and I some time to translate alone in our room. "I knew it," I said. "He's fresh off the boat." I felt a bit ashamed to be reading the entries in the gardener boy's diary, but my curiosity overwhelmed any shame I felt.

Ran flipped a few pages. "So Vandermeer's got all these illegals working for him?"

"We don't know they're illegal," I countered.

"You're so naive," he said, finding another entry in the journal.

Sea calm today. No storms. Too many people down here, though; many fights. People fight for space. People fight for food. People fight for nothing. It's something to do to pass the time. My father says English is a hard language, but schools there will teach if I want to learn. I want to learn.

Ran looked to me thoughtfully. "So you say there's always different people working at Vandermeer's house every day? And the old ones just seem to disappear?"

I nodded. "What do you think happens to them?"

Ran thoughtfully scratched his hair. "I think he eats them."

"Ran!"

"Sure. He gets people that no one will miss, has them do the yard, then cooks them up for dinner."

"Don't be gross."

"You said you smelled something cooking."

"It was TURKEY!"

"How do you know that a human steak doesn't smell like turkey? Frogs legs taste like chicken, don't they?"

I pushed him back onto his bed, and he laughed.

"That's not it," I told him, "There's something else going on there, I just can't figure it out yet."

I told him to turn to the last entry. He did. It was dated the day before yesterday.

Room enough for all of us. I have my own bed. Hot water enough for whole family. Land to grow our own food. No time for school right now. Dad works the machine twelve hours a day. I work ten. Sisters work in factory. Mom farms. No frost here—Food grows all year round. Tomorrow I work in Mr. Vandermeer's yard. A great honor. I hope I do not disappoint. Maybe then I won't have to go back to the machine.

"Oh, no! I ruined it for him!" I thought back to that fearful look in the boy's eyes when I chased him into the house. "I got him into trouble."

"What's this machine he keeps talking about?" asked Ran.

I just shrugged. "Keep reading."

Ran found his place and continued.

When I sit at the machine, I turn my eyes to the sky, trying to remember that my time at the machine will pass. Windy today. Heavy clouds blow past and melt in the corners of the world. I look to the wind-blown clouds, and the great beams beyond.

"Kind of poetic," said Ran. He turned the page. "It ends there."

I took the diary back from Ran, and looked at it thoughtfully. "I should get his book back to him. I wonder where he lives."

"I'm sure Vandermeer knows," said Ran.

There are some people who live in their own private world. They go about their business, away and apart from others, keeping guard over the things they do and think the same way they keep guard over the things they own. Their faces are no trespassing signs. Their words are wrapped in barbed wire. That was Mr. Vandermeer. But a no trespassing sign was also an invitation to explore, and find out what was so special that it needed to be protected.

The next weekend, I stepped once more into Mr. Vandermeer's world, offering him no warning that I was coming. I didn't ring the bell—in fact, I waited on my own lawn, until I saw one of his housekeepers open the door to take out the trash, then, as she went back in, I snuck up behind the bushes, and kept the door from closing. I took a deep breath, and quietly slipped inside.

Again the overwhelming smell. Turkey once more, and the table set for one. Two men stood on ladders in Vandermeer's study, carving designs into the wood molding on the ceiling. Two women, with dark circles under their eyes, carried heavy cardboard boxes down from upstairs, then went back upstairs again, and didn't come down. I could hear Mr. Vandermeer's voice—he was in the downstairs bathroom, instructing another worker. He spoke in a language that sounded European.

I slipped past the bathroom, and into the kitchen. The chef was gone for the moment, and so I dared to open the oven and peer inside, unable to get Ran's cannibal suggestion out of my head.

There was a turkey in the oven. I sighed with relief.

"What were you expecting to find, Lien?"

I jumped and the oven door slammed with a jarring bang.

Mr. Vandermeer laughed, incredibly amused at my reaction. It irked me, and made me just a little bit bolder.

"So how come you're having turkey again?"

"It's Saturday," he answered. "I have it every Saturday. Like clockwork."

"And you're eating alone. Again."

His smile didn't falter. "A party of one."

"What a waste of food."

"If you'd like to join me, I could have a place set for you."

His offer actually sounded genuine, and although dining with Mr. Vandermeer was not something I really wanted to do, I accepted. "Yes," I told him. "I love Turkey." It allowed me more time to figure out just what was going on in his house.

I called my parents, and told them I was having dinner at a friend's house—I didn't dare tell them that it was Mr. Vandermeer, as they were convinced he was the lunatic of all luna-tics, and they were probably right. We sat down in the living room, to wait for dinner. He asked me questions about my family, about school, and what subjects I liked, and through it all, he kept a sense of patient control of the conversation, that was as unnerving to me as the ticking of the grandfather clock in the corner.

Another woman came downstairs and dropped a heavy box, then went back up.

"Would you like to see what I do?" he asked, and without waiting for an answer, he went over to the box, and pulled out a blouse, handing it to me. The label said VANDERMEER FASHIONS. I looked in the box to find a whole collection of identical blouses. Nothing strange or awful was in those boxes at all.

"You import clothes?"

"In a manner of speaking, yes."

It was, in its own way, a letdown, and I began to wonder if Mr. Vandermeer was less mysterious and interesting than I had thought.

Another woman descended the stairs, and deposited a box of VANDERMEER FASHIONS at our feet. I noticed that this was a different woman than any of the others I had seen before, but her eyes were just as tired and worn. I felt a warm breeze caress my face, and searching for its source, my eyes were drawn up the stairs, to an open door. The attic door.

The woman went back up the stairs, began to climb up the steep attic steps, and disappeared into darkness. What was it about that attic . . . ?

And then it finally occurred to me what was wrong with all the workers at Mr. Vandermeer's house. There were never any cars out front, and none of the workers ever seemed to leave. They simply went into the house . . . and disappeared.

Mr. Vandermeer wasn't watching me—he was watching a butler exit the kitchen with several silver platters.

"Dinner is served," he said, and he went to the dining table, for the first time turning his back on me.

I knew this may have been the only chance I had, and so I took it without thinking. Instead of following him into the dining room, I hurried up the polished mahogany stairs to the second floor, and swung the attic door wide. If I hesitated, I knew I would have lost my nerve, so I bound up the attic steps into that warm current of air blowing down on me, until, in the darkness, I banged into a second door at the top of the steps. Air whistled beneath it. With my heart pounding in my ears, I turned the knob, and pushed hard against the door. It flung open and I fell . . . onto dirt. Not the musty, dusty dirt that coats the floors of most attics, but hard-packed earth. I quickly got up to get my bearings, and what I saw around me, to this day I have no way to explain.

I was on an unpaved street. To the left and right of me, shoddy-looking concrete apartment buildings rose five stories into the air. Clotheslines crisscrossed like cobwebs between them, across a narrow dirt alley. People on bicycles bumped past me on the uneven alley, and I heard voices, dozens of voices, all babbling in too many different languages to distinguish one from the other.

Mr. Vandermeer's attic wasn't an attic at all. It was a ghetto.

Two strong hands gripped firmly onto my shoulders from behind. They carried with them a chill as potent as an electric shock. I froze in place.

"You are a meddlesome girl," said Mr. Vandermeer, with a furious frustrated sigh.

I squirmed out of his grip, and tried to get past him, down the attic steps. "I want to go now," was all I could say. "Please can I go now?"

But Mr. Vandermeer stood in my way. "No. You wanted to see what was in my attic and now you will see what's in my attic. You'll see all of it. And maybe then you'll understand."

He turned me around to face the street again. This time I dared to look up, and saw dense billowing clouds blowing past. Above those clouds, through a mile-high haze, I could see the heavy slanted beams of the attic roof!

I look to the wind-blown clouds, and the great beams beyond. . . .

That diary entry wasn't just being poetic—that boy was writing exactly what he saw!

The sun shone through a gap in the clouds, but I realized it wasn't the sun at all. It was a single massive light bulb, dangling from a cord, a mile in the sky.

"You've shrunken us!" I shouted. "You've shrunken all these people!" But when I looked behind us, I could see that the attic door wasn't towering over our heads, it was exactly the same size as when I stumbled through it.

"I assure you that no one's been shrunken," explained Mr. Vandermeer. "I don't downsize people."

"Then how—"

"You will find, Lien, that space can be made in ways you've never even imagined."

And then he pulled me down the narrow street.

We strode through row after row of identical apartment buildings. As I looked into the windows, I could see whole families squeezed into one room. Others lingered in entryways, as if they were overflowing from the crowded apartments—and as Mr. Vandermeer passed, they all lowered their heads in a show of respect. Or fear.

"Don't be fooled by appearances," Mr. Vandermeer said. "These people want to be here. They want to live this way. Some are refugees from warring nations. Others left their homelands to escape starvation and poverty. But here, everyone works, and no one starves."

We came out of the shadows of the tenement buildings, to an open field, where dozens of workers planted and harvested crops. It was then that I began to hear the churning noise—a distant mechanical grinding that shook the ground.

"On the outside, my attic is only thirty-four feet across," explained Mr. Vandermeer, "but on the inside it extends a mile in all directions. That's four square miles of land for building . . . for planting . . . and for manufacturing."

He pointed across the field to the left. "My clothing factory," he said. "I have one hundred and fifty workers putting in an honest day's labor there."

I wondered how many hours made labor honest.

He turned and pointed to a complex to his right that spewed out white smoke from a high smokestack.

"Concrete and steel factories, for building," he explained. "I employ three-hundred and twenty-nine there."

I was still reeling from the sheer size of Mr. Vandermeer's attic space, but I tried not to show how disoriented and confused I was. "I guess you really are rich," I said. "To be able to pay so many people."

He turned to me as if I had said something in a language he didn't understand. "Pay?" he said. "There's no need for payment here. This is a perfect society, without money. If the people do their work properly, then I make sure they get what they need."

I felt that electric chill run through me again. "In other words . . . they're your slaves."

Mr. Vandermeer tossed back his head, and gave his superior laugh again. "Lien, you are so naive."

Straight ahead of us, directly beneath the mile-high dangling incandescent sun, was another factory. It was from there that the deep mechanical grinding sound came. It must have been hot, for the air around it shimmered and rippled in heat waves, like a road in the desert.

"What's that place?" I asked.

Mr. Vandermeer hesitated, as if he really didn't want to tell me. But finally he said, "That is the space-maker."

As we drew closer, it became clear how very large this factory was, and then I realized it wasn't quite a factory. It was a single, open-air machine, full of gnashing gears, and powerful pistons pumping up and down in an unrelenting rhythm, It was a beast of a machine that counted out time in perfectly metered beats.

On the fringe of this great machine, new gears, levers, and pistons were being installed, frantically welded together by workers, as if their lives depended on getting the job done.

"This is the most important part of our little village," said Mr. Vandermeer, as he led me deep into the superstructure of the clock-like mechanism. Around us, gears towered over our heads, and heavy springs coiled around themselves like pythons.

But by far the most amazing, and most disturbing part of the machine was the human part, because everywhere you looked there were workers—hundreds of them, maybe thousands of them. They pushed and pulled on massive levers. They threw their bodies against giant flywheels, to get them to turn. They turned cranks, their bodies covered in sweat, and their mouths contorted into strained grimaces. From each of their bodies, waves of heat radiated outward. Or, at least I thought it was heat.

"What does this machine do?" I asked. "What are they making?"

"They are making space," Mr. Vandermeer said, not at all bothered by the struggling workers around him.

"I don't understand."

And he proceeded to explain. "Surely you know that matter and energy are one in the same. $E5mc^2$? Matter can be converted into energy—it's the principal behind a nuclear bomb. Well, in the same way, space and time are interchangeable. That is, one can be converted into the other.

He led me up a narrow catwalk, where I could get a wider view of the immense machine. "These workers here . . . they are converting time into space. Space enough to fit an entire village in my attic. Even now, they're building new wings to my machine, making it bigger as more and more people arrive. In six months it will double it's power—and my attic won't just cover four square miles—but sixteen! And in a year from now, sixty-four! In just a few short years the area inside this attic will be larger than most of the nations these people came from!"

I let his words hit me. I tried to absorb them, but it was simply coming too fast. A machine that converts time into space? How could that be?

"The time that you're converting . . . where does it come from?"

"From them, of course." Mr. Vandermeer gestured to the sweating laborers around us, too absorbed by their back-breaking work to even know we were there. "The time comes from their lives."

They were all of different nationalities, and yet, they were all the same; nameless, faceless, like the cranks and gears they turned. But one face in that crowd did look familiar. An Asian face, hair drenched in sweat.

"I know him. . . ."

It was the boy gardener, whose diary I had come to return. Only he didn't look like a boy anymore. He looked like a man—a tired, downtrodden man. The circles under his eyes were just as dark as the gray-haired laborers around him. It was then that I truly understood what Mr. Vandermeer meant.

"This machine," I said, "it ages them doesn't it? It slowly pulls the life right out of them."

"And turns it into something far more useful!" insisted Mr. Vandermeer. "Room to live and breathe!"

"It's horrible."

"If it's so horrible, then why don't any of them leave? After all, my attic door is never locked."

I turned to look at the exhausted boy. He threw me the slightest glance but couldn't afford the energy to keep looking. He continued to pull and push on the crank that powered the engine that pulled the time from his life, radiating it outward from his body, in rippling waves of space. Waves that I had first taken for heat.

"These workers sacrifice their time for their families. They stay here because they know how much better it is than the outside world."

I shook my head, refusing to accept Vandermeer's twisted logic. "No. They stay here because they don't know how to leave. Sure they can see the door, but they're afraid of what's outside it. They're afraid of you!" I pulled the journal out of my pocket, and showed it angrily to Vandermeer. "This belongs to him! I found it when he was gardening in your yard. He has dreams. He wants to go to school and learn English."

Mr. Vandermeer just waved the thought away. "Why does he need to know English here? Why does he need further schooling at all? He knows all he needs to know."

I approached the boy as he labored at the machine. He didn't slow his pace, but I could tell that he knew what I was doing. Gently, I placed the diary at his feet. But he couldn't take his hands off the machine long enough to retrieve it, so it just sat there by the tip of his worn shoe.

"You don't own these people!" I screamed at Vandermeer, over the monotonous drone of the hellish space-maker.

The old man crossed his arms. "I own their time, I own their space, and I own every ounce of their labor,' he said. "So I own all of them that is worth having."

My words began to fail me, and I found my emotions balling up in my fists. I pounded against Mr. Vandermeer's chest. I pushed him back against his own machine, but he kept his balance, and just smiled at me.

That's when I ran. I bolted through the maze of gears and workers, out into the great field, where more workers plowed in a panicked pace, as frantically as the machinists. Did they know they were slaves? People with no wages, and no future except for whatever future Mr. Vandermeer chose to give them? Is this what they had hoped for when they left the shores of their distant lands?

I reached the overcrowded apartment buildings, winding through the maze, searching for the one door that would lead me out. I looked behind me many times, but never saw Mr. Vandermeer following. And then I realized that he didn't have to follow me. I meant nothing to him. Once I found my way out, what could I do? I couldn't tell anyone—No one would believe me. All I could do would be to sit in my room, the horrible knowledge of this place stuck in my head, just as the people were stuck in this attic.

I finally found the door. Just as he said, it was not locked, it was wide open, as more women brought boxes of clothing from the factory down the stairs, then came back up again, to return to Mr. Vandermeer's little universe.

I pushed past them on the attic stairs, ran down the grand mahogany staircase, past the elaborate turkey dinner that was still set on the dining table, and out the front door.

All those workers tending to his home—Mr. Vandermeer could have a hundred people working on his yard and in his kitchen, and in the rooms of his house, and there'd still be hundreds more anxious to take their place the next day—anxious to be used by their landlord.

I raced into my own house, into my own cramped room, which suddenly seemed so spacious, and cried for every soul trapped in Mr. Vandermeer's attic.

* * *

My parents noticed that something was wrong with me, but they didn't know what it was. They figured I was overworked at school, or I was fighting the flu, or something like that. How could they know that my thoughts had been poisoned by what I had seen across the street.

"You should do something after school, Lien," my mother suggested. "A sport maybe, or computer club, or dance. Something that will cheer you up."

I thanked her for the suggestion, but did nothing. I thought my depression was as deep as Mr. Vandermeer's attic was high. I lived like that for weeks. Until the truck came again; Its deep rumble pulled me out of my light sleep at four in the morning. This time when I heard it, I didn't waste time—and I didn't convert it into space either—I converted it into action. I wasn't sure what I was going to do, but I knew I had to do something. Quickly I dressed, and ran across the street, as the driver opened the big double doors.

A wave of people poured out of the truck, as I knew they would. This batch of desperate newcomers were Eastern European—refugees of some bloody conflict. All their belongings were packed into tiny suitcases, and the driver shuffled them out like cattle, toward Mr. Vandermeer's front door.

I ran up to them.

"No!" I screamed, shattering the quiet of the night. "Don't go! He'll use you! You'll be slaves, and you'll never get away!"

But the people pulled away from me, not understanding my words. Terrified that I meant them harm, they moved toward the warm, safe light of Mr. Vandermeer's door. But I knew that it was a false light.

Vandermeer heard me right away as he stood on his

porch shepherding in his huddled masses. He strode toward me with an anger in his eyes I hadn't seen before.

That's when I knew exactly what I had to do. I dodged him, and pushed past the crowds of frightened people. I wove around them on the grand staircase, and pushed them out of the way as I climbed the steep stairs to the attic, pushing through the door at the top, into the narrow street.

It was dark and quiet up there. It was night, just like it was outside. Then I reached over and flicked on the attic light switch, and suddenly the entire world was lit by the dangling sun-bulb above. For Mr. Vandermeer, being God was as simple as turning on a light.

I heard heavy footsteps behind me. This time Vandermeer was chasing me, but I wouldn't let him catch me. I might not be the fastest runner in the world, but I'm not slow either, and I ran with every ounce of my soul. Quickly I made it out of the ghetto, into the fields. Far ahead, the great space-maker churned away, boiling time into space. I headed straight for it, not sure what I would do when I got there, but knowing if anything was to be done, it had to be done there. All the while Mr. Vandermeer was right behind, shouting at me, cursing at me, but his words only pushed me faster.

I burst onto the narrow catwalks between the gears and slaving workers of the space-maker, searching for a way to stop the machine. Surely there had to be a button or lever that would grind the thing to a screeching halt. But the longer I searched, the more I began to despair. Why would a machine that was never intended to stop moving have a cut-off switch?

I only slowed my pace for a moment, but that was all it took. Mr. Vandermeer grabbed me by the collar, pulled me off my feet, and lifted me out over the churning gears.

"I have no use for you," was all he said, and I felt his grip begin to loosen. He was going to drop me into the mechanism without a second thought!

Then, among the many movements of the intricate machine, I saw a new motion. An iron pole arced across the air, and hit Mr. Vandermeer in the head. He let go of me, but as he did someone else caught me. The one who had swung that pole. The boy with the diary. With his machine-strengthened arms he lifted me up, over the railing, to safety.

Vandermeer lay on the floor, dazed, but was quickly recovering. If I was to do something, I had to do it now . . . and suddenly I knew exactly what it was. This machine was like a clock—and like a clock, every gear was connected to something, which was connected to something else.

And clocks break down all the time.

I took the pole from the boy. It was heavier than anything that I had ever carried, but I wouldn't be holding it for long. With all my strength I rammed it into the teeth of the great gear in front of me. Then I watched as the gear turned, and tried to mesh with the cog beside it.

A screaming metal complaint resounded from the gears, as their teeth tried to mesh, but the pole was firmly lodged in the way . . . and the machine just stopped.

Every gear, every piston, everything came to a screeching halt.

"No!!" Vandermeer got up, and tried to dislodge the pole but it was no use. The many workers ceased their labors, wondering what was going on, and the machine wailed as its last moving piece—the mainspring—continued to turn, building up incredible torque as it wound itself tighter and tighter.

All that energy had to go somewhere—and it did! The spring broke free, tearing out the gear that drove it, and that in turn tore out the gear beside that. In an instant, the entire machine was an exploding chaos of gears and springs. Massive chunks of metal tore free, gears rolled down catwalks, and everyone began to run for their lives.

Everyone except Mr. Vandermeer.

He alone stayed with his machine, mourning its destruction as it came down around him.

Together, the gardener-boy and I ran across the field, following the rest of the scattering workers. As we ran, I noticed our shadows begin to change, becoming longer. I looked up to see the great light in the sky shifting position, rapidly dropping, and saw the immense attic beams crushing the clouds into wisps of vapor as they came down. Now that the machine had stopped, the attic was losing space. The sky was falling!

By the time we reached the apartment buildings, crowds were pressing against the narrow attic doorway in panic, trying to escape the crushing roof as it came down. Somewhere along the way I lost sight of the boy, and I realized he must have gone to find his family.

How long will it take, I wondered, until the all the extra attic space is gone . . . and what will happen to everything trapped inside these walls?

As if to answer me, I heard a heavy crunch, and looked up to see the very tops of the apartment buildings crumble to dust as the roof beams squeezed down on them.

The crowd at the attic door was thinning now, as they gushed in a flood of humanity down the stairs. I was at the very back of the crowd. The farmland boiled and folded in upon itself, like a giant angry sea. I watched as the once-distant concrete and steel factory plowed into the empty apartment buildings like an ocean liner; and as the last gears of the space-time converter exploded heavenward, shattering the dangling light up above.

The ceiling continued to come down, crushing floor after floor of the tenements. The buildings pressed closer and closer threatening to flatten me between them, as the alley disappeared. Then finally I was stumbling down the stairs, carried by the panicked current of immigrants through the Vandermeer house, and out the front door.

Only when I was standing on my own curb, did I dare to look back. It seemed everyone had gotten out, except for Mr. Vandermeer. And as I looked at the house in the dim rays of dawn, I could see the walls begin to bow outward.

I knew what was about to happen.

Perhaps all the space had been taken out of the attic, but the mass remained. Thousands of tons of concrete and steel were compressed into to that tiny attic space. I suppose the space- maker machine had kept the attic from feeling its true weight until now, but without that machine, the sheer mass of everything that had been inside was too much for the house to bear.

The entire attic fell through the house below it, the walls exploded outward with a sickening crunch of splintering wood. The earth shook like the most violent of earthquakes, and when it was over, there was nothing left of Mr. Vandermeer's house, but a hole fifty feet deep, punched into the ground by the super-heavy attic.

Light came on all around the neighborhood, and as people began to come out onto their porches to see what had happened, the refugees from Mr. Vandermeer's attic began to disperse.

My family joined me on our lawn, thinking I had just come out of our house myself.

"An earthquake?" asked my father.

"No, a sinkhole," said Ran. "Look at that!"

But I was no longer interested in the hole across the street. Instead I turned my attention to the people who had escaped from the attic and were now homeless. They were all running, scurrying away, quickly disappearing into the morning in search of a new place—In search of some space of their own.

And for an instant I wasn't sure whether I had done something wonderful for them or something terrible.

I was so worried about the hurrying, disappearing faces, that I didn't notice the one right in front of me. It was the boy with the diary. He stood there, with two girls behind him—the sisters he wrote about—and a man and woman who must have been his parents. They all looked troubled, even frightened, but it wasn't the same kind of hopeless terror that seemed to fill the corners of Mr. Vandermeer's attic. It was the fear of a challenge. The wariness of a new day.

The boy turned to look at me—He looked at me with a smile in his dark eyes, and said something in Vietnamese. Like I said, I don't speak much of the language, but there are some words I do know.

"It's 'thank you,' " I translated back to him, knowing that they would be his first words in this language. "In English, we say 'thank you.' "

He reached out and heartily shook my hand. "Thank you," he repeated, in a heavy accent. "Thankyouthankyouthankyou!"

And then he left with his family, disappearing into the morning as all the others had.

"What was that all about?" asked my mother.

"I found something for him," I told her, "and I gave it back."

My younger brothers had already taken to dueling with wood fragments that had landed on our lawn, and the rest of us began the task of cleaning up the mess left in our yard, even before the police cruisers pulled onto our block to rope off the sinkhole across the street.

I don't know what happened to all of the people who escaped from the attic. Perhaps some of them were sent back to where they came from, but I'm sure many more found the dream they left their homeland for. I know, because every once in a while I'll see one of them walking in the street or shopping at the supermarket. Perhaps someday, I might even run into the boy with the diary again, and we'll talk about things and smile because we'll know that even without Mr. Vandermeer's infernal machine, there's time and space enough for everyone and everything in this world, if we only know how to make it.

PEA SOUP

······································

Death would have been better.

Nathan Richmond was convinced of it. Death would have been easy compared to the eternal torture of the drive to his grandparents' house. Eight unendurable hours cooped up in the backseat of the family Buick, with a sister on either side. The three of them sat like caged animals as the dusk dissolved into night.

"I'm hungry," grumbled Nathan.

"You're always hungry," snapped Adrian, his older sister, who sat to his right. She was fifteen and was the world's most unpleasant travel companion.

A billboard in the distance began to grow larger as they approached it, but Nathan didn't take much notice of it. Instead he tried to focus on his pocket video game, which was losing battery power and was moments from crashing.

For an instant the approaching billboard reflected their headlights, casting a pale olive light into the car, but the sign quickly passed, and the night dove back into the blackness that filled the awful crevices of the earth commonly called "the middle of nowhere."

Nathan wiggled his foot, which had fallen asleep—and even that slight motion was met by a violent shove from Adrian.

"Stop kicking me!" she complained.

"I wasn't kicking," Nathan tried to explain in a calm, rational voice. "My foot fell asleep, and I was—"

"Mom, will you tell him to stock kicking me?"

"But—"

"Ouch!" came a shout from his left. Nathan turned to see his four-year-old sister, Maggie, holding a hand over her eye. "Nathan punched me in the eye!"

"It was an accident," pleaded Nathan. "It was my elbow . . ."

But Maggie was already crying and clutching her old, mange-haired Baby-Go-Bye-Bye doll to her chest.

"You see how he's acting?" said Adrian.

"But—"

It was no use. His mom flicked on the dome light and turned to him, extending her wagging finger. When she extended the wagging finger, it always meant that all hope was lost.

"Nathan, I swear to you," she said, "if you don't change your behavior, we will find a suitable punishment and you will not be a happy camper."

"Make him kiss Grandma on the lips," Maggie suggested, and added, "Ouch!" when Nathan elbowed her again—this time on purpose.

"I saw that," growled Mom, her finger still wagging hypnotically up and down. Nathan watched the bright red nail do its little dance beneath the dim glow of the dome light up above. "You keep your hands to yourself."

"And his feet!" added Adrian—which, of course, was

impossible, because Nathan sat squarely on the hump in the middle of the backseat, and the only other place to put his feet would have been his mouth. "Maybe if you didn't eat so much," snapped Adrian, "you wouldn't be so fat, and there'd be more room back here."

"I'm not fat!" insisted Nathan. "I'm stocky." And it was true. Sure, he had a few extra pounds—but nothing like his sister imagined. And he was active, too, playing ice hockey three days a week. As for Adrian, well, she constantly fought her own weight, eating like a bird, and pecking at people like one, too.

"Can't we all just get along?" their father asked from the relative safety of the driver's seat. He reached over and turned up the radio, which dragged down a faint country-western station among violent bursts of static. "There . . . that's better."

How much longer to Grandma and Grandpa's house? wondered Nathan. *Five more hours? Six? And I'm expected to survive that long? Impossible!*

A rectangular shape appeared in the dark distance. With his video game dead, Nathan let his eyes follow the approaching shape.

Was it the square frame of a truck? No, he decided. There were no headlights. It was just another roadside billboard. Nathan squinted until he could see it clearly. On it was a picture of a bowl, and in the bowl, something steamy and green: a khaki-colored brew, thick and chunky. The words painted above the bowl read:

Pea Soup—168 Miles!

Nathan grimaced. "Yuck! Pea soup!"

Little Maggie turned to him with her brown eyes wide in revulsion. "They make soup out of pee?"

Nathan sighed, not having the strength to respond.

The sign loomed closer and brighter until their car passed into darkness once more.

Another hour of purgatory.

Dense white nebulas of fog brooded on the road, waiting to be punctured by a Buick on cruise control. Dad had shamelessly forced them to sing "A Hundred Bottles of Beer on the Wall." All hundred verses. Only they didn't sing about beer, since Mom felt it was an inappropriate beverage to dedicate so much quality singing time to, so they argued over what liquid to sing about. Nathan wanted root beer, Maggie wanted apple juice, and Adrian wanted iced cappuccino. Dad abstained from voting, and as usual, Mom sided with Adrian. "A Hundred Bottles of Iced Cappuccino on the Wall" filled Nathan's aching ears and vocal cords for twice as long as beer would have.

When the song was over, Maggie was asleep, stretching and poking her hard little black shoes all over Nathan's anatomy.

"Don't you dare wake her," said Mom, wagging her finger again.

Right about then, another rectangular shape appeared in the distance, but Nathan was distracted by a strange, silent vibration in the seat. Adrian had let one rip—and she could have gotten away with it, but leather tells all.

"Dad, Adrian's farting again!" Nathan held his nose.

"I am not!" She shifted positions uncomfortably. "We're passing through a cow pasture, that's all."

The approaching road sign loomed closer until it seemed to be directly in their path—but that was just an optical illusion. In a moment it took its normal place on the right side of the road, growing brighter. The image was familiar, a large steaming tureen of green. This time the sign read:

Pea Soup—87 miles!

As Nathan examined the image, he noticed that the soup wasn't chunky and gloppy at all. It seemed smooth and shimmering, a bright ocean-green. For a moment, as the sign whooshed past, Nathan could swear he smelled the stuff. After three hours cooped up in a car with his family's various bodily odors, the smell of pea soup didn't seem that bad after all. Of course, it was just a trick of his mind, but he tried to hold on to that smell long after the sign had passed.

"You know, come to think of it, I'm getting a little hungry myself," said Dad.

The road did not turn. It did not vary a single degree to the left or right. Beyond the dark flatlands, a crescent moon rose, anemic and uninviting. With legs bruised from an hour of pummeling from Maggie's plastic-heeled shoes, Nathan tried to see something—anything—of interest off the side of the road, beneath that anorexic moon. Every once in a while he thought he saw fields: rows of crops speckled with gray boulders. He imagined those boulders were people hunched over the midnight crops—and when he stared out the window long enough, he could make himself believe that they actually moved. Nathan wondered if this place would look as bleak in the daytime . . . and wondered if those crops were of the edible variety. He was even more hungry now. There hadn't been a single place to stop for more than an hour on the desolate highway.

This time, when the road sign made its appearance, Nathan stared at its dark shape in anticipation as it approached.

"Turn on your high beams, Dad," Nathan asked.

The headlights flicked brighter, and the bowl of soup on the billboard seemed to practically leap out at them.

Pea Soup—7 miles!

This time the bowl was larger than before, and the soup within seemed to swirl and glimmer like liquid jade. Nathan had only tasted pea soup once in his life before. He had thought that once would be enough, but now, the hunger in his belly was telling him differently. He could smell the soup now stronger than anything. He could feel it running down his throat, sweet and delicious. Suddenly there was nothing in the world he wanted more than pea soup.

"Hey, Dad! Maybe we should stop there and get something to eat."

"I was thinking exactly the same thing."

Nathan heard his father slip out of cruise control, and felt the car accelerate. Even so, they were the longest seven miles Nathan could ever remember.

A final billboard emblazoned with the words *Pea Soup—Exit Here!* greeted them at the turnoff, and there, alone in the distance, stood the restaurant. It seemed tiny as they approached down a weather-worn two-lane road, but like everything else in this flat part of the world, looks were deceiving. By the time they reached it, Nathan could tell it wasn't just a little shack, but a full-fledged restaurant, two stories high, with rooms that seemed to stretch out in all directions. The entire structure was outlined with winking Christmas lights, even though it was March, and the parking lot was packed. It seemed to Nathan that every traveler for a hundred square miles must have stopped here.

"Must be a popular place," said Mom, the Queen of Understatement.

"Just park anywhere, Dad," said Adrian, rubbing her stomach, just as hungry as Nathan.

By now Maggie had started stirring, and as she opened her weary eyes to the bright flashing lights, she quickly revived. "It looks like the North Pole!"

Maggie was right. Nathan recalled a visit to a place called "Santa's Workshop" when he was little. It was full of animatronic elves, and featured electric bumper sleighs. This place reminded him of that—bright and inviting. In fact, a little *too* inviting.

"There!" shouted Adrian. "Park there!"

"That's a red zone, dear," said their mother.

"Who cares?" Adrian unlocked her door. "What are they going to do, tow us? There's probably not a tow truck for fifty miles!"

And since the huge lot didn't have a single parking place, Dad pulled right up to the red zone. Nathan, whose hunger was making him light-headed, didn't complain. The second the car was stopped, he pushed Maggie out, took a deep breath of the brisk air, and made a beeline to the front entrance, where a crowd of people were heading in.

"That's odd," said their mother. "All these lights, and nowhere is the name of the restaurant."

"Who cares?" said Nathan. "As long as there's *food.*"

"Yeah," echoed Maggie, dragging her ragged doll behind her like a security blanket.

Inside, the crowd seemed to quickly disperse as an army of hosts and hostesses led hungry families into the cavernous depths of the restaurant. Finally the Richmonds were alone, with a single young hostess. She seemed pleasant enough, although her platinum-blond hair was pulled into such a tight bun on top of her head that it seemed to stretch out her cheeks and eyes. Still, she had a heartwarming smile, and the softest of green eyes. She smiled at Nathan, and he found himself smiling back.

"My, you look like you've come a long way."

"And a lot farther to go," responded Dad.

"Well, I'm glad you found your way to our little corner of the world," said the hostess. "Party of five?" She reached down, finding five menus without even looking.

"Yes," said Mr. Richmond. "How long's the wait?"

Her stretch-lipped smile widened to reveal a row of perfect capped teeth. "There's never a wait," she told them. "We pride ourselves on service."

She turned and led them past room after room of diners, all happily consuming their meals, and finally sat them down in a cozy oak room, with plaid carpeting and a crackling fireplace. The Richmonds settled in and she handed them the menus. "I'll also be your server tonight," the tight-haired waitress said. "Today's special is pea soup."

"Big surprise," said Adrian.

"Soup's only ten cents a bowl today," said the waitress.

"I'll have a bowl," Nathan blurted out.

His father threw him an I'm-wiser-than-you look. "Wouldn't you rather see what else is on the menu?"

"No," said Nathan, with conviction. "I want the soup."

"Me, too," said Maggie, who now understood what pea soup was *really* made from.

"So do I," said Mom.

Dad sighed, putting all pretenses aside. "I guess I do to."

"I'll have the tuna salad," said Adrian.

The waitress/hostess took their menus and glided away.

"Ten cents!" mused Dad. "What a deal!"

His wife patted his hand. "Things are less expensive in this part of the world, dear."

With Nathan's hunger growing exponentially, he busied himself watching the other patrons. It seemed they weren't the only ones who were hungry. Across the room sat a policeman, digging his bread into a bowl of soup as if mining for gold, savoring every last bit of it. At another table an elderly couple lifted spoon to mouth over and over again, faster than they ought to be able to move. And at yet another table, a businessman gave up on his spoon and lifted the bowl to his lips, pouring its steaming contents into his mouth, chugging it down as fast as he could swallow. Little rivers of green coursed down his cheeks and onto his tie.

"Gross," said Adrian.

When the bowl was empty the businessman lifted his tie and licked the soup off.

A few minutes later the waitress reappeared and slid bowls before them. The edges were delicately carved and hand-painted in soft pastels, like the finest of china. Inside rested a perfect circle of pale green soup, an inch and a half deep.

"I'm afraid we're having some trouble with the tuna salad," said the waitress. "But here's some pea soup while you're waiting." She smiled at Dad reassuringly. "On the house." Nathan wondered what sort of trouble they could have with tuna salad.

Adrian took a deep whiff of the soup. "Well, I guess it couldn't hurt to try it."

Nathan's ravenous appetite was quickly taking control. He could feel the soup's rich aroma reaching up his nostrils, taunting and teasing. The smell was so overpowering, he felt he might black out. His peripheral vision went dim. His ears began to ring. He couldn't feel his fingers or his toes.

"Bon appétit," said the waitress.

It was as if Nathan were possessed. Suddenly, he craved this soup with every ounce of his being. He craved it more than anything in the world. Nathan hungrily dipped his spoon into the bowl and brought the rich, jade-colored brew to his lips, letting its rich, velvety creaminess spill over his eight thousand taste buds.

Nathan couldn't remember how long it took him to finish off that bowl. It was as if he were lost in an ecstatic trance. He might as well have been unconscious. The next thing he remembered was staring down at a bowl, his spoon rattling emptily, and suddenly feeling very, very sad about its souplessness.

He looked up at his parents. Their bowls were empty as well. So was Adrian's. Maggie was finishing off the last bit of her soup with the same enthusiasm she usually lavished on candy.

"More!" she demanded when she was done, completely dispensing with the magic word "please." No one corrected her, because they all felt pretty much the same.

Their waitress glided up, just as pleasant as you please. "Our soup is something special, isn't it?"

Dad smiled at her dreamily. "I'll say. How about another round?"

"Certainly." The waitress gathered up their empty bowls. "Of course, only the first bowl is ten cents. Second helpings are twenty dollars apiece."

Nathan could see his dad's eyebrows furrow as he quickly calculated what the damage would be. But it was his mother who voiced dissent.

"That's robbery!" she said, extending her wagging finger. "You can't do that to people!"

"I'm sorry if our policy upsets you, ma'am," said the waitress, never losing the happy lilt in her voice. "If you'd like, I'll tally up the bill now, and you're free to go."

"But my daughter never got her tuna salad," Mom re-minded her.

"I don't want it anymore," announced Adrian. "I'd rather have soup."

Dad gently grabbed Mom's wagging finger and lowered it to the table. "It's all right, miss. We *do* want seconds. All of us. And we'll pay."

Nathan had watched this interchange with a growing sense of helplessness and panic. But suddenly he felt all the tension release from his chest. He heard his sister breathe a sigh of relief, as well. *I'm full*, thought Nathan. *But I'm even hungrier than I was before.* Deep down he knew that this should not be, but it was late, and he was tired, and he didn't want to start any battles within his own brain tonight. He just wanted to eat. Was that so wrong?

Meanwhile, across the room, a well-dressed woman plunged her face into a bowl of soup, sucking it up like a pig at a trough.

There was a motel behind the restaurant. They hadn't seen it because it wasn't very well lit. It seemed small from the outside. But once inside they realized the place was huge. It had many levels of tiny little rooms that resembled shelves in a filing cabinet. From the size of the place, Nathan figured it must have extended deep underground.

Nathan was relieved. It was good that they stay here overnight, he thought. It was the right thing to do. Especially because, after four bowls of soup, he could barely move, much less squeeze into a car.

A blond woman with a tight bun of hair stood behind the reception desk. Nathan thought she looked awfully familiar.

"Why—it's you!" exclaimed Mom, stopping short before reaching the desk.

Dad just smiled lazily at her. "You sure get around."

"Will you be staying with us tonight?" asked the hostess/waitress/hotel clerk.

"How come you're here?" asked Nathan. "I thought you were a waitress."

She shrugged. "I'm many things to many people."

"I'll bet you are," said Dad. His leering grin was the kind that would most definitely make Mom mad.

The woman held out a key ring on her finger, like the brass ring at a carnival carousel. Mom grabbed the key as quickly as she could.

"There's a free breakfast buffet in the morning," the girl advised them. "Muffins, scrambled eggs, that sort of thing."

But none of those things seemed very appealing at the moment. "What if we wanted something else?" Adrian asked. "What if we wanted . . . soup?"

The waitress lady smiled and winked. "Sure. But it'll cost a little extra."

The hotel room was not the kind of place the Richmonds were used to staying in. No framed prints of famous artists. No mini-bar. Not even a TV. Just four painted cinder-block walls, and five small beds covered with drab green military blankets, tucked in so tightly it was hard to squeeze into them. The room was not meant for so many people, and the beds were pushed so close to one another there was no room in between.

"Just like five peas in a pod," Dad commented jokingly, but the thought made Nathan shiver.

That night Nathan dreamed he was skating on a great frozen lake. He was skillfully moving through figure-skating crowds with his hockey stick. Far ahead of him was the goal, larger and less protected than he had ever seen it in real ice-hockey games. He looked down at his puck, ready to shoot it, but stopped. His puck wasn't flat. It was round. It wasn't black; it was green. Suddenly the ground shook, his knees began to wobble, and before him the ice shattered in a spiderweb fracture, like a windshield pierced by a bullet. The ice separated, twisted and bobbed—a hundred ice floes slowly melting.

And standing on one of those floes was his family. They weren't dressed in heavy parkas and winter coats. They weren't even dressed in sweaters. Instead, they all wore bathing suits, as if it were just a day at the beach.

"Come on, Nathan!" his father called. "You'll be late for breakfast!" And with that, his dad climbed a diving board that grew out of the ice floe and did a triple gainer into the water. One by one the others did the same, first his mom, then his sisters—and all the while Nathan screamed at them to stop, for once they hit the surface, they never came back up. Nathan could do nothing about it. All he could do was skate around the tilted edge of the great hole in the ice—until he realized he wasn't skating around a lake at all. It was the edge of a bowl—a hand-painted fine china bowl—and the water beneath the bobbing chunks of ice was green. Nathan lost his balance and felt himself sliding toward the edge.

"No!" he screamed, but it was too late. He had plunged into a hot, thick liquid, and his skates were so heavy he went down as if it were quicksand. He opened his mouth, and it instantly filled with the familiar taste of pea soup. Suddenly, instead of wanting to escape, he wanted to swallow, and swallow again. He wanted to breathe the soup into his lungs and sink as deep as he could go, until he was lost forever in the bottomless bowl.

And that desire was so terrifying, Nathan woke up screaming.

When his eyes cleared, he could see it was already daylight. Bright daylight—not the slim rays of dawn. He was alone in the tiny hotel room.

"Mom? Dad? Anyone?"

No one was in the bathroom. No one was in the closet. And it occurred to Nathan that this place, in daylight, didn't resemble a hotel room at all—although for the life of him, he couldn't figure out what the place reminded him of. He peered out through the small barred window, to see flat fields cut by the highway in the distance, and beyond, more fields. The farmland looked much more attractive in the daytime, but still the desolation was unnerving.

More unnerving was the parking lot, for as Nathan left the room and crossed the immense lot between the motel and the restaurant, in search of his parents, he realized that his sister had been dead wrong. There *were* tow trucks in this corner of nowhere. Dozens of them. The parking lot was now half-empty as tow trucks hauled away the cars—the old ones and the new ones, the cheap ones and the expensive ones . . . and a bright red Buick with a license plate that read RCHLND1.

Nathan's walk became a run as he burst into the restaurant. He ran past the battalion of hostesses and through one dining room after another. But then he slowed, and stopped. He sniffed. The fragrant aroma of soup beckoned to him. It filled his mind now, slicing at his fear. *Slow down,* it seemed to tell him. *Take it easy. Things aren't as bad as they seem.* That pungent smell seemed to whisper to his brain all the things that he wanted to hear. All the things that would make him stop. And eat.

His parents were at the same table they had occupied the night before. They were wearing the same clothes they had worn last night, too, but now those clothes were barely recognizable. They were covered by layer after layer of dense, green pea soup. It ran down their faces and speckled their hair. It puddled in their laps and dripped in thick pools on the floor. Nathan watched, speechless, as his mother lifted a bowl to her mouth and poured it down her gullet—most of it spilling down the front of what was once her favorite blouse.

Nathan screamed. It was the only thing that got their attention.

"It's about time you got up, sleepyhead," his dad gurgled. "Have some breakfast. It's already paid for."

"Dad—they're towing away the car! You have to stop them."

His father only laughed. "How do you think I payed for the soup?"

Nathan saw someone enter the room. No . . . he *felt* someone enter. He turned to see who it was.

"Is there a problem here?"

It was the waitress. The same one who ushered them into the restaurant the night before. The same one who gave them their room. The same one who kept bringing them bowl after bowl after bowl of the terrible, wonderful soup.

"No problem," said Nathan's father. "My son's a little cranky because he hasn't eaten breakfast." Then he grabbed Nathan's arm with a slimy soup-covered hand and pulled him toward an empty seat, where a fresh bowl of steaming soup was waiting for him. And yes, Nathan *was* hungry—hungrier than he could ever remember being—and he couldn't imagine eating anything else but that soup. It was as if his whole body had changed, and he could no longer digest anything else.

"Things will be much clearer to you, Nathan, once you've had something to eat," said Dad.

"Better sit down quick," said Adrian, "before I eat your portion."

"Mmm," said Maggie. "Can Baby-Go-Bye-Bye have some, too?"

His mother wagged her finger at him. "Sit down, Nathan, and stop making a spectacle of yourself!" But her wagging fingernail was not red anymore. It was Granny Smith–green. And so were her eyes. So were all of their eyes, just as green as the waitress's.

Nathan turned and ran, but the waitress caught him. Her arms were much stronger than anyone's ought to be. Her smile remained, but her eyes showed a deep-seated anger. When he looked in those eyes, it seemed as though Nathan could see deep into some awful place. Those eyes had depth that went far beyond the back of her skull.

"Don't make this more difficult than it has to be," she threatened. Nathan could feel her fingers digging

into his arms with bone-crushing strength as she tried
to move him back to the table. Nathan struggled. He
twisted and turned. Finally he freed one arm and
reached up to grab any part of her that he could. He
snagged his fingers around the bun of her hair and
pulled, tearing free the barrette—an iron thing with
teeth like a bear trap.

Shocked, she loosened her grip, and Nathan pulled
himself free—in time to see her hair fall out of its bun.
But it wasn't just her hair. With the iron barrette taken
away, her pretty, tight skin began to sag and fold. Deep
creases formed around her eyes. Her cheeks slid into
jowls, and the skin of her neck buckled into flaps like
the neck of a chicken. Only now did Nathan realize
that her hair wasn't platinum-blond, but stark white.
She must have been hundreds of years old!

Nathan raced past her and burst out of the dining
room, not knowing where he was headed. All around
him he saw the other hosts and hostesses, each one the
same: hair and skin pulled back to make them seem
young, instead of ancient. They were all staring at him.

Nathan burst through a door onto a catwalk, and
before him was perhaps the most horrible sight of all.

He had found the kitchen.

In the center was a pot—a *cauldron*—at least twenty
feet wide and two stories deep. It was black and bul-
bous and filled with the bubbling soup, pleasant of
smell and numbing of soul. Mindless, green-eyed
drones in drab gray rags stirred the mixture and added
pound after pound of pureed peas, carrots, and spices,
from a blender ten feet high. Nathan watched in mute
horror as one of the workers lost his footing and
slipped into the blender. No one cared.

Nathan turned and ran, even more desperate than
before to escape. Finally, at the end of his endurance,

he burst into cold daylight beneath a sky white as the old crone's hair.

He was in the parking lot, which now was completely empty except for a few buses—and beyond the parking lot were fields high with crops. He could lose himself in those crops! He could disappear, and the old witch—or whatever she was—would never find him. He pushed himself across the empty parking lot, heading for the safety of the crops . . .

. . . until he saw the nature of the crop . . . and the hunched workers who pruned, weeded, and picked. Hundreds upon thousands of workers in the fields around him, up and down every row, lovingly tending their precious peas.

"Nathan," said a gentle voice behind him.

He turned. Her face was a wrinkled mask of age—but she held out her hand and a worker handed back her barrette. As she clipped it to her hair, the skin of her face began pulling back until the wrinkles were gone and she was once again the image of youthful beauty. Her eyes sparkled and no longer seemed angry. Now they seemed compassionate and full of pity.

"Why resist the one thing in the world you want more than anything else?" she appealed to him. "Why torture yourself, Nathan?" Several workers in tattered garments grabbed hold of him and pulled him closer to her. In one hand she held a thermos, and in the other, a fine china bowl.

"Nothing in the world is as satisfying," she said, with a musical, hypnotic cadence to her voice. "Nothing sticks to your ribs and fills you up like a nice bowl of soup."

She took a step closer, opened the thermos, and poured the silky liquid into the bowl. Nathan shook his head, trying to prevent the intoxicating fragrance from reaching his brain. "No!" he shouted through gritted teeth.

"It's all you'll ever want. It's all you'll ever need. Come, be with your family," she said. "Right now they're boarding a bus, bound for some new farmland we've just acquired. Two thousand acres. We need you to help plant the crop, Nathan. Don't you want to be with your family?"

She held the bowl out to him, and Nathan fought his hunger with every ounce of his spirit. *I can resist it. I can resist it,* he told himself, but as if reading his mind, she told him:

"No, Nathan. You can't."

At last the vapors rising from the soup reached up his nostrils like two fingers, pulling him toward the bowl. He felt his face lower, closer and closer, until the tip of his nose touched the surface of the soup, and the moment it did his will imploded and he gave himself over to the hunger. He pushed his face into the soup and began to drink.

"Very good, Nathan," he heard her say. "Soon you will join your family in the fields."

Yes. Yes, that's exactly what I'll do. He drew in another mouthful and swallowed.

"You'll labor day and night, planting and reaping, resting only to sleep. And at the end of each day you will be rewarded with a hot bowl of soup."

I'll work all day, every day. For the soup. For the soup. The smooth liquid filled his mouth and nose. He could feel it warming his stomach. He needed it now, more than he needed air to breathe, and so he kept his face deep in the bowl.

"And after a few years, if you're a very good boy, you'll get to work in the kitchen."

Yes! The kitchen! The shallow bowl had become bottomless. Nathan's face was pressed into it all the way up to his ears, and still he felt there was farther to go.

"And if you're very, very good, you'll get to hand-paint the china bowls."

Nathan finally drained the last of the soup, licking the bowl like a puppy, until not a drop remained. *It's soooo good. . . .*

"And if you give your life over to your work, some-day, a very long time from now, you'll receive the highest honor of all . . ." Then she wiped the soup from his forehead and cheeks, and whispered into his ear, "You'll get to be a waiter."

Some time later, a bored boy stared out the window of his parents' car. It had been a long trip and there were many hours left to go. He watched the afternoon scenery pass by, endlessly.

"Day laborers," explained his father as they drove past one patch of cropland after another. In each field workers swarmed over the crops like drones. "Hard work and low pay. It oughta be against the law to treat people like that."

For a moment the boy thought he saw a kid in the crops looking at him. A boy about his age, a little bit chubby, with a sad look on his face, and his lips smeared with something slimy green. But before he could get a good look, the car sped on and the laborers passed out of view.

"Hey, how about we stop and get something to eat," suggested the boy's father.

"Good idea, Dad." The boy glanced at a billboard looming up ahead. And he smiled. He knew just what he was in the mood for.

THE ELSEWHERE BOUTIQUE

. . . .

ONLY THIRTEEN SHOPPING DAYS UNTIL CHRISTMAS.

A giant sign at the entrance to North Bluff Plaza proclaims the words in big block letters. People rush across the slush-filled parking lot into the mall, as if their lives depend on getting inside. I guess my brother and I are no different; we're on a mission as well. We still have one Christmas gift left to buy.

"We'll be waiting in lines all day," whines my younger brother, Paul, who would much rather be watching football. "Can't we just do it some other time, Georgia?"

"There is no other time," I tell him, and drag his complaining little butt across the melting snow, into the mall.

Once in the wide, warm corridor of the mall, we try to figure out which way to go. Should we go to the department store on the east end, where you need a gas mask to make it through the perfume department, or should we go to the department store on the west end, where the clothes are so cheap, they tear when you try to take them off the hanger?

That's when we first notice a shop we haven't seen in all of our previous shopping expeditions. It's just a tiny store, nestled between a card shop and an art gallery. A small neon sign over the entrance reads The Elsewhere Boutique. Even though every other store is crawling with customers, no one ventures into the odd little place—perhaps because they're not advertizing any Christmas sales.

"You want to check it out?" I ask Paul. He wrinkles his nose, clearly not wanting to set foot in anything called a *boutique*.

"I'd rather go to the video arcade."

Still, I nudge him in, and we cross the threshold onto the clean tile floor of the empty shop. On the wall I can see row after row of little jars—tiny things carved in crystal. They're shelved floor to ceiling and the shelves stretch back as far as I can see. Apparently this store is much larger than it appears, recessing deep into undiscovered regions of the mall.

"It's perfume!" says Paul. "That's all, it's just a perfume store. Let's go."

But as I sniff the air, I don't smell the slightest hint of fragrance. If it isn't perfume, what *is* in those little vials?

"May I help you?" says the clerk—the only one in the store. He's a tall man, with a polished dome of a head so void of hair it actually shines, reflecting all the colors of the vials on the wall.

"We're looking for a Christmas present," I explain, "something for our father."

The shopkeeper smiles warmly. "How delightful! It's usually the parents, hurrying about to buy things for the children. Nice to see things reversed."

"Yeah," sighs Paul, "and we can't just go out and get any old thing—we have to get something *meaningful*."

The bald man nods, knowingly. "I see. It certainly is hard to find meaningful presents nowadays."

"That's for sure." I think back to Dad's birthday. We got him a birthday card that featured dead flowers, a pipe, and a wooden duck. None of the things on that card had anything to do with our dad. In fact, come to think of it, none of those things have to do with any-one's dad that I know. As for the present, we got him a sparkling socket wrench—which was about as mean-ingful as the wooden-duck birthday card.

"Well, if meaning is what you're looking for," says the shopkeeper, "then you've come to the perfect place."

"So what is all this stuff?" Paul asks.

"It's everything!" the man says. "And nothing." Then he smiles with a grin of complete satisfaction. "It's elsewhere. Perfect and absolute."

He looks at us as if what he's said makes sense—as if it's all very obvious, and we'd have to be fools not to understand. I look at Paul, Paul looks at me, we both read the cluelessness in each other's eyes, and then turn back to the shiny-headed man, saying what is per-haps the only thing that can be said in this situation: "Can we have a free sample?"

"Well, I suppose," he says, "but it will have to be a very small sample." He turns to the wall behind him, moving his fingers in the air as if he's playing the piano. "What to choose, what to choose . . ." He scans the rows of tiny bottles and finally pulls one off an eye-level shelf. It's green crystal, but the sharp cuts in its pattern reflect a deep blue. He hands the bottle to me, Paul pulls it away, and I pull it back from Paul, giving him a dirty look. As the older sister, I do have some privileges, and one of them is inspecting fragile things first. I hold it up to my eye, watching how it reflects the light. I can't see anything through the refracting pattern of its design. There seems to be nothing inside—no liquid, no powder . . . nothing.

"Exactly what is it?" I ask. Paul pulls it from me again and examines it himself.

"Read the tag," says the man.

I look at the small tag tied around the bottle's neck. The tiny printing reads:

Binary Alternative Reconfiguration

Finally I dare to say the words that I know will make me feel like an idiot, but I have to say them anyway. "I don't get it."

The man looks at us with mild pity in his eyes, and proceeds to tell us something that I don't quite understand, and probably never will. "I deal in events that never occurred," says the shopkeeper. "Situations that might have happened but didn't, choices that were never made, moments that were lost. All the might-have-beens, large and small—those are the things I sell." Then he gently takes the jar from us, holding it up to the light. "Here's a particularly small might-have-been: '*binary alternative reconfiguration.*' It sound complicated, but it's really rather simple. It merely means that the 'elsewhere' contained in this bottle will only effect the two people who open it." He hands it to me. "Go ahead, it's your free sample."

I look at the bottle once more, trying to decide if this strange, looming man is trying to have some fun at our expense—yet he seems so sincere and so serious that it's hard not to believe him . . . and both Paul and I are desperately curious.

"Go on, Georgia." Paul's eyes dart nervously back and forth. "Go on, open it up."

I hand him the bottle. "You hold it, I'll pull the stopper."

Paul holds the bottle carefully, and I reach for the delicately carved crystalline stopper and pull it from the tiny bottle. It makes no sound. I look inside it . . . Empty. Nothing inside. Nothing at all.

"There!" says the bald man, with excited satisfaction in his voice. "How do you like it?"

"How do I like what?"

"Why, your free 'elsewhere,' of course."

This guy's beginning to make me mad. I turn to my sister. "Paula, do you have any idea what he's talking about?"

Paula plays with her pigtails and shakes her head. "I don't see anything."

"Ha ha, very funny," I tell the shopkeeper. "Do you like making kids look stupid?"

"You misunderstand, George," he says. "That is your name, George . . . isn't it?"

I try to stare him down. "Free sample, my butt! I guess you get what you pay for."

He laughs at that—a deep, hearty laugh that seems far too resonant for a man so painfully thin. Now I'm really getting mad. It's bad enough I have to miss an afternoon of football to go out shopping. I don't have to stand here being laughed at by a scrawny, funny-looking man.

I grab my sister's hand, fully prepared to walk right out of the shop, when the creepy shopkeeper says, "Of course, you won't be able to tell the difference. That's the whole point!"

I turn to him. "The point of what?"

"Don't you see? Once 'elsewhere' becomes 'here and now,' it's not elsewhere anymore."

"Just stop the double-talk and speak English," I demand, not wanting him to get the last word.

He holds the little bottle, plugging it up with the stopper once more. "Your old reality is now contained in this bottle. But since it's no longer real, you can't possibly remember it." Then he puts the bottle back on the shelf. I have to admit, as much as I want to shrug it off, I can't keep my eyes off that green bottle. I can't stop wondering what it contains. I want to leave, but I can't. Not yet.

"OK," I say, "how about another free sample?"

"How can I do business if I give things away for free?" says ol' Chrome Dome, not as friendly as he was a moment ago.

I cross my arms stubbornly. "Do you want us to buy something from you or not?"

He sighs, "Very well," then he turns to the wall behind him.

"No," I say. "I want to pick."

He tosses me an irritated gaze, then waves his hand, gesturing to the rest of the store. "Help yourself, George."

I begin to browse. Each delicate crystalline bottle has its own shape and texture—and each one has a small tag on it. While Paula keeps looking at the bright, shiny ones, my eyes are attracted to a row of jagged ones—shiny, black obsidian bottles. I pick one up and hold it carefully in my fingers.

"You have expensive tastes," the shopkeeper says. "But a promise is a promise. You may sample this one if you like."

I look at the tag. It says, in that tiny, ballpoint-pen printing:

Thermonuclear War—1982

"Hmm!" says the bald man, raising an eyebrow. "Nineteen eighty-two, a very good year."

I take a firm grasp of the black stopper, pull it out, and glance inside. Nothing. Empty again. I blow into it and my own breath comes back to meet me.

"You know, someone really oughta put you out of business," I tell him.

They say there's a sucker born every minute, and I guess I'm one of them. I glance outside to the shredded remnants of the old mall. My parents say it once had a roof, but that shattered years ago. Now the cold snow of the nuclear winter just pours in night and day. I hear it was a real nice place once—but that was before I was born, before the war in '82. I've seen pictures, though.

I take a glance at my radiation gauge, and get mad at myself for wasting time in this store. I'm almost at my radiation limit, which means I won't have time to look for something for Dad today. I'll probably have to get him an apple again, like last year—and those things are so darned expensive. Christmas presents. That's one of the things I hate about being an only child, I don't have anyone to help me pick out gifts.

I prepare to zip my radiation suit closed and head out through the store's air lock, but the bald man grabs me by the scruff of the neck and pulls me back.

"Not so fast, George," he says. "I've given you two free samples. The least you could do is offer to purchase something."

Now I begin to get scared. Mom and Dad were right, I should have never ventured to the surface. People are crazy up here, their minds rotted by fallout. Now I can think of nothing but getting to the safety of my home. I reach into my pocket and pull out a wad of bills and throw it at him.

"Here!" I say. "Here, take whatever you want, just let me out of here." Still, he holds me firmly, and tallies the bills on the counter.

"Thirty-four dollars. Very well. You can choose anything from this display case." And he points to a shelf on the wall filled with bright, colorful bottles. I grab the first one I see: a sky-blue one, with glimmering purple refractions. Anything to get out of his bony grasp.

"Good choice," he says, still holding on to me tightly. "Now there's only one bit of business left."

Then his hands seem to reach across the room. It has to be an optical illusion, but still, it seems as if they're stretching—as if they're rubber. He grabs the sample bottles I had opened, and since he doesn't have a free hand, he puts them into his mouth and pulls the stopper with his teeth, like a grenade—first from the black one, then from the green one. At last he lets me go. I lose my balance and slip to the floor. When I get up again, he has already stoppered the bottles and put them back in their places.

I shake my hair out of my eyes and grasp Paul's hand—there are very few times Paul will let me grab his hand, but he's just as shaken as I am by the strange man and the empty bottles. For once, Paul doesn't mind his big sister protecting him.

"Come on, Paul. Let's just go home. We'll find something for Dad some other day."

"But you've already got a gift for your father," says the shopkeeper. "A perfect one."

"Yeah, whatever!"

Then the shopkeeper smiles far too broadly, as if his mouth is made of rubber as well. It's as if everything about him is changeable and can stretch to any shape he likes.

I hurry with Paul out of the store and back into the busy shuffle of the stuffy, overheated mall, and then out into the cold, clean air of the parking lot.

Out on the street, we sit at the bus stop, lost in our own thoughts, watching the steam of our winter breath drift into the air and disappear.

I try to get The Elsewhere Boutique out of my mind, but the more I think about it, the more it troubles me. What if it were possible to bottle up all the things that might have happened but never did? And if those things were ever released into the world, how would we know that anything ever changed?

"That guy was weird," Paul says, and shakes his head as if trying to shake all the weirdness out.

"He sure played a head game on us, didn't he?" I take a look at the little bottle I'm holding. Thirty-four dollars for a bottle of nothing. Well, at least it's pretty. Then I notice the little dangling tag, and curious, I turn it over to see what is says. The card reads:

Billionaire Businessman

"Yeah, sure," I say aloud, barely able to believe that I wasted my money on this dumb little bottle. Well, maybe it won't be a total loss. I'm sure Dad will find some use for it.

RALPHY SHERMAN'S BAG OF WIND

•••

The bag sat innocently on the library table between my sister Roxanne and me. A brown paper bag—the kind of sack you get at the grocery store. The kind you can cover your school books with. The kind of brown bag you'd like to drop over the heads of some of the *really* ugly people out there. Just a plain brown paper bag. The mouth of this one was folded over, so you couldn't see inside.

Roxy and I had left it unguarded. We hadn't thought much about it. I mean, who was going to bother it in the library? But I guess when you leave a single brown paper bag alone in the center of a big round table and walk away, some bozo's bound to wonder what's inside.

We were racing stealthily around the aisles, playing one of our favorite games: Psychotic Librarian. The game involved misshelving books in unlikely pairs, while the Librarian ripped her hair out, searching for us down the narrow, maze-like aisles. I had just shelved *Breakfast at Tiffany's* next to *Naked Lunch*, when the Librarian made an exhausted lunge at me through the stacks, from the next aisle. "I'll get you, Ralphy Sherman," she growled, "if it's the last thing I do," and it might just have been, considering the way she was huffing and puffing.

I slipped out of her desperate grip, and took off down the science aisle, where I ran into Roxanne. She held a copy of *Moby Dick* in one hand, and was searching for a suitable match on the anatomy shelves.

"This is going to be a good one," she said, "I just know it."

That's when we caught sight of Marvin McSchultz. Beyond the end of the aisle, we saw him leaning over our table, his hands slowly trying to open the curled lip of our bag to get a serious look inside.

"Can you believe him?" I said. "Somebody oughta call pest control!"

We stormed out of the aisle to catch him red-handed. He turned to us, his beady little snake-eyes trying to feign innocence, but we knew better.

"Oh, hi, guys." Marvin was the kind of kid who might as well have had a "Kick Me" sign tattooed on his forehead. He had ears like a pair of amphitheaters on either side of a zit-cratered moon face. If he had a good personality, it would have redeemed him, but his personality was like a wet sock on a cold morning. His twin amphitheaters were always stretching their way into other people's conversations, so he could spread unpleasant gossip, and his dirty-nailed fingers were little crowbars prying their way into everyone else's belongings. Just like they were right now.

Roxanne put her hands firmly on her hips. "Have my eyes deceived me, or were you daring to touch our stuff?"

"Who me?" blurted Marvin. "No, I was just going to move your bag over. Yeah, that's it, I was gonna move it to the other side of the table."

I grinned because I can always spot the amateur liars in any given situation. "Well, it's a good thing you didn't open it," I advised him. "It could have been disastrous."

Marvin's amphitheaters pricked up. "Whadaya mean 'disastrous'?"

"Don't tell him," warned Roxy. "If you do, he'll tell everyone, and we'll never keep it to ourselves."

"C'mon please," said Marvin, taking the bait like a hungry little trout. "Please, I promise not to tell." He was practically drooling.

I checked the aisles behind us. The librarian had not yet emerged, obviously still wandering the maze of aisles in search of us. She could be there for hours—it was a pretty big library. I sat Marvin down, while Roxy began to read her copy of *Moby Dick*.

"This isn't any old bag," I whispered to Marvin. "It's a receptacle for a supercell mesocyclone vortex tube."

"Huh?"

Roxy sighed, but kept her eye on her book. "I knew he'd be too thick-brained to understand."

Marvin looked from me to her, and then to me again for further explanation.

"Okay . . . in layman's terms," I said, running my finger gently down the edge of the sack. "there's a tornado in this bag."

Marvin stared at me with uncomprehending reptilian eyes. "Whadaya mean a tornado? You mean one of those science kit things, where you can make a twister in a bottle? I seen those. It's just water pouring from one soda bottle to another."

"No, Einstein," said Roxy, with infinite impatience.

"We don't go for cheap imitations. This is the real thing."

Then Marvin quirked his lips in disbelief. "Yeah, right," he said, "and I'm a green space alien in disguise."

Unruffled, Roxy tossed her hair. "If you are, then please tell your people to bring back our mother. It hasn't been the same at home since you guys abducted her."

No doubt Marvin had heard that particular story, but obviously had a hard time believing it.

"You're just a couple of losers," he said, which, coming from Marvin McSchultz was too comical a comment to take seriously. "You two can't even come up with something clever to say—like telling me there's a rat inside, or a tarantula, or some animal you found runt over in the road that your mom says you gotta bury or else you can't come home for dinner—" Marvin grimaced, recalling some unpleasant memory "—no matter how hungry you are."

"Actually, Marvin, all those things might be in the bag, too," I offered. "You never know what gets swept up inside a tornado."

"I wouldn't be surprised," added Roxanne, "if there were a few farm animals swirling around in there."

"Ha, ha," said Marvin. "You're nuts, you know that?"

Roxanne raised an eyebrow, and turned a page. "That's exactly what they said to Ahab when he first told people about the great white whale." Roxanne slammed the heavy cover of the book with an ominous thud, and pushed it across the table to him. "But nobody's laughing now." The book caught the very edge of the big brown bag, and it rocked slightly back and forth.

"And then again, maybe there's nothing inside it," I told Marvin. "Nothing . . . but air."

Marvin slowly turned his eyes to the bag, watching it closely until it stopped rocking.

"If you don't believe us, why don't you peek inside?" I suggested.

He called my bluff and began to reach for the bag.

"Of course," Roxanne added, "you might end up like something 'runt over' in the road—but don't say we didn't warn you."

Still Marvin refused to listen to our own special brand of reason, and he poked his crowbar finger in the bag's folded edge, beginning to pull it up . . . and a breeze blew across the little hairs on the back of our necks.

"Did you feel that?" I said.

Instantly Roxanne and I both dove off of our seats taking cover under the table. Marvin was a microsecond behind us.

"It was just the air conditioner," he insisted, his head beneath the table, and his butt sticking up into the air like an ostrich. "It *was* just the air conditioner, right? *Right?!*"

"Are you certain of that, Marvin?"

By the tone of his voice, we could tell he wasn't certain of anything anymore. "It's . . . it's impossible," he blathered. "Wind can't stay in a bag!"

"It can if it's charmed," I said.

"Charmed?"

Roxy picked up where I left off. "Yeah. You know, like a snake?" She pulled on his collar until the rest of his body fell under the table to join his big old moon face. "You can control it, if you know the secret incantation."

"Incantation?" echoed Marvin. "It sounds spooky."

I peered out from under the table to make sure we were unobserved, then I leaned closer and whispered into Marvin's oversized ear. "The twister was charmed into the bag a hundred years ago by some guru in India, and as long as you say the incantation right, it will never harm the person who opens the bag."

"We got it last year from an old lady in a trailer park," Roxanne continued. "She told us that she spent the last forty years moving from one mobile home to another, and when she got tired of living in one, she opened up the bag, wiped the whole place out, and collected the insurance."

"Trailer parks!" shouted Marvin, as if some grand mystery of the universe had just been solved for him.

"We took the bag on vacation with us," I told him. "We used it for skydiving."

"No way!"

"Way! Have you ever skydived down the mouth of a tornado funnel?"

"It's a real trip!" said Roxy.

Marvin just shook his head as if trying to make it all go away. "No," he said. "No, no, no!" He crawled out from under the table, bumping his head on the way up. We followed. Around us, the library seemed even quieter than before. No one had noticed our little foray under the table, and no one noticed us come out.

"Forget you guys!" he said, dismissing us with a wave of his hand. He tried to leave but couldn't, for although his feet kept walking away, his eyes kept staring at the bag, pulling him into a weird elliptical orbit around the table. "Okay," he said, pushing forth his last question. "If it's in there, how come I can't hear nothing inside?"

I just shook my head. "Don't you know Marvin? It's always dead quiet before a tornado."

At last our logic broke though his thin wall of resistance, and he finally looked at the bag with fearful respect, and a flesh-searing curiosity. Curiousity enough to kill the largest of cats. We knew we had him.

"We've grown tired of it lately," I told him.

"Yeah, too much responsibility," said Roxanne.

"And too much to clean up."

"And it eats us out of house and home—literally."

"We were hoping we could get rid of it."

"To the right person, of course,"

"And for the right price."

Then Marvin "Moonface" McSchultz, eyes locked on the silent paper bag, shoved both his hands deep into his stuffed pockets, and jingled them around.

"How much you askin'?"

I smiled. "How much you got?"

Ten minutes and twenty-three dollars later, Marvin left the library a happy man, with one extremely light brown-paper bag in his hands.

"Remember," Roxy reminded him as he pedaled away, "don't open it until you're out in a field far away from here."

"Far, *far* away," I emphasized. "And don't forget to swing your hula hoop while repeating the magic incantation."

"And if it doesn't work the first time," added Roxanne, "try it again without any clothes on. That usually does the trick."

"I'll remember!" shouted Marvin, as he hurried off, steering with one hand, and holding the bag gingerly in the other as if it contained a small nuclear device.

We watched until he disappeared over the hill, then we hurried off to spend his twenty-three dollars at the mall.

* * *

We thought we'd heard the last of it until dawn the next day. That's when the storm came. No one predicted it. It wasn't on any weather map. It just showed up on the doorstep of our town like an uninvited guest. I awoke to the sound of rattling windows, and Roxy frantically calling my name.

I stumbled out into the hall, where Roxy was standing in her nightgown. "Where's Dad? Where's Whatserface?" Whatserface was our new nanny. As we went through nannies too quickly to count, we rarely bothered to learn their names.

We heard the front door open as Whatserface went out to retrieve the morning paper. With umbrella held high, she stepped out onto the porch, and was promptly pulled up into the skies by the wind, and we haven't seen her since.

"Ralphy, I think it's a tornado!"

"Here? We never have tornadoes here!"

And in response, the wind growled, and hurled a minivan through the living-room window. Well, that was enough to wake up Dad. He shuffled out of his bedroom, and took a long hard look at the beached car, its upturned wheels still spinning.

"Is that ours?" he asked.

"No," I told him.

"Oh. Good," he said, and returned to his bedroom, hit the snooze button, and vanished beneath the covers.

Then, as quickly as the storm had begun, the raging, roaring winds fell silent, and we heard a loud *thump* on our roof, followed by what sounded like sheets flapping in the wind.

What the? But before I could finish the thought, our broken living room window became shrouded in a red flutter.

Something rolled off the roof into the fluttering fabric, with a clumsy-sounding *Ooof*, as it hit the lawn. That's how we knew it wasn't a some*thing*, but a some*one*.

Roxy and I pulled open the door, which was almost off of its hinges, and were met by a sight even stranger than the minivan on the couch. A lump bobbed and bumbled beneath the slick-red fabric, like a rat under a rug. Finally the lump emerged. A moon face, with amphitheater ears. Marvin McSchultz.

"Wow!" said Marvin, more hyped-up than I'd ever seen him. "Wow! That was great!" He struggled to free himself from his parachute harness. "It pulled me off the ground, spun me higher than the clouds. Heck, I thought I was on my way to Oz! But then it just dropped me down the middle! I was spinning, I was tumbling, then I pulled the rip cord, the chute came out, and suddenly I'm floating while the whole world's spinning all around me. It's true what they say— there's no wind in the middle of a tornado. Every-thing's nice and still. A'course I had to pull on these here steering ropes, to keep myself right in the middle. It was just like you said: the twister didn't hurt me, because I did the incantation, just like you told me, hula hoop and all!" His eyes were wide with excite-ment. His hair, which was usually a greasy bowl on his head was teased into wild tornado-twisted tufts. Then I noticed that in one hand, he clutched the brown paper bag we had sold him—making sure to keep it closed.

"Thanks, you guys," he said, shaking my hand so hard it almost pulled right out of its socket. "You changed my life! Thanks for selling me this fantastic bag of wind!"

Roxanne's jaw had dropped so low, I thought it might fall off completely. "But . . . ," she began. "But it can't be! We made up the whole—"

I closed my hand over her mouth so quickly, it made a popping sound, but it succeeded in shutting her up. "Sold it?" I said to Marvin, keeping completely calm. "We didn't sell it to you—we *rented* it to you."

The smile began to drain from Marvin's red-cheeked face. "What?"

Roxanne struggled against my grip, but still I held her mouth closed.

"You don't think we'd part with something like that for a mere twenty-three dollars, do you?" Finally Roxanne stopped struggling, and when I released my hand, she fell right in stride with me.

"That's right," she said. "You paid us the one-time usage fee, and now the bag comes back to us."

Marvin pursed his lips, and tried to tame his wild hair. "No fair!" he said. "You guys are Indian givers. That's what you are!"

Roxanne's face, which a few moments ago was wild with shock now narrowed into an indignant scowl. "Indian givers?" she repeated. "That's very insulting to Native Americans, you know."

"But . . . huh?"

I took a step forward. "You know I have a mind to report you to the principal."

"Something like that won't look good on your permanent record," warned Roxanne.

Finally Marvin caved. "Fine," he said, handing me over the bag. "Be that way." And he turned and left, dragging his parachute behind him.

When he was gone, we looked at the bag for a very long time. We put our ears up to it, and heard nothing . . . but then it's always quiet before a tornado.

"What do you think?" I asked Roxanne.

"I don't know. What was that incantation you told him?"

"Owah . . . Tanass . . . Siam . . .

Roxanne raised an eyebrow and shrugged. "Go figure." Then she turned and went back into our wind-blasted house in search of a broom, dustpan, and hydraulic winch, so she could clean up. As for me, I went straight down to the basement on a mission.

All things considered, I suppose there really are stranger things in Heaven and on Earth than we dare imagine. Maybe even stranger than Roxanne and me. Now if I can only find that hula hoop. . . .

LOVELESS

••••••••••••••••••••••••••••••••••••••

The dead frames of ancient brick buildings loom all around you as you trek through the worst part of town, in the worst hour of night. You're cold, you're alone, and your body aches, but you must force yourself on. You have no choice. On every side of you, windows are boarded up, and walls are tagged with layer upon layer of graffiti.

No one lives here anymore—you're certain you won't find her, but you have to try.

Finally the number on the building matches the number scrawled on the slip of paper you carry. Upstairs, behind a broken window, is a hand-painted sign. You can barely read it in the moonlight. It says: **Madame Loveless, Psychic. Palms read. Futures revealed.**

You've already been to three psychics, all phonies, but those psychics were visionary enough—and terrified enough—to see that you needed the real thing. That you needed the services of Madame Loveless. It took half the night following poor directions, but you've finally found her.

But if she's such a good psychic, then what's she doing living in an awful place like this?

Suddenly a voice behind you makes you jump. "If you're looking for Madame Loveless, you won't find her here," the voice says.

You spin to see an old man crouching in the shadows of a dim doorway. Beside him is a shopping cart filled to the brim with trash and trinkets.

"Building's been condemned for over a year," says the old man. "Rats are the only tenants now."

The old man steps into the pale streetlight. His skin is covered with layers of grime, and the grime covered by layers of clothes. He speaks in a high-pitched, raspy voice, ruined by disease and cigarettes. "Just a second," he says, then rummages through his cart, coming up with a cracked, bulbless flashlight. He aims it at you, as if it works.

"Look at the likes of you! You certainly need a fortune-telling, don't you?"

"Do you know where Madame Loveless has moved?" you ask.

"I might and I might not," says the bag man with a smile. Knowing what he wants, you reach into your pocket and hand him five dollars.

He aims the dead flashlight at the bill, obviously hoping for more, but in the end he grunts and says, "Follow me."

He heaves his slight weight against the overstuffed cart, and it rattles across the broken concrete.

About five blocks away, you come to a wrought-iron fence around a park. The old man chains his cart to the fence, then squeezes through a gap. He leads you across a field of untended grass and ivy. As the street disappears behind you, you notice dim gray shapes all around.

"This park sure has a lot of benches," you mumble, but the old man offers you a dark chuckle. "Those aren't benches," he says. "And this isn't a park."

You look once more and finally realize that you are surrounded by tombstones.

"It's a shortcut," says the old man, waving his broken flashlight. "This way."

You stop dead in your tracks, not wanting to take a single step farther. The moon has slipped behind a dark cloud, and there is no light up ahead. If you turn and run, you can follow the glow of a distant streetlight back to the deserted street . . . but that would mean crossing back through the cemetery alone.

"A lot of people are scared of cemeteries," says the old man, "but there're no spirits here, only bodies. Spirits hate graveyards, because they don't like being reminded that they're dead." Then he pauses for a moment. "Of course, every now and then someone comes back to rest in their old body for a while, and they moan with whatever's left of their vocal cords."

You can almost feel the ground shake from the power of your own shiver.

"Oh, don't be so spooked," says the old man. "It's not like they can haul themselves out of their graves or anything, they barely got any muscles left, if they have any at all. Most they can do is scratch a little."

Somewhere far away you hear something scratching.

The old man makes his way up a hill toward a solitary family mausoleum. The name on the mausoleum is Loveless.

"I . . . uh . . . didn't need a *dead* fortune-teller," you tell the old man.

"She's not so dead that she can't tell your fortune," he answers.

You have no intention of following a crazy old man into a mausoleum, but then something occurs to you. This creepy person is wearing a heavy woolen hat, and in the dim light you can barely see beyond the wrinkles. That nasty, raspy voice doesn't necessarily belong to a man.

Only now does he take off his ski cap to reveal that he's not a man at all.

"Are you . . . Madame Loveless?"

The old woman smiles. "In the flesh."

The way you've figured it, Madame Loveless has little or nothing left of her sanity—which may or may not make her a good psychic. But she had better be good, because you must have your fortune now. You must know the truth.

"Please come in," says Madame Loveless. You step into the dusty stone room.

The small family mausoleum smells awful. It's cluttered with heaps of gnawed chicken bones and stinks of rotting food. A greasy crystal ball sits on an old wooden table in the center.

"This place is the only property my family owns," says Madame Loveless, as she pours herself some imaginary tea from a cracked, empty teapot.

"They kicked me out of my apartment, but I won't let them kick me off family property."

Another shiver echoes through your body as you wonder how crazy a person has to be to start rooming with the dead. Then you begin to wonder how desperate you must be to have come here at all.

Madame Loveless replaces the pot on the ledge above Claude Loveless, beloved father, who has been a resident of the wall for over thirty years. You shift uncomfortably in your seat as you watch the woman sip from her empty cup. Steam beads on her forehead as if the cup at her lips is filled with hot tea. She offers you some, but you don't want to share in her insanity.

"Are you real or another fake?" you ask. "I've seen plenty of fakes."

Madame Loveless puts down her teacup and looks you in the eye. She's the only one who has dared to do that for as long as you can remember.

"It's an honest question," she says, moving toward the iron door of the stone room. "The answer is yes and yes. I'm real and a fake at the same time. You see, most people who want their fortunes told are imbeciles who want someone to change their luck. Since I can't take away their troubles, I take away their money." And then she smiles. "But I can see you're different."

"Prove to me you're for real," you demand, and the old woman looks at you as if reading the truth right off of your eyeballs.

"You come not only seeking to know your future," she tells you, "but to know your past. For many months you have wandered the nights alone, because the sight of you strikes fear into people's hearts. They don't understand what you are. But what's worse is that you don't understand either."

Somewhere far off in the forest of gravestones, you hear something moan. *This doesn't bother me,* you chant over and over in your mind. *This doesn't bother me at all.* But the truth is, with each passing moment, you are becoming more and more terrified, and you begin to feel that Madame Loveless isn't really insane at all . . . because the stone room around you has some-how changed. The dead flashlight is now shining a bright beam on the wall ... and the old woman's teacup is full of steaming tea.

"Shall we begin?" says Madame Loveless.

There's no turning back now. You hold out your hand and brace yourself for whatever she has to tell you.

The old woman runs her fingers along the lines of your palm, her fingertips like old parchment.

"A well-crafted hand," she tells you. "Fine as any I've seen."

"What does it tell you?" you ask, trying not to sound as anxious as you really are.

Madame Loveless smiles. "What is it you want to know?"

You begin to anger. She knows what you need. She knows why you came here. She only has to look at you to see the awful state you're in.

"I'm not here to play games!" you tell her sternly.

She nods solemnly. "Few are," she answers, "but your questions must be specific, if you want the answers to mean anything."

You swallow hard, and voice aloud the questions that have plagued you for as long as you can remember. "Why is my skin so pale and gray?" you hiss at her.

She flips over your hand, running her rough palm across the back of your fingers and up to your wrist. "Because your skin is as old as the land and sea," she answers. "As old as the mountains."

"Why am I always so cold at night?" you ask. "Why do I burn with fever in the day?"

She touches a hand to your icy forehead. "Because you rise and fall with the sun," she tells you.

"Why do my bones creak? Why does it hurt each time I move?"

The old woman grabs your arm and flexes it. You feel the grinding, and grit your teeth from the pain—

the same pain you feel with each grasp, each footfall, each breath.

"Because the bones you speak of do not exist," she says. "And you feel the pain of a spirit not born to move."

And finally you ask the question you are afraid to have answered—the question that means everything, and may just destroy you if the answer is known.

"Who am I?" you ask.

The old fortune-teller leans in close and speaks in a whisper. "Not who you think you are."

You close your cold eyes and try to deny it. You have memories. You remember friends and a family. You remember a life.

"But that life is not yours," says the woman, as if reading your thoughts. "That life belonged to someone else."

You put your head down into your hands and weep, feeling stone-cold from the top of your head to the pale bottoms of your feet. There are no tears when you cry. And now you must admit to yourself that there never have been tears.

"It's not true!" you say.

The old woman reaches out her cup of hot tea and pours it across your arm. It should burn you, but it does not. Instead, it just rolls off your pocked, hardened flesh.

"You see?" she says. "Your body tells the truth, even if your heart won't." Then she gently takes your hand. "Come, I'll take you home."

You stand, spirit broken, and she leads you out of the dark stone mausoleum, into the wind that slithers like a serpent through the endless hills of the grave-yard. She leads you past tall stones, so old that the names cannot be read. At last you arrive at a dark pedestal. You can no longer deny the truth, for the memory comes back to you as you stare at it.

There used to be a statue on that pedestal. The perfect likeness of a child who died much too young. For a hundred years the statue stood over the grave as a monument for friends to remember. Until friends no longer came. Until family aged and were buried before the statue's unmoving eyes. Until the world moved on, and the rains and winds etched off the name carved in the gravestone beneath your feet.

And you forgot who you were.

So you stepped down from that place, forgetting that you were stone, searching for someone who could tell you your name.

"Your place is here," Madame Loveless tells you. "Guarding the child beneath."

"But the child's forgotten," you tell her, mournfully. "I'm forgotten."

The old woman considers this, and says, "I've given you the past. Now I'll give you the future." Then she looks into your eyes and tells you this: "Years from now, when I am nothing but dust, and time takes over this graveyard, you *will* be remembered. You will be taken from here, and will stand in a warm place of honor. You will have value too great to measure. And people will visit you. They will not know who you are, but they will come just the same . . . if only you can wait."

You know the old woman speaks the truth, because in this world of change and lost memories, time brings all things full circle. That which was discarded becomes priceless. Those who were abandoned will someday be loved—if you can hold on till that day.

And so you hope, because hope is all you have as you climb the granite pedestal and take the pose you know so well. Hope of a new life beyond the boundaries of time. Hope of a special place and purpose beyond this lonely grave.

Hope enough to give you the courage . . . to wait.

Where They Came From . . .

• •

I am often asked where I get my ideas, so I thought I'd share the origins of the stories in *MindQuakes*.

Yardwork

I was giving a workshop at a school I was visiting. The task was to come up with an unlikely title, brainstorm story ideas, and then try to develop the most unlikely idea. The title we began with was "The Man Next Door." Someone suggested that he's burying something in his garden, and everyone tossed out the usual possibilities: His money, his family, his boss—and then someone shouted out "he's burying himself." The classroom laughed, but I thought the idea was just quirky enough to work. The question is, why would he do such a thing? My goal was to take a potentially morbid idea, and turn it into something as heartwarming as it was creepy.

Caleb's Colors

There's a painting in my living room by Eyvind Earle, a favorite artist of mine—a surrealistic landscape draped with a bough of leaves, redder than red. You can stare at its unearthly beauty for hours, and never get tired of it. It's as if you can walk right in. . . .

Ralphy Sherman's Jacuzzi of Wonders

My six-year-old son Brendan thinks the Loch Ness Monster is just about the coolest thing in the world, and can tell you all there is to know about it. Once, when we were all sitting in a particularly murky Jacuzzi, Brendan said, "I'll bet this Jacuzzi is about as cloudy as Loch Ness," and then he smiled, because we both knew it was going to end up as a story. As for Ralphy Sherman, he's the one and only character who appears in all of my books. Someday he'll get a book of his own.

Number 2

What if inanimate objects had hopes and dreams of their own, just like us? As I thought about that, it occurred to me that a classroom pencil led a pretty miserable life. Sharpened and gnawed on, then sharpened again. All the worse if you're a pencil with dreams of greatness.

The Soul Exchange

Ever since Veruca Salt went down the garbage shoot in Willy Wonka's factory, I've loved stories about unpleasant kids who got their just desserts. With that in mind, I wanted to see what would happen to a self-absorbed kid who found a way to trade in bodies as easily as people trade in cars. And what if our greedy kid found herself taken in a used car scam?

Damien's Shadow

I awoke one night to see a heavy tree branch casting a dark shadow on my wall. While the tree itself was unimpressive, the shadow of the branch made it look like a "hanging-tree," the kind they used to dispense justice in the old west. But a shadow was all you could hang from a shadow-limb, right? Then I began to wonder what would make someone want to hang a shadow? I was too spooked to sleep, so I got up and spent all night writing the story.

Terrible Tannenbaum

True story. Or at least part of it. A few years back, we had this unfortunate Christmas tree. It would loom all day long, then every night keel over, and shatter ornaments all over the piano. We had to string it up to our wall and upstairs banister in three places to keep it from falling. But this tree was like Houdini—because it pulled free from its bonds, and fell again. The kids were terrified of it—they kept looking at, afraid it might fall on them as they passed. They feared for Santa.

Dead Letter

With all the horror movies about the living-dead, it occurred to me that no one has ever come forward to complain about how the living-dead are portrayed in the media. After all, everyone else complains, why not them?

Boy on a Stoop

I saw this kid when I was in New York, sitting on the stoop of an abandoned building, like he belonged there. He was reading *Catcher in the Rye*. For some reason, it seemed downright creepy to me, and it stuck in my mind. Then, recently I read a book with my sons about strange sea creatures, like the anglerfish. I began to wonder what a creature that was angling after humans might have as its "worm." Well that all depends on what it's trying to catch. . . .

Retaining Walls

We recently had a patio put in our backyard—which is not as easy as it seems, I found out. Part of the job required putting up a retaining wall to hold back the hill from mudslides, earthquakes, nuclear war and Alien invasions. Or so you would think, considering the amount of work that went into building the thing. With walls on the brain, I couldn't help but write this story!

Dark Alley

I always try to include a story that came about during a school visit. Last year, while visiting Whitehorne and Grover Cleveland middle schools in New Jersey, I was running a creative brainstorming workshop. Of the many settings the kids brainstormed, I had asked them to take the idea of a bowling alley and the things in a bowling alley. We narrowed it down to the ball return, and I posed the question, "what might the ball return send back instead of a bowling ball?" Some kids said a head, others said a rock, and then someone shouted, "a dinosaur egg!" While the egg turned out not to be a dinosaur egg, it was that idea that sparked this story.

The In Crowd

For some time I wanted to write a story about a character whose mind was so powerful, that he absorbed people right into it. Elements of that idea were in my novel *The Eyes of Kid Midas*, but I wanted to explore it in a different way, and so I came up with the characters of Alana, who didn't know how to get close to people, and Garrett who got too close.

Special Deliverance

This began as a one-joke premise—a delivery boy having to deliver a pizza to the place down under . . . however, the more I wrote, the more I felt I wanted the story to have more depth than just a cheap twist at the end. Then I began to consider this: What if our delivery boy was delivering more than just pizza? What if he were also delivering souls from that awful place. Suddenly the story took on a whole new perspective. As for the location of the ghost town of giant apartment buildings, that was inspired by a true-to-life abandoned city called Pruitt-Igoe. It was torn down a few years back, but you can see scenes of it in a weird but fascinating movie called Koyanisqaatsi. (Don't even try to pronounce it.)

Mr. Vandermeer's Attic of Shame

I was trying to come up with a concept for the cover of MindStorms—my previous story collection—and I thought of the idea of an attic roof covering a stormy sky. Ultimately the artist didn't use that idea, but the image stayed in my mind. I began to wonder who would live—or be trapped—in an attic the size of a small world, and what type of person would own that attic. Then, after seeing a news story about illegal imigrants who were practically enslaved in secret sweatshop factories, right here in America, I felt a need to tell a story about their plight. That's when I knew what this story had to be about.

Pea Soup

Anyone who's driven the lonely stretch of road between Los Angeles and San Francisco knows exactly where this idea came from. Everywhere you go, your eyes are drawn to signs for a place called Pea Soup Anderson's. Eventually, with each passing sign, you begin to count the miles by your distance from the restaurant, and that innexplicable craving for pea soup starts to take control, whether you like pea soup or not. Any time we take the trip, it's a family tradition to stop there and devour a few bowls of pea soup, which is actually very good. But I wondered what might happen if there were another pea soup restaurant where the soup was a little too good. . . .

The Elsewhere Boutique

Malls are just full of bizarre specialty stores, aren't they? Some stores just sell rubber stamps, or calendars—I even saw a store that sells little jars of sauces, and nothing else. Well, there are lots of things you can buy in a little jar, aren't there? I figured, why not squeeze a whole universe inside? The problem is— once you opened it, and the bottled universe replaced the real one, how would you know that anything has changed, or if you've changed as well?

Ralphy Sherman's Bag of Wind

Ralphy Sherman makes a guest appearance in almost every book I write. He's just a fun character, and I always like to come up with strange and absurd adventures for him and his sister. I wanted to tell a tornado story in this book, and since tornados are strange and absurd things, who better to be a part of a twister story than Ralphy?

Loveless

Madame Loveless (originally Madame Bayless) had appeared in an early draft of my novel *Scorpion Shards*, but I ended up cutting her out. Still, I always liked the idea of the fortune teller who happily resided in the graveyard. The question is: who would be so desperate that they'd follow her into her creepy lair? Since the story is told in second person, the answer is: you! And you just happen to be a lonely statue.